I0664425

Escape from Siberia

The Richard Jackson Saga, Volume 12

Ed Nelson

Published by Eastern Shore Publishing, 2024.

Table of Contents

Other books by Ed Nelson

The Richard Jackson Saga

Book 1 The Beginning
Book 2 Schooldays
Book 3 Hollywood
Book 4 In the Movies
Book 5 Star to Deckhand
Book 6 Surfing Dude
Book 7 Third Time is a Charm
Book 8 Oxford University
Book 9 Cold War
Book 10 Taking Care of Business
Book 11 Interesting Times
Book 12 Escape from Siberia
Book 13 Regicide
Book 14 What's Under, Down Under?
Book 15 The Lunar Kingdom
Book 16 First Steps

In the Richard Jackson World

Mary, Mary

Stand-Alone Story

Ever and Always

Cast in Time Series

Book 1: Baron
Book 2: Baron of the Middle Counties
Book 3: Count
Book 4: Earl
Book 5: Earl of the Marches

Dediation

This is dedicated to my wife Carol for her support and help as my first reader and editor.

Thanks to my Editors, Ernest Bywater, Lonelydad57, Old Rotorhead, Lon, and Antti.

Also, the Bellefontaine High School Class of 1962, just because.

Professionally edited by Janet E. Rupert

Quotation

That's the way it happened, give or take a lie or two.

James Garner as Wyatt Earp, describing the gunfight at the OK Corral in the movie *Sunset*.

Copyright © 2021

Chapter 1

I held Nina in my arms. I didn't want to let her go. I don't know how we will work this all out, but work it out we will. I still don't know how she could have gone with that prince behind my back, and I would probably never understand.

It didn't matter. Nina was back where she belonged. I had been a lifeguard and pulled some desperate people out of the water. They hadn't clung to me like she was.

It took me a moment to realize that she was sobbing her heart out. We were standing in a room full of people, some family, some I had never seen before.

I saw Mum; I mouthed to her, get us a room. I had to give Mum credit; she didn't take the cheap shot she could have. She just steered us to an open doorway. It was to somebody's office, but it wasn't occupied, so she gently led us in, and left, closing the door behind us.

We stood in that office for the longest time wrapped in a hug.

She finally pulled away from me and looked up into my eyes.

"Rick, how can you ever forgive me?"

"I don't know that I have to forgive you. All I know is that I need you in my life."

She hugged me again and started sobbing.

I held her gently. She had lost weight, and it felt like I could break her if I hugged her too tightly.

After a while, there was a knock on the door. It was Mum.

"Rick, we need you out here to talk to people, and it looks like Nina needs to wash her face. I will take care of her."

I went back out to face a crowd of well-wishers, at least that is what I thought they were. My emotions were so jangled that I had no idea what was said to me or how I answered.

My answers must not have been too bad because no one fled crying or challenged me to a duel.

5

There was the inevitable press conference where I was asked intelligent questions, such as, "How does it feel to be a duke?"

"It's too soon to tell."

"What are your plans now?"

"Go to Disneyland? No, just kidding. I have to figure out what this new title means, and I have work to do with the North and South Vietnamese governments and two golf tournaments to get ready for."

I wasn't about to tell them, "And sort out my relationship with Nina."

The empress and queen both avoided the press. I had to learn their tricks. I was summoned, never asked, always summoned, like, "Here Rover, good boy, good doggy."

Elizabeth started with, "Thanks for being a good sport about this. We knew if we asked in advance you would try to weasel out of this. We do need help here in the long run and when we get closer to the transition."

Empress Ping continued, "In the shorter term, you can help Hong Kong become the window to the world for China. As our ports expand, they will help our economy, but we need to get trade moving now so the people are happy with the new government."

"I can see that, but could you make it something like, oh I don't know what, anything but this high-sounding title?"

"The high-sounding title will get people to listen to you who otherwise would have shrugged you off. The title shows the regard in which you are held by the empress and me. It is not the title; it is the connections."

"That makes more sense to me. Do I have some sort of duke uniform I have to wear?"

"You won't have to wear your robes until you give your maiden speech in the House of Lords. You can't do that until you are twenty-one."

"Do I have to do it then?"

"Some never give a speech, so they are never seated."

"That sounds good to me."

"You will change your mind by then."

"We'll see."

After that, I spent the rest of the afternoon with the Governor of Hong Kong and his staff. They gave me an overview of the problems facing Hong Kong. I assured them that I would have little involvement, if any, with Hong Kong other than investing in areas that could help the colony.

From their faces, you could tell that they were skeptical, but I meant it. I wanted nothing to do with running a country, a colony, or even a township.

My takeaway from that meeting was that the sooner they could handle the cargo containers the better and that they could use help in bringing up their manufacturing to modern standards.

My company was upgrading the port, so that was just a matter of time. As far as modernization was concerned, I wanted to check on a project in Pittsburgh, and if it was going as well as I had heard, then a source of help might be available.

Dinner was a formal event with the queen and empress. I wore my Coldstream uniform as I didn't want to go to the bother of all the nonsense in formal dress.

Nina was my table partner. You could tell she still was uncertain of our relationship and was noticeably quiet. A dinner like this was never the place for a personal conversation. Anything said would make the tabloids within a day.

The expected comments and questions were directed at me from up and down the table. Some of them were bold like the guy asking for a business meeting as his company would be a good investment for me. The one that took the cake was the woman who tried to set me up with her daughter, with Nina sitting beside me!

Some aide to the governor asked the woman an innocent question. "Oh, has she had those buck teeth fixed?"

I managed not to spew the glass of wine I had been sipping. It did shut the woman up.

Early the next morning, my family and I had a private meeting with Queen Elizabeth. She assured us that the dukedom was to be seen mostly as a reward but that any good I could do for Hong Kong would be appreciated.

My being made a duke was an English title, not a Hong Kong one. They didn't do that in the commonwealth or colonies.

I made a private decision to purchase land and companies in Hong Kong so that I would have a real part of it.

My interests would be vested in upgrading their manufacturing and bringing in new business. The governing would be left to the politicians. I didn't have the stomach for it.

Empress Ping had departed for Beijing after dinner the previous night. Her hold on power was still tenuous.

We boarded my 707 for the long flight back to LA.

Nina and I spent many an hour in my office talking. There was much to say. Most of it I can't remember. One conversation did stick in my mind.

"Why that scumbag of a prince?"

"Rick, I think I fell into the trap that is built for all American girls. We have read stories all our lives about a nobody-American girl meeting a handsome prince, and they fall for each other and live happily ever after.

"We have been conditioned is the best I can put it. He was good-looking and certainly a good actor. I didn't realize how badly I was being used until you showed up and smashed your car.

"My world came crashing down at that point. I don't know what was going on in my head. I was so bedazzled by the prince that you went out of my mind. If I thought about it at all, it was that my romance with the prince would soon be over, and you and I would be back to normal.

"How could I be so naïve? How can you ever trust me again?"

"Nina, you are right, you breached that trust, but that doesn't mean that we can't rebuild it. It will take time; maybe years, but we can rebuild it."

I could see her eyes light up with hope. I also felt hope but was scared to death of what would happen if she failed again. It would crush both of us.

I would like to say those thoughts went through my mind immediately. It took days for me to think everything through—also, a couple of serious conversations with my parents.

We did have a few light-hearted moments on the flight. Mum and Mary had been shopping. They came to dinner on the flight dressed as traditional Chinese coolies, funny straw hats, and all.

I had become proficient with chopsticks, the rest of the family, not so much. It was funny to see Eddie wrestle with them trying to eat rice. He did it, one grain at a time. You have to give him credit; he is very stubborn or very hungry.

Chapter 2

It was the first of July when we landed at LAX. Traffic was terrible getting home. We talked seriously about flying in and out of Ontario airport in the future. That way we could even fly a Cessna to the Forest Service station.

We had talked about using that as our escape route if there was ever a problem at Jackson House, but we had let it slip by the wayside. We needed to revisit it even if only for convenience.

Not that it would have worked this trip. There were too many of us for my small aircraft. Even taking a limo from Ontario would be better than this Los Angeles mess.

Nina was riding with us; we would drop her off at her house on the way home. I got out with her when we reached her home.

"Nina, the past is the past. Would you like to have lunch tomorrow?"

"I would love to."

"Okay, meet me at the Forestry Service station. I have to practice putting on the Troon greens."

She gave me a funny look but didn't question it.

The family retired early; these trans-Pacific flights were exhausting. There was also the jet lag factor. We hadn't been there long enough to get turned around; but still, it was enough to cause problems.

At breakfast the next morning, I knew I was in trouble when Mary came in wearing a "Save the People" t-shirt.

"Good morning, Ricky. How much are you paying me for infringing on my trademark?"

"Nothing. I'm not the one who made or who is selling them. Go back to China and find those people. Sue the heck out of them."

"Pooh, you are no fun at all."

"Sorry, squirt. Did you want me to throw myself at the mercy of the court?"

"Oh, would you!"

"Your honor, I have most foully infringed upon the trademark held by my little sister. I will pay the penalty."

Mary tried to put on a deep-sounding voice.

"You shall buy her ice cream every day for a month."

"I won't be here for the entire month. I have to go to England and Scotland."

"Then you shall buy her ice cream every day that you are with her."

There was triumph and glee in her voice. Then another voice was heard.

"And she will ask for Mum's permission every day that you are here. If Mum says, 'No,' then it will still count as a day off Rick's sentence."

Dad has a very deep voice when he wants it.

Mary stomped her foot.

"Well, I tried."

"Not a bad effort. A tear or two when you first came in might have helped."

She got a thoughtful look, "I think you are right. I will work on that."

This is Mary at eight. I can't imagine her teen years. If I'm lucky I will be married and out of the house.

The movie turned out to be a big disappointment for me. I thought I would have a better part. I was shown riding around a lot and passing messages, but I had few scenes with any meat in them. The Charles and Molly story was a side issue in the movie.

The one good thing was that I hadn't ended up in a water trough, yet.

I rode George over to the Forestry Service station and worked on my putting. The greens at Troon were going to be murderous. I was most concerned about how the smaller European ball would act on the different grass used. Two variables were two too many.

I expressed that to Sam. He told me to man up.

I went back and forth all morning, putting and driving. At noon I looked up to see a beautiful young lady standing there.

I did the natural thing and kissed her.

My Nina was back. I hoped and prayed it was to stay.

We had lunch together at the little FS canteen. It was only a hamburger and fries, but it was heaven. It might have been the company.

I had gotten to know some of the rangers who worked there all the time. They stopped by and wanted to know what they should call me now. The Duke of Hong Kong seemed too formal.

I agreed and told them to call me, "Rick."

That set our world back in its orbit. I was asked what it all meant. I told them it was a political maneuver and that I was a pawn in the game being played by the queen and empress. It probably was the truth.

Nina had driven over, and I had ridden George, so we parted company until this evening. We were going to the Hamburger Hamlet for dinner.

I was running late when I got back to the house and cleaned up to head out to the studio. I was careful not to speed. I didn't need the publicity right now.

On the set, I had my big scene with Molly. I asked her to be my wife and she consented. After she said, "Yes!" I was to jump up and shout "Hurray!" I did jump up.

The blankety-blank people had put a water trough behind me to fall into.

It was bad enough when I was surprised. Try drying off and changing clothes five times. The rest of the cast enjoyed this too much.

Even the real "Duke" made a point of being there to laugh at me.

I did the best acting of my career. I kept smiling and pretended it didn't bother me while I was thinking about using fire arrows on their houses.

Later I picked up Nina, and we had dinner at the Hamburger Hamlet. It was a quiet event as we both felt like we were starting over to get to know each other.

We were open in our feelings, me wondering about trust and she wondering about the world I was moving in.

To me, it didn't seem like anything special. It had crept up on me, and I got used to it a bit at a time. She was seeing it all at once, and I could see where it would look scary.

I told her to remember that everyone I was dealing with was a person just like us. Maybe they had titles and power, but in the end, they were people.

She asked me how I would help the people of Hong Kong.

"There are two things the Governor and his staff told me that I could do. Modernize the harbor, which is already in process. Then any help I could give in bringing their manufacturing techniques in line with the rest of the world would be good.

"I have to make a phone call in the morning, but if what I have been told is true, we might be able to do better than bring their manufacturing to world standards. We might be able to set new standards."

"How is that?"

I told her about meeting a consultant named Ed Deming in Japan. He was trying to find work there. He had some success, and after a conversation, Todd Goodson and I asked him to go to Pittsburgh and see what could be done at our plant.

"From what I have heard, it has been miraculous. I'm going to confirm it with Todd. If it is true, I'm going to hire him to help Hong Kong. That is if the Governor agrees."

"I doubt he would have the nerve to disagree with you right now."

"You are probably right."

"What else do you have going on?"

"Well, I have two golf tournaments coming up. After that, the movie will be finished, so I guess I will have to find something to do."

About that time her good friend Tuesday Weld and her latest boyfriend came in the door. As expected, there were the hugs and squeals two girlfriends gave each other when they had spent more than a half-hour apart. Maybe I exaggerate a little but not by much.

Tuesday excitedly shared that she had been asked to do a movie with Elvis which would start filming soon for a release in 1962.

I told them how I had bailed Elvis out of jail in Mexico several years ago. Since then, he has refused to go back there, no matter how much the promoters offered.

She asked how Nina and I were coping. We told her we were taking it slow but thought we could work things out.

Her boyfriend seemed like a nice guy, better than that jerk at the dance. His name was Charles Harz, and he was a new screenwriter. Have I told you I don't like most screenwriters? They come up with scenes that end up with me in water troughs.

Tuesday and Nina spent time talking about their mothers. Nina was positive because Mom was getting back together with Dad. Tuesday complained that her mother thought that Tuesday owed her everything in the world.

I didn't envy Charles. If he married Tuesday, he would have mother-in-law problems for certain.

After all that I took Nina home, where we parted with a chaste kiss.

Chapter 3

After my run and workout, I called Todd Goodson in Pittsburg.

"Todd, I have heard that Deming guy has been a tremendous help to our operations. Is it true?"

"More than true. Just being able to recognize what is a stable process has been a big help. We have spent a lot of time trying to fix things that can't be fixed."

"What do you mean?"

"If a process is stable, you have to improve the process to get better results. We were trying to adjust processes, rather than improve them. Using statistical control charts, we have been able to identify which processes aren't stable. Those we can fix.

"He also makes a point that having to inspect your work for quality is a failure. "You should have a system in place to make a good product the first time.

"Another good idea he pushes is to break down the barriers between departments."

"What do you mean?"

"I would guess you have never sat in a meeting where the engineers have come up with a wonderful design. The only problem is that manufacturing can't make it."

"Wow, I would go ape, well, I would have a hard time at that meeting. So, do you think his ideas would help industries in Hong Kong?"

"His ideas will work anywhere in the world. They are based on facts, not opinions."

"Can he effectively communicate these ideas?"

"Most certainly; for example, he has what he calls his red ball experiment. It involves dropping a red ball into a large funnel. It is almost impossible to drop it dead center straight down. So, the ball rolls around the funnel until it drops down.

"Below is a rifle target with the rings. He offers money to anyone who can achieve a better score. They can't because it is a stable fixed process. The only way to do better is to physically change the funnel setup. No matter the language, people can understand what they are seeing."

"So, you think we could use him in Hong Kong?"

"Yes, whoever integrates his thinking will do better than anyone who doesn't. It's based on real science, not a consensus of how things should work."

"Okay, I will arrange for him to give demonstrations to manufacturers in Hong Kong."

"I'm all for it as long as we have access to him."

"That right there tells me what I need to know.

"As usual, Todd, I have jumped right to business. How is your family doing?"

"Thanks for asking, everyone is doing fine. I just wish Mary wouldn't keep coming out with new collections. My daughters buy every new release. I think I'm working for Mary, not you!"

"That's funny. I will tell Mary that. How old are your girls?"

"The oldest is ten, the youngest seven going on thirty."

"That sounds like Mary."

"People think it is the job giving me gray hairs. It is those two girls. I don't know what I will do when they start dating."

"Buy a shotgun and be sure to be cleaning it when the boy shows up for the first date."

"Yeah, my father-in-law is part Cherokee. He was sharpening his tomahawk on my first date."

"That would do it! I have to go; I need to practice for the upcoming golf tournament."

"We wish you the best. When you are playing, we announce how you did on each hole on the plant PA system. You should hear the cheers when you do well. Jackson Enterprises employees are proud of you.

"When your dukedom was announced, t-shirts saying, 'I work for the duke,' started showing up."

"Wow, well I got to go."

"Later, Your Grace."

I gave a "Bah," as I hung up.

From there I rode George over to the golf course. The new tennis courts were in, and several baseball diamonds were in place. You could see where a walking trail went off into the woods.

When completed this would be considered a luxury resort, at least by Forest Service standards.

I spent my time on the practice green setup for Troon. I was looking forward to playing the course.

I had lunch at the canteen on the grounds and then went back to alternating between the driving range and the putting green. I wasn't going to lose the upcoming match due to lack of effort.

John had been over in Scotland scoping out the course. He told me that the course was deceptively simple-looking when you viewed the course map.

The first six holes on the old course went almost due south, running parallel to the Firth of Clyde. They were the easiest holes on the course and where you would have to go for it to break par.

Holes 7 and on moved inland with hillier dunes and deeper bunkers. This is where those birdies made on the six holes went home to roost. To make it even more fun the rough was covered in gorse. This grass was about six inches tall and overlapped each blade so much that you could lose a ball a foot off the fairway.

They had spent generations fine-tuning this course, starting in 1878, to make it one of the best in the world. Read best in the world as being as difficult as possible while still being playable.

He told me from records it would take about 10-under par, maybe an 11, to win the tournament. It was doable but involved some luck. Like no wind to knock the ball down at the wrong time.

Later, I returned home to clean up to go to the wrap party for the movie. As I had told John Wayne and Mr. Monroe, this was my last B-movie, especially Westerns. I was afraid one more Western would have me typecast forever.

I would consider taking a part in a spy movie. They still sounded like fun, but it had to be in a leading role. I still thought my movie career was about over. I was doing movies for the fun of it and the comradery on the set. This movie was a disappointment in all departments.

I had dinner with my family before going to the party. I asked Mary if she was going to let Nina model again.

"No, I haven't forgiven her for what she did to you."

"I'm working on forgiving her, so you should too."

"I will as soon as I see that she treats you right. I saw a picture of her 'Prince McDreamy.' He looks like a jerk. How she could pick him over you I will never know."

I related how Nina had been raised on stories of the prince showing up and sweeping the commoner off her feet to live happily ever after.

Mary thought that was nonsense. That was when I remembered that this eight-year-old had been raised on stories of the common girl rescuing the dumb prince, then meeting a real man, and living happily ever after.

Mum's stories had a different slant. I think they were based on her real life. I wonder who the prince was? Maybe one from Morocco? I still wanted to find out what went on there during the war.

Looking back and forth between Mum and Dad, I could tell there was something there, but no one was talking.

Denny proudly announced that the third franchised studio had been opened. Both he and Sam Nielsen, his former boss and now partner, were doing well. This was good to hear.

After dinner, I headed over to the Beverly Hills Hotel where the wrap party was being held.

At the party, there were the usual gag gifts. They had a photographer there so everyone who wanted could have their picture taken with the two dukes.

They had outtakes to show, and they had to highlight me ending up in the water trough. If nothing else, I wasn't making any more of these movies and ending up as a joke in the outtakes.

When did I become such a crotchety old man?

There came a point where the alcohol level had risen in the room so that inhibitions were being discarded. I had nursed a beer all evening and decided it was time for me to leave.

I mentioned to the guys I was standing with that I needed a restroom. They just nodded and one pointed to a doorway. Now if it had been a group of women, they would have accompanied me.

Thankfully, guys don't do that. When I got to the restroom door, I kept on moving and retrieved my T-bird from the valet. I considered going over to Nina's as it was only nine o'clock but thought better of it and went home.

At home, I called Government House in Hong Kong. I had been given the name of the governor's chief aide as my contact. I caught him just as he was heading out to lunch.

I told him that Jackson Enterprises was making marked improvements following the advice of a consultant by the name of W. Edwards Deming.

If they were interested, I would sponsor a trip to Hong Kong where Deming could share his ideas with any industry leaders who would care to come.

He thought that was a great idea but had one reservation.

"They won't want to come to hear a consultant they have never heard of, but if the Duke of Hong Kong were present...."

I sighed, as I started to realize what I had started.

"I will plan to attend. Keep my LA office Manager Jim Williamson informed of the dates."

That did make me think that it was time to give Jim a new title, vice president of something, and a large raise.

Chapter 4

Even if you own the company, some formalities must be followed. I wrote a letter to my Board of Directors recommending that Jim Williamson be elevated to the title of Executive Vice President of Operations, Jackson Enterprises, with a commensurate salary. It would be approved, but done this way there could be no legal repercussions.

They would vote on it at our quarterly meeting. There is no doubt it would be approved. Since the meeting was the next day, I sent Jim a copy as he would be attending the meeting, and I didn't want to blindside him.

On second thought, I also called him and told him how much his work was appreciated and what promotion I was putting him in for. There was strong emotion in his voice as he thanked me.

In the morning after my normal workout, I donned a suit and tie and made one of my rare appearances at my office. Mum, Dad, Mr. Wingate, Jim, Todd, and Don were all present. Mark Downing couldn't make it—something about Sharon having a baby.

I would have to ask Mum what an appropriate gift would be, but that would wait until after the meeting.

Popeye was among the missing. He was in South Vietnam right now settling some dispute on the docks.

Thinking of Popeye reminded me of something. When it came to new business, I had an item.

"I have scheduled the *Pride of Liberia*, to be at the intersection of the International Dateline and the Equator on September 23 at midnight."

That got some raised eyebrows. I explained about the Order of the Purple Porpoise and that it was the one sailor's honor that Popeye didn't have. That made sense to them. Popeye had done so much for the company, we owed him. Besides, everyone present, even Mr. Wingate, wanted to go on the trip.

There were two more items that I brought up on the new business agenda.

"As some of you know, I made an extremely lot of money off the people attacking Jackson Enterprises. More than half that money is being invested in a new bank in China. It is the Bank of Guangzhou.

"I have done this to try to keep the region stable as their government transitions. It is a commercial venture that I expect will make a profit. I'm also underwriting bonds to upgrade their infrastructure with the same goal in mind, the long-term stability of China."

Dad joked, "China seems to have followed you home; are you going to keep it?"

I didn't reply to that; it was too dumb to consider.

I continued. "Our freight forwarding business is extremely profitable. We created it to even out the cash flow when container demand was down.

"Maybe I have been sitting on an airplane for too many hours, but what if we created an airline system for freight forwarding? I call it a system because it won't be your typical, pick up at point A and deliver to point B. I'm thinking of bulk delivery of many small packages.

"It can be done by creating a series of hubs. For example, if we started here in the US, I would have a major hub around Memphis, as it is centrally located based on population distribution.

"Any package going from California to Florida would be picked up at a local airport by a light plane and flown to Ontario, where the packages from all California airports would accumulate during the day.

"That night they would be flown on a 707 or other large aircraft to Memphis. From Memphis, the package would be flown to

Orlando, where it would be broken down and delivered to its hub airport. From there we would need a fleet of trucks to deliver it to the final address."

What I thought was a wonderful idea got shot down unanimously by my board. It would cost too much to set up and there was no guarantee of success.

I still thought it was a good idea and I would figure out a way to do it, even if I had to set up a new company with a different board of directors. Unlike my early days in business, I was now a known commodity and was of age.

Maybe I should have started with a local version in California and expanded from there. That is what I should have pitched in the first place. Oh well, too late now for that meeting.

Dad reported for Dennis Lawson and his business reporting. It was in the black and picking up stations weekly.

The financial report showed us making a ton of money as usual. I hope I wasn't pouting because no one went along with my idea, but I was bummed out when the meeting ended.

I did remember to ask Mum about a gift for the Downings and their new child. She said she would take care of it from the family. It would be something like a paid-up college fund.

That sounded good to me. From my days in Bellefontaine, I thought you gave things like an outfit for three or four-month-olds, knowing full well they would outgrow it in weeks.

I went out to the practice green for one last round before heading to Scotland for the real thing. John and Sam were all packed and ready to go. John had finally talked Sam into leaving his beloved greens for a week to see the tournament.

Several of the rangers had volunteered to make certain the water came on when it was supposed to, which was what kept Sam awake at night.

What was keeping me awake was the fact that I hadn't got in any early practice rounds at Troon. I would only have three days, Monday through Wednesday, to practice on the course.

The whole family was going, but not on the same plane. Dad and the boys would be on one airline. Mum and Mary on another. I would be on my own.

We had started doing this so that if a disaster happened, the whole family wouldn't be lost.

After golf, I drove over to Nina's house where I had been invited for dinner. Her parents had finally reconciled and gotten married. It was by a Justice of the Peace with Nina the only other person plus the hired witnesses. They had talked of having a "small ceremony of only a couple of hundred people," but had given that up as too much work.

The dinner was low-key. I think Nina's parents were tiptoeing around our recent breakup. I could see why; I was still trying to sort out things in my mind.

Mr. Monroe asked me. "What are your duties as the Duke of Hong Kong?"

I told him I was making it up as I was going. I felt I shouldn't have any direct involvement but provide opportunities for improvement.

I went on to tell him what I was hiring Dr. Deming to do. I would lead them to water but not attempt to make them drink.

"Rick, ever since you helped us restructure our studio's business flow, I have known you have a good feel for these things. Now you are doing it for what is essentially a country."

"Oh, I'm also working with the government of South Vietnam to eliminate the corruption in their government."

"How are you doing that?"

I went on to explain how the new South Vietnamese President Trần Văn Hương was contacting the groups I had recommended around the world, like MI5 to set up their FBI equivalent."

"Why not the actual FBI?"

"I'm trying to spread the different agencies around the world. Also, I have heard some disturbing things about J. Edgar Hoover. Not corruption in the money sense, but how he tracks people he considers enemies."

"We in Hollywood know about that full well."

"Anyway, I am doing this hands-off. Trần asked for contacts for whatever agency he wanted to work on. I gave him a list of groups that could do the job. I don't begin to know all the various groups and their records, but I do know people who do."

"In doing so you are increasing your contacts and influence around the world."

"I never looked at it that way, but I think you are right."

"What is the downside of what you are doing?"

"That one is easy. It's about time for the Soviets to try to kill me again."

I was being flippant, but it didn't come across that way. I could see two parents re-evaluating their daughter being around me.

I tried to backtrack, but the damage had been done. Nothing was said right then, but there would be fallout.

Nina walked to my car with me, where we smooched a little before saying goodnight. She didn't say anything about my Soviet comment, but you could see the wheels turning.

The next morning, Saturday, it was wheels up for John, Sam, the ever-present Harold, and me for Glasgow, Scotland. This was the nearest to Troon. The landing pattern crossed the south end of the golf course. It would be two rented limos for the rest of the trip. One for John, Sam, and me. The other was for Harold and my clothes; hey, this was Harold's idea.

The trip was okay as far as trips go. We played hearts for most of the trip. As usual, the stewardesses won the most money. I think they are all card sharks.

I did go up front and get another two hours in my logbook. At this rate, I might have a hundred hours on 707s in twenty or thirty years. The aircraft might even be obsolete by then!

Mum had taken care of our housing arrangements. I think what she did was call Grandmum, who in turn brought in the Queen Mum, who told some lackey to find us a nice place.

It was nice. I'm not sure we needed forty bedrooms for the week, but in case people dropped in, we were ready.

Chapter 5

We arrived in Glasgow on Saturday morning. The time change wasn't as bad as going to China or Vietnam, but it still was prudent to adjust before a major effort like this tournament.

Mum and Dad had arrived the previous day, so the family was standing out front as we arrived in front of Mum's small rental. The castle even had a moat and drawbridge!

This castle was a private residence and was not open to the public. The roads in the area were left in mild disrepair to discourage visitors and tour buses.

It was a royal family getaway. Kept low-key, Castle Firth was one of the better-kept secret royal residences. This is where alcoholic royals were sent for recovery or mad ones were locked up.

Our limo driver was aware of the turn-off road but had never been down it. His comment when he saw the castle was, "Och!"

We were shown our rooms, which thankfully had been modernized; well, they were in 1930. At least there was electricity to light the 20-watt bulbs.

I think candlelight would have done as well. Still, it was a nice place to spend the week. There would be no problem with the paparazzi taking pictures through the window.

If any of them made it behind the castle walls, there was a dungeon. We were shown this on a group tour by the staff. They didn't get that many visitors, so they were glad to show off their castle.

I think it was more the staff's castle than the royals'. The staff lived on-site; the royals came rarely. We all agreed it was a cool place to visit but we wouldn't want to live here.

Not only was it out of the way, but according to the staff, it was cold, wet, and dark in the winter. They stated this as though that was normal. I think I know where that thousand-year-old richest vampire in the world lives. One of the graves in the crypt we were shown probably houses him.

I wisely kept my mouth shut; Mary would have us awake all night.

Monday, John and I were at the golf course at our appointed tee time. We arrived early, as usual, to get the gear settled, signed in for the tournament, and spent some time on the practice greens after loosening up on the driving range. For an eleven o'clock tee time, we had to be there at eight o'clock. This golfing is hard work.

I was given a warmer welcome at the sign-in tent than I had received in America. The Scots loved amateurs. They rooted for the underdog even if I was an Englishman or Sassenach.

Sassenach translates to Saxon. This shows how far back their memories went. The Saxons lost power in England in 1066 when the French Normans invaded. The Hatfields and the McCoys were beginners at this feuding stuff.

The first six holes on the course made me think this would be a walk in the park. I was 5-under, going up to hole number 8, the Postage Stamp, a par 3, 123 yards. I loved the way every hole had a name.

The Postage Stamp was named for its small putting green. The tee shot was from the high ground over a gully onto a green set into a sandhill. There were five deep bunkers, hills, and gorse protecting the green.

There was a wind blowing and I selected a 9-iron, I should have chosen an 8 or even a 7 as I came up short. I felt lucky to get away with a double bogey.

I managed to par the next two holes. Then came the tenth hole, Sandhills.

Sandhills is a par 4, 451 yards. It is dead into the prevailing wind. It starts with a blind tee shot. You must aim for the side of a hill on the left side of the fairway. Gorse in the rough gets any drift balls. If this happens say goodbye to par. I said goodbye. My 5-under turned into 2-under.

Next was the eleventh hole, a 482-yard, par 5. The Railway's name is because it runs next to railway tracks, with a four-foot stone path. Hit that and you are out of bounds. I didn't go out of bounds. I hit a safe 3-wood leaving a 200-yard shot to a tight landing area. I went to the left into a bunker and felt good about getting a bogey, leaving me 1-under.

Hole 12, The Fox, is a par 4, 430 yards. I hit a driver down the right side and then a wedge to the green. This resulted in a par.

Then came the eighteenth hole, Craigend, a par 4, at 458 yards. All it took was a long shot up the middle right, easily clearing a bunker at 307 yards. The pin was set in the back. I was told to stay short of the pin as anything long is out of bounds. The clubhouse is close to the back of the green. I was long and ended up with 1-over for the practice round.

That evening John and I had a long talk about the day's play. I had to treat this course with more respect than I had today if I were to win.

Day two was better. I managed a par on the Postage Stamp; Sandhills had a bogey; the Fox another par. This time on Craigend, I stayed below the pin for a par. I had a 3-under for the day.

If I did that every round, I would be on the leaderboard, but probably not the winner.

On the third day of practice, I managed a 4-under so felt like I had a chance in the tournament.

My partners in the practice round were all amateurs like me. No disrespect intended but this wasn't my competition. We were polite with each other, but we were from different worlds. I was a bloody duke!

That evening I spent as I had before every tournament. Quietly at home. Not that the castle was homey. It felt more like a combination of museum and mausoleum. No parties had been planned while we were in residence.

I noticed my brothers and sister were sticking close to our parents tonight. This place was spooky. The staff had retired for the evening to their little cottages behind the castle. We had the tremendous pile of stone to ourselves.

There was no radio or television. There was an old windup Victrola with a selection of pre-World War II records. They were so thick you could use them as clay pigeons, the only problem being that a direct hit wouldn't break them.

We would take turns winding the machine just to have some noise. When it was time to go to bed, no one argued when Mary went with Mum and Dad, while Denny and Eddie shared a huge bed.

That left me. There was no way that I would say that I was scared, but I did sleep with the low-wattage light bulbs on.

I lay there for the longest time waiting for things to go bump in the night, but they didn't. Suddenly, my portable alarm was going off.

A fog had settled in overnight, so I put off my run. No way was I going to run in the strange countryside when I couldn't see more than twenty or thirty feet in front of me. No, I wasn't scared that something would jump out and get me. Really!

Despite all that I felt rested from a good night's sleep. John told me that he felt silly, but he had left his light on all night. I replied that the place didn't inspire confidence. I didn't see a need to tell him I also had left my light on.

At breakfast, Harold looked tired like he had no sleep. I asked him how he felt. He told me that he was good until going to bed. It was only then that he realized he was staying in the castle that was the center of all the ghost stories of his childhood.

I teased him a bit, "You were scared of a few ghosts?"

"No, I was scared of all the unexplained deaths that have occurred in this castle."

"You mean the ghost got them?"

"No, people have been shot, stabbed, and hanged here, with no explanation of how it happened."

Mum and Dad looked at each other across the table. I thought they would be looking for another place to stay.

This was confirmed when Mum instructed Harold to make certain everything was packed. We wouldn't be returning.

As we were driving through the main gate to leave, I noticed that the stone had words engraved above the exit.

You have left the Hous...f.... sher.

I wondered what the missing letters were. All of us were extremely glad to be leaving that gloomy place. As we were going back to town, we were stopped by the police. They had been looking for us all night as we hadn't turned up at the royal residence.

The limo that John and I were in continued to the Troon golf course, while the rest of the family followed the police to the correct residence. I wondered where we had stayed last night.

Chapter 6

After last night's strangeness, I was glad to be in the real world. The golf course seemed like a haven to me.

My tee time was in the middle of the pack. It appears that my chances of winning have moved up, at least according to the pairings committee.

I was paired with two other amateurs. They took their golf seriously. They concentrated on each shot. Not that it helped them. They fell victim to every nasty this course had available.

It was a good thing I was playing against myself. Their dismal showings would do nothing to make me play better.

I ended the first round one stroke behind Keith MacDonald who was 3-under.

I would have tied him, but I left myself too long of a putt on the Fox and took a bogey.

Our driver now had directions to the correct house, so we went straight there after I filled in my scorecard. I pored over it as I had read tales in *Golfweek* about players who were disqualified for filling out their cards incorrectly.

The other two players in my threesome were gracious in their loss and wished me luck in the tournament. They both had done so poorly they wouldn't make the cut.

The correct place was more of what I called a mansion rather than a castle. It was brilliantly lit up and was warm and cozy inside.

I expressed the thought to Mum that this was a much better place to stay than that pile of stones from last night.

She told me that she had asked the staff about the place, but no one seemed to know of it. One incredibly old staff member crossed herself when I mentioned it but wouldn't respond when Mum asked about it.

She just mumbled about tales from her youth and left the room. We never saw her again. That night we all slept in separate bedrooms with no night fears.

At breakfast, John again cautioned me about trying to beat the course, just play it as it was meant to be played. The first six holes are where I could hit the ball long and straight and try for birdies. After that, respect the course because certainly, it wouldn't respect me.

Dad had been keeping track of the international news. Last year the Cubans in Miami had talked about nothing but taking Cuba back from Castro. They had funded a paramilitary group called Brigade 2056. They had thought they could gain US support through the CIA.

Ike had allowed the project to start, but JFK was reluctant to continue with it. It was just as well because when I was in Miami last year, everyone on the street knew when and where the invasion was to take place.

The CIA wanted to go ahead, but JFK wouldn't let them. Now it appears that the invasion was only delayed. The additional year or so had given the Cuban freedom fighters time to train their pilots for air support rather than depend on the US.

This time with the element of surprise, a beachhead had been established and the Brigade was moving towards Havana. Their success would depend on them being joined by locals.

They had a large supply of weapons and ammunition to hand out but no tanks or heavy artillery like the Cuban army. Not that the army had much, but any could make a difference.

I cleared my head of this news as we drove to the Troon course. The last thing I needed to be thinking of was an invasion. I had my own invading to do today.

Round two went better for me than round one. I went on a streak and made four birdies in a row on the first four holes. I parred out the rest of the holes to end the day in the lead at 6-under. Arnold Palmer had moved up to 4-under, so I didn't dare to let up.

That evening we learned that the Cuban tanks and artillery had been taken out by the insurgent's air. The Cuban Air Force was almost nonexistent. They had plenty of MIGs, but the Russian support group spent more time drinking rum and Coca-Cola so the MIGs weren't safe to fly.

The few that the poorly trained Cuban pilots flew were easily knocked out of the sky by prop-driven Mitchel bombers. That was sad; well, at least sad for Castro and his Soviet backers.

By the time I went to bed, the Cuban freedom fighters were within ten miles of downtown Havana. The army resistance was stiffening as their interior lines shortened.

Dad explained what interior lines were to us kids as we listened to the radio. Live reports were coming in on the short wave. This was exciting hearing a war live, as it were.

It was also scary because a lot of people were dying, and we didn't know how it would end.

Mum put Mary to bed early as she was getting upset by the reporting. She didn't like people shooting at each other. Someone might get hurt. Why didn't they fight with their fists?

No one even tried to answer her.

In the morning, the fighting had advanced into Havana and the TV and Radio stations in town had been seized. Word was that Fidel and Raul Castro had fled the country, taking a boat in the night to Venezuela. I wondered how that would work out with Romulo Betancourt in power.

It appeared that the freedom fighters had taken back Cuba. The next question was who would run the country?

While the fate of Cuba was being decided, John and I headed to Troon to decide the fate of the British Open, or the Open

Championship as they called it. They didn't deign to recognize that the colonies had an Open of their own.

This was Saturday and we had two rounds today. I was glad to be in the lead because this meant I got to tee off in the last group. This gave the morning breezes time to calm down.

What the Scots called a morning breeze would be called a Force 7 near gale on the Beaufort scale. The 28 to 33-mile-an-hour wind would send the ball back to you if hit directly into the wind.

I managed to have a run of six birdies on the first six holes but had one bogey after that on the Railroad. This made me 5-under for the round and 11-under for the tournament. Arnold Palmer was in second at 9-under.

We had a short break before teeing up for the final round. Arnold and I were in the last group. He was a gentleman as ever and told me that he was going to make a run at me. I agreed that was his right, but he wouldn't mind if I did the same.

"No, Your Grace. Go for it."

It took a moment to realize he was talking to me. This duke stuff was new to me. I didn't know if I liked it yet. It certainly got me a good table at the restaurants, so it wasn't all bad.

Arnold Palmer made good on his promise of making a run at me. He made birdies on the first six holes to my four. This tied us at 15-under, going into the heart of the old course.

We both parred the seventh hole known as Tel-el-Kebir. I never did learn what that stood for. The next hole the Postage Stamp took back two strokes from both of us, so we were even at 13-under.

The Monk and Sandhills yielded pars, and then we came to the Railway. Arnold pushed his ball left into a bunker. This cost him a stroke and he had a bogey. I managed par, making a fifteen-foot putt by having it hang upon the lip and then dropping after hanging on for an eternity. Well, maybe a split second but it seemed an eternity.

I now had the lead by one stroke.

Palmer came back on the Fox with a par, but so did I.

On the thirteenth hole, Brumah, I came a cropper. What should have been a respectable par turned into a double bogey. Now Arnold Palmer had the lead at 12-under while I was at 11-under.

We both managed par on all the holes up to 18. I had to make a birdie to tie if Arnold parred or he would have to mess up. I didn't think he would mess up.

I hit my longest drive of the day up the middle. I was in a particularly good position to hit a wedge onto the green just below the hole.

Mr. Palmer must have been feeling the pressure because, while twenty yards short of me, his wedge hit the green and didn't stick. It ran up the green and over the edge going out of bounds.

The penalty cost him the tournament as I was able to land just shy of the pin and put it in for a birdie.

I won, while Arnold got the prize money, all fourteen hundred pounds or a little over three thousand American dollars.

Chapter 7

The PGA Championship was the next week, so we flew to Philadelphia immediately after the closing ceremony at Troon. I did have to give a press conference before I left.

The tone was completely different from all the others I had on golf. Before it was, do you think an amateur like yourself is a serious golf player?

Now I was Bobby Jones reincarnated. That didn't make the questions any better. I got the normal, are you turning pro now, or waiting until winning the PGA?

As I was leaving the course, I was handed a stack of congratulatory telegrams.

The queen, the empress, and the US president along with the leaders from Germany, Hong Kong, South Vietnam, and surprisingly North Vietnam. There were a host of other countries which sent telegrams, but they were the important ones.

Then there were the personal ones like Nina, Popeye and Sybil, John Wayne, and all my corporate executives.

One was puzzling; it stated, "I told you it is a gentleman's game, and there is still no money in it. Carlo."

I knew who it was from, but why?

On the return flight, I felt a little tired from the last week. I went to bed on the plane and slept almost the whole flight. I was feeling better when we arrived.

I wondered what shape my competition like Arnold Palmer would be in. Sleeping in first class was nothing like sleeping flat in a real bed.

By the time I settled into the rented house in Radnor, it was Saturday afternoon. I did the intelligent thing and took another nap until dinner time.

The whole family had caught up from our different flights, so we boarded a train on the Main Line and went into Philadelphia for dinner at the Old Original Bookbinder's Restaurant.

During dinner, we talked about how the PGA had almost shot itself in the foot over its Caucasian-only clause. This championship was scheduled to be played at the Brentwood Country Club in Los Angeles, but the California attorney general threatened to shut down the PGA in California until the clause was removed.

The PGA moved the Championship here to Newtown Square but had second thoughts on its policy and changed its position late in 1961. By this time, it was too late to move back to California and the commitment had been made in Pennsylvania. The winds of change were blowing throughout the country.

Mary and Eddie both wanted to know what a Caucasian was. When told it was white people, they both were shocked. They had friends around the world of every color, race, and creed.

Through Mary's modeling, she had many girls of different races to model her collections. She couldn't understand why the PGA would cut out most of its potential audience. Didn't they know there were more red, brown, and yellow people in the world than white?

She seriously recommended that I not turn professional in such a self-limiting organization. The PGA would never be a success. I agreed with her but pointed out that they had relented. Now it was to be seen if anyone of color would ever become a member and win tournaments. That would be the true test.

Sunday afternoon I went out to the course to register for the tournament. My name was on the list as entered. Previously my showing up was ho-hum at the best. This time the club and PGA officials all wanted to meet me. Reporters were hanging around, but they were kept at a distance.

The club people were considered old money, incredibly old money. I was nouveau riche by their standards. I was nouveau riche by my standards.

But and this is a big but, I'm also British nobility, the Duke of Hong Kong. That wiped out the sin of making my money in this generation.

Several of the people who introduced themselves seemed nice. Most were snobs of the first water.

I loved the guy who told me to give the queen his best the next time I saw her. Somehow, I doubt Elizabeth would know him, or even know of him.

The PGA officials told me that even though I wasn't a pro or even considering turning pro, I had raised the profile of the game. Their TV ratings for last week went through the roof as compared to previous tournaments.

The TV people were even talking about helping to raise the tournament's prize money and their payout if the rating stayed at this level.

They did ask me if I would be kind enough to be interviewed by Jim McKay. I agreed. McKay had always come across as level-headed to me.

The first question was, "Rick, may I call you Rick, or should it be Your Grace?"

"We are in America, so let's go with Rick."

"Rick, what made you take up golf?"

"When I was going into high school, I wanted to play a sport. I went out for football. During tryouts, I proved to be too slow of a runner for any position. Coach Crowley was very upfront with me and told me that I could make the team but would never get any playing time.

"He didn't send me away, but he told me that there were other sports. I could run track cross country as I did have good endurance, or I could try something like golf.

"I had never touched a golf club but thought it might be worth a shot. It turns out I'm a human lever, and my height gives me an advantage. I also have a lot of upper body strength which I work to keep. Those made my first attempts successful. We won't talk about my first putts.

"My golf coach, Mr. Stone, always encouraged me to take my game as far as it could go. This week is the culmination of this journey. I owe both of those men a lot."

"Win or lose this week, you have made a mark in the game. Where do you go from here?"

"I will continue to play golf for fun. I have no intentions of turning pro."

"I have heard you say that you couldn't take the cut in pay. How true is that?"

"Last week Mr. Arnold Palmer won 3360 dollars at the British Open. My business income was more than one million dollars. I must pay attention to my business interests. On top of that, I have had Hong Kong dropped on me. The British and Chinese both are holding me responsible for improving the lives of the citizens and preparing the colony for its handover in 1997."

"You are what, eighteen years old?"

"I will be nineteen in October."

"It is incredible that you have accomplished what you have at such a young age."

"I wonder myself. It has been a lot of hard work, and a huge amount of luck, time, and place."

"Maybe not as much luck as you imply. Your fortune has come from your inventions, which has nothing to do with luck."

"It was luck that my Mum made me work my way across the Atlantic as a deckhand. That is where I got the cargo container idea. Shift enough of them, and you will invent something to make it easier."

"What sort of mother makes her son work his way across the ocean on a freighter? I understand the rest of the family flew first class."

"The sort of who wants her children prepared for the real world."

"We know that your sister Mary has her clothing collection and charities she supports. Your brother Denny has franchised a chain of photography studios. What about Eddie?"

"Eddie is concentrating on Eagle Scout now. His turn will come."

"Speaking of your mother, she has quite a mysterious past. Parts of Countess Jackson's career are well known. But several years during the war are blacked out."

"When you find out about those years, please let me know."

"I see our time is up. Thank you, and I wish you the best for this week."

"Thank you, Jim, and no, you do not have to kiss my ring."

It is a good thing his mike was turned off as he invited me to kiss a nether part of him.

We shook hands, and he thanked me for the interview. If all reporters were like him, I would do more press conferences.

The PGA people were happy with my interview. They thought it was a good start to the viewing week.

John Jacobs had been waiting patiently for me to finish up so we could get on with the real work of the week. All play had been suspended until after the tournament, so we were able to walk the course.

It was an eye-opener. Looking at maps of a course was one thing, seeing it from ground level was another. The trick to this course, like almost any other, was not to look for the obstacles where your ball might end up but to look for where the ball should go.

Those traps, hills, and tall grass in the rough were all distractors that wouldn't come into play if you hit the ball where the course architect designed it to land.

Chapter 8

On Monday, we played our first practice round. Instead of being put in a group of amateurs who wouldn't make the cut, it was Player, Palmer, and me.

They were all business, polite as all get out, but they were here to win, not make friends.

After a good drive on the first hole, I came up short on the two-tier green and took a bogey.

I parred the next three holes and got a bird on Comanche, the sixth hole. I was beginning to think this course wasn't so bad after all. That was reinforced by a birdie on the seventh hole, called Shawnee.

Coming up to number eight, Sitting Bull, a long par 3, I could taste another bird. Instead, I ended up on the wrong side of the mound in the middle of the green and took a double bogey.

Nine was a par, then came 10 with another bogey. My game was falling apart.

On 11, named Kiowa, my approach shot was short, and it rolled back off the green for another bogey.

I managed to settle down and collect pars on each hole up to 18, named aptly enough Aronimink. I did well until the green. My approach shot left me with a challenge which I failed. I took another bogey.

Playing like this would not win the tournament.

While everyone else in the Jackson family was out on social visits, I sat in my room. I had to get my act together if I didn't want to disgrace myself.

Tuesday it sprinkled rain on and off, not enough to stop play, but enough to make the greens unreliable. I managed to get around with a 72 on the par 70 golf course.

At dinner, I heard about everyone's previous evening. Mum and Dad had attended a party given by the governor. Denny had been invited to a teen party at a member's house. Eddie attended a local Scout function with the son of another member.

Even Mary had her evening out. She was asked to be a judge at a local beauty pageant for preteens. She was pleased because the first and second-place winners were wearing outfits from Mary's Princess Collection, but the other judges' opinions outweighed hers, so she thought it was a fair contest.

Mary was a surprise judge, so no one could say the girls wore her dresses to influence the judge.

Wednesday was bright and sunny with a dried-out course. I had gotten my act together and was hitting the ball consistently where I wanted it. I posted a 67 for the day. If I could do those four days in a row, I would be in good shape.

On Thursday there were some clouds but no threat of rain. I had moved up significantly in the eyes of the tournament directors. I was in the third from the last group to tee off. I was used to an early tee time in my other matches.

I started with a par on Hole 1, Apache. I kept to the right on the fairway. Normally I would have used a 9-iron to get on the green. This time I up-clubbed to an 8 to ensure that I ended up on the higher tier.

After that I went on a tear, obtaining birdies on Pueblo, Navajo, Seminole, Mohawk, and Comanche to be 5-under.

I pushed the ball on Shawnee and felt lucky to walk away with a par.

The eighth hole, Sitting Bull, a long par 3 did me in. I landed on the wrong side of a large mound bisecting the green. I ended up with a bogey. Now I was 4-under.

Nine, Kickapoo, which made me think of Lil' Abner, was an easy par.

Then there was the tenth hole, Cherokee. It was trouble with a capital T, as the song goes. I put the ball in the water. This gave me a double bogey. Now I was 2-under.

Eleven through 15 were pars. I got a bird on 16 to move to 3-under. Then I parred out for the rest of the holes to end the day at 3-under.

John Barnum at 4-under led the day. I was second at 3-under, with George Bayer in third with 2-under. None of the big names were in the first ten places.

Round two was better for me, much better. I had five birdies, one bogey, and the rest pars to lead the pack at 7-under and a score of 133. Doug Ford was right behind me at 134.

Round three on Saturday was a different kettle of fish. Gary Player came alive making par for the round. This gave him a 208. I hit a rough patch by having multiple bogeys. This brought me in at 208. Gary and I were tied going into the final round on Sunday.

Saturday night was another quiet night for me. After a catered meal, the family was out and about again. At least they were out and not having a party at the house. They did seem to remember why we were here.

Sunday morning, I was up and got my run in followed by my exercises. I found it best if I kept to my routine every day. After getting cleaned up, I dressed in the clothes Harold had laid out.

The pants were a light grey flannel. A white shirt and tie went with a dark grey sweater. It was a very conservative look. Later I was to learn it was remarkably like what the great Bobby Jones wore.

After breakfast, John and I headed out to the course. There I loosened up. No one talked to me. This was bothersome at first. Not that I wanted to talk but people usually insisted on it. Wanting money or just being able to say they had a conversation.

It dawned on me that I was like a pitcher who had a no-hitter going. No one wanted to jinx it.

Gary Player and I were the last two of the day to tee off. Our gallery was huge. The people were there to see history in the making if I won; they would also see history if I lost.

It was a quiet respectful crowd, not like what they did to Jack Nicklaus in Pennsylvania.

As we went to the tee box, the South African commented that this was the largest group that had ever followed him. I agreed that I had seen nothing like it before. After that, we both ignored our followers.

We both had good drives, keeping to the right on the first hole. I outdrove him by ten yards. It didn't matter as we both ended up on the higher tier on our second shot. We were both over twenty feet from the pin, so settled for pars.

Pueblo, the next hole, was a dogleg left, and we both parred.

On the third hole, Navajo, Gary faded the ball correctly, and it ended up rolling off the mound to end up near the pin. I was left short. Gary parred and I had a bogey.

We both parred the next hole, so I was still one down.

I caught back up on the fifth hole by landing in the middle of the green and putting it in for a birdie. Mr. Player was not in the middle and had to settle for a par.

You could tell the pressure was building on both of us as we went for it on Comanche, the sixth hole, and both had birdies. We were still tied at one under.

The next hole, Shawnee, a dogleg left us both at par.

On number 8, we both used 1-irons. All the other holes were named after tribes. This one differed as it was called Sitting Bull. No one knew why. The 1-iron is perhaps the hardest club to use. For me anyway. Gary ended up exactly where he wanted to be for an easy par.

I ended up exactly where I didn't want to be. I was in the little strip of the fairway that separated the eighth and tenth greens. I had to do a pitch and run to save a bogey. Gary Player was now at par, and I was 1-over.

We both had pars on the ninth hole, a par 5.

The next hole was the toughest on the course. Gary made it look easy as he placed his shots precisely. He had a textbook par. I had to scramble for an ugly bogey. I was now 2-over-par and in a bit of trouble.

The golf gods smiled on me, or they frowned on Gary. He bogeyed on 11 while I birdied. That put me in a little better position.

We weren't the only players on the course. Neither of us was the leader. Mr. Player and I exchanged looks and without a word, we got serious about our golf. Not that we weren't serious before, but now there was an urgency in both our plays.

Despite that urgency, we both parred the twelfth hole.

I had a birdie on 13 to tie with Gary.

Gary used a 3-iron on Iroquois, while I hit a 3-wood on this long par 3. My choice was better as it left me an easy putt for a birdie while he 2-putted for par. I was now even for the day, and he was one over.

Lenape, a par 4, is the longest par 4 on the course. My longer drives paid off as I hit a boomer out to 330 yards after its roll. Gary's was a respectable 305 yards, but it would take him two shots to get on.

Knowing this and the fact I was not the leader, I went for it. Using a 3-wood, I hit 185 yards to land almost next to the pin. It was an easy tap-in for a bird. Now I was 1-under and the new leader. Gary Player made a bird and was even for the day.

We both had birds on 16 so I was now 2-under, and he was 1-under.

On hole 17, Seneca, we both parred.

There was no drama on the last hole, Number 18 was named appropriately, Aronimink. We both parred the hole. This left me at

2-under and Gary at 1-under. I had won the Grand Slam of golf as an amateur and Gary Player had won 13,000 dollars.

Chapter 9

There was a great commotion. I saw the replay of the last hole on TV later. I couldn't believe my reaction, or I should say lack of reaction. After making the final putt, I calmly handed my putting iron to John and walked off the course like it was any other round of golf.

After carefully filling out my scorecard and triple-checking it before I signed it along with a countersignature from Gary Player. I signed his in return after checking it. I then emerged to the waiting pandemonium.

There was the PGA committee to whom I handed my card. It only took them a few minutes to confirm I had filled it out correctly. I was officially declared the winner.

I was given a replica of the Wanamaker Trophy. Gary Player was given the actual trophy for one year, and a replica to keep for life.

It was a little weird that I, the winner, didn't get the big trophy, but the tournament was really for professional golfers. The only way I was able to get in was by winning a major. Since I won three majors this year, they were almost forced to let me play.

It was just as well I didn't get the trophy; Mary might hock it for the money. Maybe not hock it, but she could stain it by serving tea in it.

After the official presentation, I had to do interviews. Jim MacKay was first up. He had a surprise for me. His network had flown in Coach Crowley and Coach Stone.

We had a brief reunion. You could boil the interview down to one phrase, "Who would have thought?"

I asked them how the athletic programs were doing at BHS. It was strange to think I would have just graduated last June. All was fine with the school. Golf was now an immensely popular sport at the high school and even at the junior high level.

I was asked if I would give a talk if I was ever in the area. I said I would, but the chances were slim.

Coach Crowley presented me with a BHS football autographed by the players from the class of 1962. Written on it was thanks for not playing football and best of luck in golf. Smartasses.

Coach Stone had brought a new box of golf balls and asked me to autograph them, he would hand them out to the golf team and any supporters who deserved one. I thought it was over the top but signed them.

After that, it was the reporter wolfpack. Now that I had a Grand Slam and proved myself to be the best golfer in the world, what were my plans?

"I need to fly to China and check on port construction, followed by a trip to Vietnam for the same reason. After that to Australia to buy a station, then to England to rob some dogs for the queen."

The last had them talking to each other. I used the slight silence to thank them and ducked out.

Back at the rental house confusion reigned, and a celebration had started. There was a slew of telegrams from world leaders.

I loved the one from North Korea, their leader for life told me if I came there, he would beat my ass in golf. I didn't doubt it. He would win even if he had to have my legs cut off. I think I will pass on that match.

People who none of us knew were coming in the door. Dad finally let out one of his piercing whistles, which I had never been able to do. It got everyone's attention.

"Everyone out right now. I've called the cops."

That worked. The only people left were our group and a young couple. Dad asked them why they stayed. They explained they were the Bacons, and it was their house which they had rented to us.

They were staying with friends across the street and were scared to death that the house would be destroyed. They had come over to see what was happening.

Now they knew it was under control, they would go back across the street. Their baby Kevin needed his parents.

There were all sorts of phone calls and more telegrams. I was asked to do the complete round of TV shows but didn't accept any of them. I needed some quiet time to decompress and remind myself that I wasn't the best golfer in the world.

The best golfer was one of those professionals who would do this day in and day out for years. I truly was an amateur.

The next morning, we took separate limos to the airport. We had a hard time getting out of the neighborhood. The police had blocked off access to the street we were on, but there was a line of TV trucks and reporters from all over the world waiting for us.

There had been one telephone call I couldn't ignore. JFK wanted me to stop by the White House.

I took a limo down to DC. My 707 would be flown to Baltimore to pick me up for my trip to LA. The ride down took the better part of three hours. This gave me plenty of time to worry about my future.

My immediate future was in DC. I was certain the Kennedys just wanted to congratulate me in person and have a photo op.

My concern was what I was getting into on the world stage. So far, I had been acting on impulse and had been lucky. As much as I hated to admit it, John Kennedy had been correct when he said I wasn't devious, but the Chinese were.

This could be true of every world leader and their staff that I dealt with. Each leader owed their allegiance to their country and should try to get the best for the country. If Rick Jackson got caught in the middle, oh well.

This included those I trusted the most. Namely Queen Elizabeth. Now Empress Ping was on the list of those that I trusted but had a country to take care of. I knew the empress could be ruthless.

Then there were those that I owed my best. My family of course, but also the Jackson Enterprise employees.

Now I was the Duke of Hong Kong. I had been told to take care of those people. Did I owe it to them?

Through my businesses, I was helping England, China, Germany, and the United States. What if it became a choice of my business or a friendly country? Should I go with my feelings or the cold calculations of accounting? What if there is no happy medium?

I had recently played hardball with the Kennedys, and it came out okay. Did I have it in me to do this regularly? Would I lose my soul in the process?

Faking it in the movies is one thing, real life another. Thinking of my recent school days, they were a permanent holiday compared to what I was now facing.

On reaching the White House, I found that I was half right. There were congratulations and a photo op. There was also a more serious discussion.

JFK started with, "Rick, you have proved adept at dealing with world leaders. For someone your age, amazingly so. I would like you to continue what you are doing but with a limited ambassador's portfolio.

"Your primary mission would be to gather information."

"What sort of information?"

Thoughts of James Bond went through my head. When it had been a daydream or movie part it sounded fun. This was scary.

"In your conversation with leaders, you will be told what they want, not only from you but the United States. I would like you to report what you are told directly to me. Then the State Department can match that information up with what we are trying to achieve and come up with a win-win situation.

"When we try to gather this information through formal channels there are so many filters that the message doesn't always get through."

"I can see that. If it does not break a confidence, I will do that. But I can see conflicts arising if I'm given information that would benefit the US or England, but not both.

"If I get a reputation as being a tool for others, I will not be able to see to my business interests. I have to decline your request Mr. President, but I will freely pass on any information which is not in conflict with my goals or it is something that could harm America."

The president was gracious, but I could tell I hadn't won any points today. This was exactly the sort of thing I was worried about on the trip down. Was I up to this?

It was a funny flight from Baltimore to LA. Everyone was up about my golf win. Suddenly, the Grand Slam looked like a childish game. I was playing with the possible fates of millions of people. I sat in my office with the door closed and brooded while John and the flight crew whooped it up.

Chapter 10

By the time we landed in Los Angeles, I had made several decisions. First, if I was going to do a lot of business in China, I had to learn to speak Mandarin. It was the most widely used.

I had to spend serious time in Asia and the various countries I had committed to help. On top of that, I needed to pay more attention to my business operations on a routine basis.

It wasn't that I didn't have good people taking care of things. It might be that they were too good and insulated me from the problems that came up.

Not the minor stuff, but I thought some large issues had been handled without my knowledge or input. Not that I would have been able to help, but I would have been able to learn.

When I got home, the first thing I did was to call Jim Williamson and ask him to consider how to set up a daily brief for me of large issues that faced the company and what was being done.

He told me that he already had that in place for himself and all the other company-level managers to keep them apprised of the business in general.

I told him that I wanted to be included in the distribution as part of my business education. They were doing a great job of running the company, and I would be a fool to think I could do better at this stage of my life.

He replied that I might surprise myself, but in general, he agreed. The truth of the matter was that things had grown so quickly that every member of the management team was stretched in their growth.

I asked him if he knew of any Chinese immersion courses in the area. I shouldn't have been surprised when I found out that our company already had a contract with one for our engineers going to China and other points in the Orient.

There also was a group that taught our engineers Spanish. That I didn't need. There weren't any schools that taught Russian. I asked him to have a look around for one. It also was on my list. That and German.

From wondering how I would spend my time, now I didn't have enough.

Dr. Deming's trip to Hong Kong had been set up for five weeks from now, and I had agreed to go, so I had time to spend one month in the immersion course. There was a side benefit to taking the course. I would disappear from the public eye for a month. That would allow time for my current notoriety to settle down.

I did take the time to drive over to the Forestry Service station, sorry George, to thank Sam for all his good work.

He told me he was happy that I had won and that I was paying to keep the practice range up for the Forestry Service. He and the head ranger were talking about setting up a nine-hole course with the goal of having eighteen in the future. Some hardship post this would be!

That evening Nina and I went out to dinner at the Brown Derby. We both knew the result would be our pictures in the tabloids with lurid headlines. So be it.

We had a nice time talking together. Things had changed between us. There was no groping in the backseat at a drive-in now, and we were more serious about getting to know each other.

We were both afraid of each other. Before, we had a natural acceptance of each other. Now we examined our thoughts and actions. It was a slower but truer learning experience. Who was this person and how did we relate became the unspoken question behind almost every comment. The more I learned about Nina, the more I liked her.

I'm not going to use the love word because I'm not certain what that is, but I knew I liked her, and she was my best friend in the world. Did I mention that she is very good-looking in every sense of the term?

The next week the tabloids had their field day. The most common theme was, "Reunited, pregnant?" We both had many phone calls and were badgered in public to deny or confirm the stories. We both knew better than to say anything but, "No comment," and not even that if possible.

If there were witnesses available it was no comment, in private nothing.

Jim Williamson got back to me; a slot had opened in the Chinese immersion course. I grabbed it and started immediately. It would get me out of the public eye for a month.

I imagined that I would go to this office building and be immersed in the language eight hours a day and then go home.

In reality, I was told to pack a week's change of clothes, as laundry would be done on-site. When I went for registration, it was at a hotel that was one step up from a fleabag. I was told it was a typical Beijing hotel, very upscale compared to those out in the country.

Instead of going home every day, I would be living here for the month. When they said immersion, they weren't kidding. It started at check-in.

The verbal questions were in Chinese. I could answer in English. That was almost fun as I tried to guess what they were asking. I was glad there was no line because it took over half an hour to give my name and address and to be assigned a room.

The course was intense. The company had paid for me to have one-on-one training. There was a rotating group of instructors that would start on me when I woke up and keep at it until I went to bed.

There was truly little downtime. Meals were the only place where I interacted with other students.

Even there the rule was Chinese only. I had just thought I knew how to use chopsticks. Within a week I could have snatched a fly out of the air if there had been any flies.

My first impression was a dump, but the place was as clean and neat as a pin. Everything was old and worn but clean.

I continued to hate the hole-in-the-ground toilets and vowed to fill the hold of my 707 with rolls of American paper.

After two weeks I realized that I had dreamed in Chinese and was thinking in Mandarin during the day. We talked, we watched movies, and we played games. They had their act together. When I began to look stressed with an exercise, they changed what we were doing.

It was working. One characteristic that I had that few others had was that I could change my accents at will. I could go from speaking Chinese as a native of Beijing, to that of an American, then a Brit from Mayfair to a Spaniard from Madrid.

My instructors would get a pained look when I switched on them. This was the only small revenge I could get. It was funny when one of them would try the accent change. They all sounded over-the-top fake.

One takes one's victories where one can, large or small. From being hailed as the world's greatest golfer to pestering language instructors within a month was extreme even for me.

Each morning, I could go through my exercise routine and take a run. Of course, I was accompanied by an instructor who would talk all the way. The run was always the same guy. He was the only one who could keep up with me and talk at the same time.

One thing that worked in my favor was that Chinese Mandarin was a tonal language; the way a word was pronounced could change its meaning. My facility with accents was a saving grace.

They had a list of three thousand characters which I had to learn. In the time I had, I managed almost fifteen hundred. I was told it would take the three thousand to be able to read a daily newspaper. To come across as educated I needed eight thousand.

By living on-site and working sixteen hours a day, I had almost five hundred hours of instruction. The US State Department considered Mandarin a category five language, the hardest to learn. They calculated that it takes eighty-eight weeks or twenty-two hundred hours to become proficient.

I would like to say I was a wonder kid; I wasn't. What I was, was a doggedly determined student. Just like my school days, I spent my time working.

Since I had one-on-one instruction, it was at my learning pace, not that of the slowest student in the classroom. When I served my thirty days and was released, I was told that I was rated at ILR Level 2 with limited working proficiency. I could get through a normal day without causing an international incident.

With another thirty days, I would reach ILR Level 3 professional working proficiency as rated by the US government. I don't know if that was a sales pitch to spend another thirty days, but if so, it didn't work.

I was so glad to get out of there. I had my driver stop at a Carl's on the drive home. I was dying for a greasy cheeseburger and fries.

Chapter 11

It was mid-August when I got home, and it was time to fly to Hong Kong. Dr. Deming had already flown over and was touring some manufacturing plants to find out what the state of art is in Hong Kong.

I got a call from the company that was providing my flight crew. One of the hostesses was getting married and was giving up the flying business. Because of my problem with the one who climbed into my bed, they wanted to know if I wanted to interview her replacement.

While they were telling me this, I had a bright idea.

"I'm putting another requirement on the job description. This stewardess also needs to be a native Mandarin speaker. And yes, I would like to interview the person."

"Why do you want a person who speaks Chinese?"

I explained that I was learning to speak Mandarin and thought that having someone to work with on those long flights would be a bonus.

They found a lady in LA who fit the bill. She was about fifteen years older than me. She had just finished a degree in pharmaceutical medicine. Like all graduate students, she was dead broke. She was looking for any job until she could find one in her native China.

Tu Youyou was a delight to talk to. Mostly because she didn't make fun of my limited vocabulary. She was the only one of the three candidates sent that suggested I always have the latest Chinese newspapers on board.

That way I could work on my reading vocabulary, and then we could talk about the content of the stories so I could learn about the realities of Chinese life.

Her one weakness was she knew absolutely nothing about being a stewardess. I called Hastings Aviation and told them to go ahead and hire another hostess. I was hiring Tu as my interpreter to accompany me on my trips.

She happily agreed to the job offer. It seems she has a boyfriend in China, an old school classmate that she hadn't seen in a long time.

Halfway through the flight to Hong Kong, I began to wonder if I had made a mistake. The lady was merciless. She drilled and questioned me in Chinese on everything.

I had to read the Chinese newspapers she had brought on board from cover to cover. She would question me hard on the political and financial sections. The depth of her questions made me think she had grown up in that world. The political world had changed; the empress was now in charge.

When you got down to how the country was run, there were few changes. It was very much top-down. Just a different person at the top.

I did find out that being born in the year 1943 made me a Sheep. My lucky numbers are 1 and 7. My mantra is "I am complete all on my own".

I had never won anything with those numbers, and I know darn well I'm not complete on my own. I need others to be a success. Heck, I wasn't even that wild about eating grass. So much for Chinese astrology.

Tu told me it was okay not to believe but be careful about sharing that. Many Chinese took it seriously and would be offended.

She was very curious about the new empress and had many questions about her, which I couldn't answer. That gave me food for thought. What were the empress's real plans for China, and where did I fit in?

Right now, I looked like a court favorite, but like any other royal court, one could fall from grace quickly.

Our deplaning in Hong Kong was different than any I had experienced before. You would have thought I was royalty from the reception I was given.

There were a red carpet and all the Hong Kong high officials waiting for me. This included the governor. I rode in his limousine on the way to the Peninsula Hotel.

I asked him why all the hoopla.

"Your Grace, may I call you Richard?"

"Rick would be better."

"Thank you, Rick. The British population isn't that impressed. It is the Chinese here who love and respect you. I have to put on this show, or I will lose their support."

"Why do they love me?"

"It is well known that you are Empress Ping's and China's benefactor. You have created a stir in the sporting world, and even though golf isn't well known in China, it has gotten their attention. Young men now carry a golf club instead of a cane. You will see thousands of t-shirts with your picture on them."

"Your movies are being shown in China for the first time. Newsreels of your bull riding are shown in every theater. You are the man of the moment here and on the mainland."

"I hope this doesn't cause me a problem with the empress."

"It won't at least right now. If your popularity continues to rise and she thinks you are a threat to her throne, all bets are off."

Talk about cold water being thrown in your face! Me a threat to the Chinese throne. Being thrown into a water trough suddenly sounded better.

I changed the subject.

"I am thinking of buying a suite at the Peninsula Hotel. What do you think of that?"

"Don't. Security would become a problem for you and the hotel. Buy a compound at Clearwater Bay. It is a beautiful area, not fully developed yet, but close to the Clearwater Country Club, which would be delighted to have you as a member. It is only a half-hour drive to the city."

"I will have someone start to look for a place."

"I have taken the liberty of having a shortlist of compounds for you to look at."

"Exactly what are you talking about when you say compound?"

"In Hong Kong, a compound is a walled-in area with a gatehouse, and with a large mansion as the main living quarters and outbuildings for the staff and extras such as a stable."

"Oh, very much like Jackson House in California."

"Yes, I have seen pictures of Jackson House in the newspaper."

"In the newspaper?"

"Right now, the public wants to know everything that they can about you. The only thing that hasn't impressed them is your singing."

"A discerning public then."

"No, a total lack of appreciation and understanding of Western music. I find your songs delightful."

Who knew? Time to change the subject.

"What do you think of Dr. Deming?"

"The man is brilliant. He gave a short talk and demonstration of his ideas. I think he will be a great help to us."

I was due to meet him in three days. This would give me time to recover from the time change.

At the hotel, I was hustled through the lobby, which was lined with Hong Kong police to hold the crowd back. One thing the governor was right about was seeing people wearing a t-shirt with my picture on it, labeled the Duke of Hong Kong.

That was only plain weird.

Tu and Harold were riding in the car behind us, so my clothes and interpreter were at hand. At Tu's suggestion, I wasn't to let people know that I had a rudimentary understanding of Mandarin. It would be better if the first words out were fluent. It would give me great face.

Plus, if I made errors, I could lose face. I still wasn't comfortable with the concept of face but had to play the game.

The next morning a car from the embassy took Harold, Tu, and me around the island to look at the compounds they thought would be appropriate.

The one I chose, and the others agreed with me, was the hands-down choice. It was on top of the tallest hill overlooking Clearwater Bay. It looked down on the country club.

It consisted of fifty acres with a seven-acre compound in its center. The main compound had a ten-foot wall with the main gate at the front and a back gate letting out to a backroad down the mountain.

The main house was a forty-room mansion with ten-bedroom suites, plus another ten bedrooms. All had baths included.

It had a familiar feel to it. It reminded me of Jackson House. I asked about the history of the house.

It was built in the 1920s by an American railroad heir by the name of Jason Talmadge.

I didn't let on, but I decided to buy the place then and there. Who knew what secrets it could hide?

The last owner, a rich Chinese, had the facilities updated and the whole place painted, and then promptly lost his fortune on the gambling tables of Macau.

After the tour, I asked how much the asking price was. It was four hundred thousand dollars. I thought that was a bargain, but the aide apologized. He knew the bank had that much in it, but they would be glad to break even.

I told him I would like to make an offer.

Instead of going directly to the hotel, we stopped at the bank which owned the mansion. I offered their asking price which made the deal easy.

That is how Jackson House Hong Kong came into my possession. I called Mum and Dad later and asked Mum if she would like to oversee the furnishing of my new house.

She suggested that I needed a local person for that job and that I was to explore that place very carefully.

Chapter 12

While I was anxious to explore the new house, I had other duties that came first.

In town, I met with Dr. Deming.

"Doctor Deming, how was your visit to the various plants? Can you help them?"

"Not by myself. They lack profound knowledge and resources."

"What knowledge, and how can it be provided?"

"They do not have any understanding of statistical principles, so they cannot tell the difference between a process that needs to be repaired or adjusted and one that can only do better by being improved."

"Can you impart that knowledge?"

"To only a few; there are too many for me to instruct."

"Are there any additional instructors available?"

"I don't know any who know statistics and can teach it in Mandarin. They would have to be bilingual so that I could talk with them."

"I will see if there are any students in China at one of their universities who meet these criteria."

"That would work if they have enough. I would like to have fifteen or twenty of them."

"I will see what I can do. Now you mentioned resources. What do they need?'

"They need to modernize their machines; I even saw one factory that was belt-driven with no safety guards on the belts. I couldn't get out of there fast enough."

"I bet. I could set up a series of long-term low-interest loans at the Bank of Hong Kong. I would guarantee them so the bank should be willing. Do you think fifty million dollars would do it?"

"I have a hard time wrapping my mind around the fact that you have this wealth at your disposal. Fifty million in guarantees could result in half a billion in loans. That would be more than enough.

"Rick, if I were you, I would negotiate with the bank about a share of the total interest rate. You stated you would stand behind any losses; you should share in the overall profit from all the loans."

"I like that thought. I will tell my people to work on that. If you'll excuse me, I will make a phone call to Beijing to see what I can do about student instructors."

"Go right ahead. I need to call a friend, Joe Juran, about an idea I have just had."

We both made our calls and set things in motion. It turns out there are some reputable Chinese schools that might be able to help us.

Zhejiang University, Beijing University, Shanxi University, Nanjing University, Fudan University, Tongji University, and Tsinghua University all had possible candidates.

Empress Ping's education advisor would canvas them and have likely candidates from Beijing for Dr. Deming to interview. The advisor was interested in what we were doing and would consider Hong Kong as a test case for doing the same in China.

When I met back with the good doctor, he had some news of his own.

"There is a group in America, the American Society for Quality Control. They have been trying to develop a course to certify Quality Engineers. Due to infighting among some of their officers who are consultants as to which one of them will get to run the program, nothing has happened."

Deming continued, "Joe has access to their body of knowledge and textbooks. We could use it as the foundation of my course and institute a program of certified trainers. As the concept grows, we could add trainers at need."

I built on that thought.

"If it works, I bet that some of the universities would include it in their curriculum."

He replied. "Whichever country does that will lead the world economically."

"Now I will call my new headquarters in Beijing and have them start the negotiations with the Bank of Hong Kong. Can I impose on you to write this up to present to the governor?"

"I will be glad to. Tell me, why didn't you call any American Universities? They have many Chinese students attending."

"Politics. The Kennedys would not appreciate me upgrading a competitor's capabilities."

"Doesn't it bother you to help another country?"

"If it were us or them, yes it would. As I see it, I'm helping people. What about you?"

"Much simpler. American companies haven't woken up to those things that are changing. I have to earn a living, so I follow the money."

"Don't we all?"

From there I went on to my next appointment. It was why I asked Dr. Deming to write the report. I had to check out the Clearwater Bay golf course.

I live a hard life.

The golf course was nice, nothing compared to the tournament courses I had just played, but a nice course to relax on.

I had my tee time reserved under another name, Ed Bowsher. This was to avoid a lot of commotion.

That lasted until I walked into the pro shop. At 6 foot five inches and having your face on lord knows how many t-shirts, I never had a chance.

What got me was the other three players in my foursome immediately put their places up for bid.

This didn't sit well with me, so I told the pro I would come back some other time. There were screams of outrage. Not from the original players in the foursome. They had their money and left.

Now I was in an ethical quandary.

I decided I would play but told the others there would be no pictures of us together. I had not been asked if I would do this, and they had lost face by trying to buy time with me.

The fact that I told them this in Mandarin took them aback. Two of them bowed picked up their bags and left. I returned their bows with respect.

The other defiantly teed up a golf ball without even tossing a tee to see who would go first. He hit a straight long ball. I hit one farther, much farther. I made it to the apron of the first hole.

From there on I was on a holy tear. The course record was 64. I carded a 62. My course-provided caddie had given me good advice on every hole.

The other player and I never exchanged a word. In the end, when he signed his card and handed it to me to sign, I tore mine up and walked away. I know I was acting like a jerk, but his arrogance in thinking he could buy his way with me left me angry.

My caddie chased me down and asked why I hadn't turned in my card with a new course record. I asked him why; and then said, besides, I can come back and do it again tomorrow. Now, who is arrogant?

From a good start on the day to a bad finish, at least a stressful finish, was more than I wanted. I was driving my Bentley so was able to go where I wanted. I ended up having dinner at a little fishing shack-type restaurant down on the docks.

I know I was recognized but no one approached me. What a refreshing change. This being public always was tiring.

The next day I had a meeting with the Hong Kong governor. He had talked to Dr. Deming about the report and liked what was proposed. He went even further and told me that if a business were successful, the government would pay off their loan after five years.

This would cut into my potential profits but would benefit the businesses, so I had no complaint.

The North Vietnamese had sent an emissary to Hong Kong to talk to me. There was no advance notice. He walked up to the front door of Government House and asked for me.

This happened while I was with the governor, so I was told that the emissary was asking for me. The governor and I exchanged puzzled looks. Things were just not done this way!

The governor excused himself from his own office so the emissary and I could talk privately.

"Your Grace, thank you for seeing me. I know this is not normal, but we didn't want anyone to know of this meeting. I have come directly from our leaders in Hanoi. Nothing is in writing or has been talked about on radio or telephone."

"We do not want the Soviets to know of this conversation. They want us to go to war with the South in an attempt to bring the United States into the fray. This would leave China in a bad position as they would have to support the North, leading to problems with the US.

"We were prepared to do this, but events have overtaken us. China has changed their type of government and you have brought South Vietnam together and are turning their army into a real army.

"We could not win such a conflict even with direct Soviet support, which they would not give. Since we will not attack the South, the Soviets have cut off our aid. As such we cannot repay you for the modernization of our port. Is there any way you can help us?"

"There is, but there will be a price."

Chapter 13

The emissary asked, "What will that price be?"

"I need to talk to several people to make sure it is a reasonable price. I am planning on going to South Vietnam next week. If it is all right, I will stop in Hanoi and talk to your leaders."

"It must be soon as the Soviets are pressuring us."

"It will be and tell your leaders we will come to a deal to keep the port operations going. I just don't know what that deal is yet. I will charter a plane for the trip and not even tell the pilots we are stopping in Hanoi until we are almost there. Please make certain your air force doesn't shoot us down."

"There is little danger of that; our air force is a disaster. However, our missile defenses are strong."

The emissary left and the governor asked if I could share what that was all about. I told him.

"What is the price you will be asking?"

"I have absolutely no idea. I will be asking the empress, the queen, and the US president for their thoughts."

"The sooner you ask the better because they will have to run it by their advisors. You really should be asking the prime minister rather than the queen."

"Yes, I should, shouldn't I."

I left it at that.

I was loaned an office in a secure area of the building to make my phone calls. I made them in the order I had given the governor. I told the empress's chief of staff my question and who else I would be asking. Next were two other calls of a similar nature.

The next day I had my answers. Amazingly, they were all the same, normalized relations between North and South Vietnam. Have them open to trade with each other. It was thought if they did that, the Vietnams would eventually reunite and lessen the chances of war in Indochina.

I also made a phone call to the pro shop at the Clearwater Bay Golf Club. I spoke to the pro. I asked if he knew the two men who had won the bid to play with me but bowed out when they realized I hadn't agreed to it. He did. They played on the days that the public was allowed in. I asked him to see if they could join me in a round as my guests tomorrow.

He told me he would check with them. I did it for two reasons. One, they had been gentlemen in a bad situation. Two, it was another poke in the eye to that jerk who insisted on playing. Someday I will grow up, but not just yet.

That evening, I called Nina back in the States. She was starting school at Stanford in a week and was extremely excited about it. We must have talked for an hour. We concentrated on the risks of long-distance relationships. We had both seen firsthand some of the dangers. It wasn't going to happen again.

Our biggest concern was that we would grow apart as we traveled in different circles. We had no ready answer, just an awareness of the potential problems.

Next, I called my parents. They were both at home, so I got to speak to both on their speakerphone. I updated them on my international events and what Dr. Deming and I were attempting in Hong Kong.

They thought it was a bold program. Dad asked me what products we were concentrating on. I told him that we hadn't talked about that.

He suggested that we review what they made in Hong Kong compared to what was manufactured in the US. To pay special attention to US products which didn't have the best reputation.

It wasn't late here in Hong Kong, so I spent several hours with Tu discussing the day's events reported in the Chinese newspapers.

She told me she was pleased with my progress. I could now hold a conversation with a Chinese fifth grader. Shot down in flames!

The next day I brought my dad's suggestion up in a telephone conversation with Dr. Deming. He told me the Hong Kongese were discussing that very issue. They felt that consumer items like radios and televisions were a good target. The US market for the new color TVs was huge, and the quality of the current TVs wasn't that great.

They already had a small presence in that market, so they were considering putting huge efforts there. I told him that was way beyond the scope of my knowledge and would trust him and the Hong Kong manufacturers to make wise decisions.

He told me they were also looking at making precision measuring instruments such as vernier calipers. Again, I told him they all knew better than me.

After that, I went to the golf club to play a round of golf with Mr. Wong and Mr. Lee. They were waiting when I got there. We had handshakes and bows all around.

My Mandarin was good enough that we were able to carry on a normal first-tee golf conversation. That is, we made our excuses why we wouldn't do well today.

When I tried, they laughed at me. I guess it was funny.

I shot another 62 to officially break the course record. This time we all signed each other's cards and had pictures taken. I was assured they would appear in the newspaper.

My scorecard was kept by the club pro to be framed and posted at the clubhouse entrance.

I felt good about myself for doing the right thing by those gentlemen. The next morning, I didn't feel so good. The late editions of the newspapers had carried the story and pictures of me with Mr. Wong and Mr. Lee.

The morning edition reported that Mr. Shen, the player I thought arrogant, had committed suicide because he had lost so much face. I was in a different world.

I had a meeting with the governor later that morning. I told him I felt that I had messed up big time. He knew right away what I was talking about.

"No Rick, Mr. Shen messed up big time. He caused his problems and came up with a solution that works in this society. If he hadn't taken his own life, his family would have paid a price for his loss of face. If he had children, they would have been ridiculed in school. His wife's friends would no longer call.

"If he owned a business, his customers would have gone elsewhere. If he worked for someone, they would fire him; he would not be able to find a job.

"To us Westerners it is horrible. To the Chinese, it is taking personal responsibility for his mistakes. If he had stepped back like the other two, there would have been no problems, but he didn't. Then he compounded his error by asking you to sign his card.

"The Chinese view your actions as proper, both in your treatment of him and the other two."

"What about Shen's family?"

"I don't know his family situation, but any family left will now be socially acceptable."

"What about their financial situation?"

"That, my friend, is not your problem, and you should stay out of it."

I didn't say anything, but I couldn't let it go. I called my Beijing headquarters and asked that Mr. Shen's surviving family be investigated. If there were any financial issues, I wanted them resolved discreetly as possible. If there was a Mrs. Shen who needed a job, they were to find her one.

I don't care about the Oriental values in this case; I grew up in Ohio and this wasn't how things were done.

I would never again take the issue of face lightly. I think I had been thinking of cultural differences as a game. It wasn't, and I needed to pay attention.

The next day, I gave instructions to the pilot to land in Hanoi, where we were expected. I reflected that the issue of face probably extended to countries. I couldn't march in and demand that North Vietnam normalize relations with the South. It would be a delicate dance.

I had to lead them to suggest that was the solution, their idea, not mine.

We were intercepted by old Soviet MIGs. The way they burned fuel, I was surprised they could stay in the air. Their contrails were black.

I was met by the same 1930s limo from my first trip, so I knew it hadn't been an insult before. This was the best they had.

Tu Youyou acted as my interpreter because she spoke YueYn, which is like Vietnamese.

We met in the same conference room as before. After several long conversations in which I told them that I had talked to several world powers and that they had suggested that any price be determined by the North Vietnamese leadership.

We spent the next four hours of them making suggestions and me saying that sounded interesting, but not making any positive signs.

Finally, one of their officials mentioned that the South Vietnamese would be easier to deal with than me.

"Why don't you do that? That sounds like the most positive item you have put on the table."

They hadn't put it on the table. The statement was a complaint of how difficult I was being. That didn't matter now that the issue had been opened.

Chapter 14

I would like to say things went fast after that. There was progress at a glacial pace. First, every complaint they ever had against the South had to be reviewed. Seeing how the French had been in charge not that many years ago, you wouldn't think there would be much to talk about.

Wrong, issues hundreds of years old were rehashed. The upshot of this revisitation of the past was that there was no possible way to work with the South.

I told them I understood, and since nothing could be worked out with the South, my hands were tied. No one asked how my hands were tied or who tied them. It was just as well; I was just trying to get them to move from their position.

"Gentlemen you have presented a serious case of why you can't work with the South. Now please present to me the conditions and reasons that you could work with them."

This was a novel idea. They circled this revolutionary thought for a long time. Since they were the People's Revolutionary Party, I mistakenly thought they would welcome new ideas.

It neared dinner time, and we adjourned for dinner. I was asked what time I wanted to meet in the morning.

I acted surprised.

"Aren't we coming back here after dinner?"

You could tell they hadn't planned on it but would lose face if they said no, so we agreed to take up where we left off in an hour.

After dinner, we went back to the room. As they quarreled within their group, I sat back and watched. It became apparent it wasn't that they didn't want to do something, they just didn't have a clue as to how to start.

"I have to go to the South next. Could I request for talks to begin on what trade or business items they might agree on?"

"But where would we meet? Whoever hosts the meeting will be in control."

I was ahead of them on this one.

"We will do it as North and South Korea do, a building or tent set up half in each country. That way each will host themselves."

They thought that was a wonderful idea. They thought this would get them home, but I wasn't done with them yet.

"How many people are in your delegation? What rank will they be? What authority will they have? What hours will they work? Who will speak for you?"

I went on with these questions for several more minutes.

They had a dazed look.

"I need answers so that the South can make similar arrangements. If we don't present a good plan, we will lose face."

This brought them up in their chairs—no face to be lost here!

It was obvious while they were autocratic leaders, they had never faced anything like a Boy Scout Senior Patrol Leaders meeting. There everything had to be nailed down so a viable plan could be presented to the Scoutmaster.

It was necessary to do this, or you could end up out in the woods without a way to start a fire or no toilet paper.

I have seen both events, so I knew it was critical to have a firm plan. I had also noticed their inability to come to a decision all day long. I had a simple remedy. No sleep until there was a plan.

I had been a Senior Patrol Leader for two years with about eighty camping trips involving fifty or more boys and adults each trip.

It was 4 a.m. by the time they had a written plan that was agreed upon. They thought they were done. I held them until I used one of their old typewriters to type the plan up and had each one sign it.

I have been with twelve-year-olds who whined less.

Another thing that became obvious was that they were in a bind, or they would have told me to leave. They couldn't do as the Soviets wanted, so their only other option was me.

As we filed out of the room, the leader turned to me. "You are a right bastard, aren't you? We thought you would be easy."

I shook my head and walked away. If he thought I was tough, wait until he meets Mum.

Wasting no time, I continued my journey to South Vietnam. After being up all night, I slept the whole flight and still was tired when we landed. I was picked up in the same limo as before. Maybe I should gift both countries new cars to pick me up. These things had no springs or shocks to speak of.

At my hotel, the same fine establishment as before, I crawled back into bed. As I drifted off, I thought about gifting hotels to them, but that was a bit much. Maybe I could talk Mr. Hilton into putting up a hotel in Hanoi.

I met Trần Văn Hương for dinner in a private room at the hotel. Tu joined us to make certain I understood anything said in Vietnamese, though he kept it to English the entire conversation.

Things were going well. The nations he had contacted to help rebuild his city police, countryside sheriffs, and national investigation service were working out well.

He was impressed with the training the deputy sheriffs were receiving. It seemed to be based on common sense and not a strict interpretation of the rules. That sounded like George Burrell to me.

The school system was getting up and running and promised to be better than anything the French had provided. One heartening piece of news was that the local farmers were creating co-ops to leverage their buying and selling power.

Corruption was down across the country as those who were involved were removed from office and frequently, their lives. A strong message was being sent.

My construction projects were on time and under budget, so all was well from my point of view. The army that I was funding was becoming a more unified force.

Trân told me that he had reached an arrangement with the Australian government that they would leave their leadership cadre in place indefinitely.

In exchange, they signed a mutual defense pact. This now made Australia a true regional power. This in turn led to increased trade between the two countries.

The talk of trade gave me the opportunity to bring up North Vietnam and their proposal which I had with me. He read it through three times before he commented.

"This is wonderful. Between their mining in the north and our rubber plantations here in the south, we will have a strong diverse economy."

This will encourage other growth in our countries.

I told him that my long-term hope was that the two countries could reunite but didn't see how that was possible currently.

"We could end up just like China. The Vietnamese live in small villages with few large towns. The small villages are not communing. They are run on a capitalistic basis. It is only in the North's large towns that the Communists hold sway.

"When they see everyone's standard of living increase, they will change, or they will have to build a wall like the Berlin Wall."

I asked him if there was anything else I could do for the country.

"Keep a low profile. The more the Vietnamese people see this as their doing, they will increase their efforts. Right now, there is more pride in this country than I have ever known. I would like to keep that going."

"That is fine with me. As you know, I'm doing this to prevent the Soviets from creating a war here that would involve the US. For some reason, I think our current administration would fall into the trap. I know President Eisenhower almost did when he sent advisors here."

"Why the US would want to be in a war in Asia, I have no idea. I'm glad your peacemaking efforts are working. When are you heading back to Hong Kong?"

"Since there is no reason to stay, I will leave tomorrow morning."

"Could you take three extra passengers with you? They are US citizens, and we want to return them to the US Embassy in Hong Kong."

"What is the story?"

"They deny it of course, but they are CIA operatives running a heroin operation out of the Golden Triangle. They are raising black funds for disruptive operations here and in Laos.

"I hope the US Government is embarrassed enough that they abandon the operation."

"I will see how I can help that along. I can't believe that a US agency would be involved in such an operation. A lot of the heroin would end up in the US."

"These people have no morals. To them, any means justify the end."

"Invite the BBC news crew to take pictures of them being handed over to me. I will arrange for news crews in Hong Kong. We will let the world press report this and see what happens."

Chapter 15

The next morning waiting for me at my aircraft was a BBC motion picture crew and three men in handcuffs. Their accompanying guards had me sign for them.

I kept a serious look on my face and did not indicate that I recognized them. The BBC talking head wanted to ask me a question.

"Your Grace, why are you taking these drug dealers to Hong Kong?"

"I was asked to by Mr. Trân. You will have to ask him why this is happening. I am just providing convenient passage."

"Be careful, your Grace, these are desperate men."

"I will. I see they are in chains; they will stay there."

We boarded my six-passenger charter. When they were settled in their seats and the pilot was ready for take-off, I handed the keys to one of the prisoners.

I turned to the oldest-looking of the three.

"Rip Robertson, what in the heck are you doing here?"

"I was sent here to shut down a rogue operation and was betrayed. The real drug dealers got away. These two and I were picked up instead."

I also recognized the other two. I didn't know their names, but they were two of the ones that got burned in the Soviet operation.

"Why are these guys out in the field? I thought they had been burned."

"They have, but the powers that be thought this would be a simple in and out with no false identities needed. Since we have been recorded by BBC, all three of us are done in the field."

That seemed like a good idea to me. Every time I had run into Robertson, it was in a failed operation. I didn't tell them the press would be waiting for them in Hong Kong.

As I thought about it, I decided that it was not a good idea. They had been outed, but it was all on the South Vietnamese who couldn't be blamed for arresting three suspected drug dealers and kicking them out of the country.

It would be different in Hong Kong. I didn't want to be associated with any part of their arrest and deportation. Not that I cared about that, but I didn't want the CIA to be mad at me for exposing their agents. I was the one that suggested the publicity. Trần just wanted them out of his country.

I went forward and asked the pilot if he could arrange a landing in Macau. He told me that they would want a reason for our visit.

"Tell them it is for a little gambling."

Macau loved gamblers; it was their main support.

I returned to the rear of the aircraft and told Robertson my plan. There was a US Consulate in Macau. I would take them there and then they were on their own. Maybe the agency could explain things away.

After landing, I was approached by immigration officials. This was one of the few times I was glad of the Asian propensity to accept bribes. Three Ben Franklins and my diplomatic passport got us into the country with no questions asked.

I then got a cab for the four of us and went to a middle-class hotel. There I left the guys to take showers. On the plane, it was very noticeable that they hadn't had a shower in days.

I wrote their sizes down and went to buy them clothes. I also picked up shaving gear and toothbrushes. These guys were a mess. Their hair was long, but we didn't have time to get them haircuts.

Several hours later they emerged from the hotel looking almost respectable.

Rip had even come up with a pair of sunglasses. It was nighttime, but he had them. Something in the spy psyche, I guess. After seeing what happened to these guys, I figured my James Bond days were over.

I gave Robertson five hundred dollars and dropped them off at the consulate. He assured me they could make their way home from here. The jerk never even said thanks or acknowledged that I had helped them.

As they were walking into the building, one of them did turn and mouthed, "Thanks." I guess they aren't all jerks.

From there I went to the Hotel Lisboa and Casino. I didn't check in, but I let my name and title be known at the front desk. I wanted a record that I was in Macau to gamble. Now, I wasn't old enough to gamble which was simply fine. I got to make a big stink when security wouldn't let me in.

This established beyond a doubt that I had been there to gamble. I took another taxi back to the airport where we proceeded to Hong Kong.

When we landed, I was met by police and reporters.

When the police asked me for my prisoners, I made a deal of looking around.

"What prisoners?"

"We were told to be here as you were escorting three drug dealers out of South Vietnam."

"Oh, those guys, big mistake. They weren't prisoners for drug dealing, they were an embarrassment to the country and South Vietnam just wanted them out. I dropped them off in Macau. I have no idea how they embarrassed the South. I just gave a courtesy ride."

The press wasn't so easy.

"Duke Richard, does this mean you work for the CIA and helped them rescue their men when their operation went bad?"

"First of all, you address me as Your Grace. Only my peers can call me Duke. Second, I do not work for the CIA, never have, and never will. We leave that sort of stuff to my mum."

Sorry Mum, but I must get them off the scent.

They badgered me some more, but I gave them nothing.

A car and driver were waiting for me to take me home. It was late, but I still had to make some phone calls.

My first was to the White House. I left word with the duty officer that I had dropped off three CIA agents in Macau and that they may want to get them home quietly. I did this because I know the CIA would have got them home quietly, telling no one, not even the president.

I didn't think they should get off cleanly. I don't know if I bought Robertson's story about them being there to shut down the operation.

From what I had read about the drug trade in the Golden Triangle, it would take more like an army brigade to shut it down, and that for only a short time.

The next was to Mr. Norman to have him let MI6 know what the cousins had been up to. If anyone thought I was going to let the CIA get away with drug trafficking, they were crazy. The only reason I let those guys go was to lower my profile in this mess.

I also called home, and since they were asleep, left messages that I was okay and that Mr. Norman had the entire story. Mum would get it in short order.

The next day I rode into town to Government House. I was resigned that my days of driving around by myself were about done with. The driver and another guard were up front.

Tu and I were in the back discussing the stories in the daily newspapers. It turns out that Mr. Trần is very sharp. He clarified that the men that I had taken out of the country had been rescued during the raid.

The reason they were in chains is that no one had a key. How he said that with a straight face is beyond me. I thought I was the actor.

I could see that the CIA would be contributing to South Vietnam's treasury.

At Government House, I shared the real story. The governor got a laugh out of Mr. Trân. He said he would like to meet such a consummate politician and blackmailer one day.

I thought blackmailers and politicians were synonyms.

We changed the subject to more serious matters. Dr. Deming was well-received in the colony. The first of his instructors had arrived and they were developing a course syllabus based on the ASQC body of knowledge.

While we were meeting, we were interrupted by a phone call. The president of the United States wanted to speak with me.

I had a childish thought about having them tell JFK that I would return his call when I had a chance. Luckily, I caught myself in time.

When I picked up the phone, it was, "Mr. Jackson, please hold for the president."

The call was transferred immediately. At that point, I might have hung up. I hate it when someone is a better game player than me, just ask my sister Mary.

"Rick, I wanted to call you and thank you for how you handled those three agents. There will be an investigation at the agency. Something smells to the high heavens. You have saved the US public embarrassment. We owe you."

I thought briefly about doing the ah-shucks routine, but settled for, "Thank you, Mr. President."

Chapter 16

I decided to play golf the next day. My driver and bodyguard accompanied me to Clearwater Bay, and I left them and joined a threesome that was waiting. They were a strange group. They looked more like musclemen rather than the doctors that I normally played with. I didn't give it a second thought.

Each of them had a caddie and they were just as out of place, looking like the others. Not exceptionally so but enough that I noticed. One thing was none of them looked familiar.

At least my caddie was one I had used before. We teed off on one and I could tell these weren't world-class golfers. They weren't terrible but you could see they were occasional players rather than regulars. That didn't matter as I was just out to enjoy the day.

There was little talking going on, and once I swore one of the caddies said something in Russian. All went well until the fourth hole ran next to a side road off the main road.

As I looked at my line on a putt, I was jumped. One of the guys even had a syringe in his hand.

I swung my putter, hitting the syringe guy in the face. Another guy jumped on my back.

I turned quickly into him, and he lost his hold.

Another man was coming at me, but I managed to get a kick into his knee. It was a losing battle. I hit one guy in the face with the palm of my hand and probably broke his nose.

Another got a solid punch into my stomach that doubled me over. My caddie had joined the fray, but I saw him go down quickly.

I backed away as much as I could. The only good thing going on was that there were six of them and they were getting in each other's way. I had two of them down. Syringe guy and broken nose guy.

Unfortunately, this left more room for the others to come at me. The guy who punched me in the stomach was good as he followed up with a kick to my knee. I barely dodged that but in doing so collected a punch in my right kidney.

That hurt. I could barely stand. One of the other guys had picked up the syringe and was coming at me. As I saw that, one of the others jumped on my back and took me to the ground.

I was lying face down as I felt the syringe jab home. There was a moment where I thought it did nothing, then the world faded to black.

I came to with a tremendous headache, and I felt like I had been beaten, then I realized I had been beaten. There was a familiar vibration going on, I was in an airborne aircraft.

I tried to move and that was when I found out that I was handcuffed and shackled both arms and legs, with a chain running around my waist and joining the sets of handcuffs. To think I had smirked at Rip Robertson in a similar situation.

Someone leaned over and looked at me. I didn't understand what he said, but I did recognize that it was in Russian.

My old friends the Soviets were up to their old tricks. I wondered if I would survive this one.

The guy held a bottle of water to my lips and let me drink. I think that meant they weren't going to kill me right away.

We landed about two hours later, but it was only a fueling stop. I was taken off the aircraft and motions were made that I was to pee on the ground without going into any buildings. Rather than messing my pants up, I managed to do so.

We soon refueled and were in the air again for another three hours. I didn't recognize the aircraft type, but it was a twin-engine about the same size as a DC 3. It had large red stars on it so there was no doubt as to who had me.

We landed again and I was taken through a hangar man door and locked in a barren room. Several of the airmen were awake and tried to ask me questions in Russian.

"I don't speak Russian."

One of them replied in English. "Are you American?"

"Yes."

"Oh, KGB caught you and bring you to Moscow for trial. We see several times."

"Has anyone got away?"

"Nyet."

I thought hard about how I could get out of here, but even if I did, where would I go?

A meal was brought to me. It wasn't that bad or else I was that hungry. I hadn't eaten in the last eighteen hours.

I thought hard about how to escape, but this wasn't like the movies where they would fall for, I'm sick, and then I could jump the one guard and sneak out. They always showed up in twos.

The armed one stood back. The one who slipped the food tray under my door carried no weapons. They had done this before.

If I were going to Moscow for a trial, maybe I could hire a high-priced Russian lawyer to get me off from whatever faked charges they would come up with.

Or maybe real charges, like, Your Honor, this horrible person in front of you prevented our brave Russian pilots in their Blinder bombers from dropping nuclear bombs on American military installations.

Or maybe, Your Honor, our man in Los Angeles was peacefully spying on CIA agents when the nasty person exposed them and resulted in our valiant commercial attaché being declared persona non grata.

Or better yet. This filthy capitalist helped kill and behead four of our agents who had merely kidnapped his sister so we could trade her for him.

He had the nerve to put the heads in a bowling ball bag and throw them onto our embassy ground. We had to put the heads on ice and ship them back to Russia. He should be charged with murder and be forced to pay for the shipment of the heads.

Okay, I was getting desperate in my thinking. If I understand correctly, my mind was trying to compensate for my current reality and change it.

Not that it would work.

After a restless night of sleep in which someone was peeing, puking, and farting every five minutes, I was fed a breakfast of stale bread and cold greasy sausage.

I offered my jailers ten million dollars to set me free. You could see the avarice in their eyes, but they turned me down out of fear of failure and its repercussions.

At that point, I was chained and returned to the aircraft. After another two refuelings, we landed in what appeared to be an extra-large military airport.

I was then taken in a closed van, which reminded me of the Black Marias in old movies, to a building. Since we drove into a bay and the overhead door was promptly closed, all I could tell was that it was a building.

One of my KGB escorts spoke up, the first words I had heard from any of them since I was woken in my cell.

"Welcome to Lubyanka."

My heart sank as this was the dreaded KGB headquarters where people died. It was famous in all the spy movies. I thought that not even James Bond could get out of my situation now.

I was taken to a room where my handcuffs, chains, and all my clothes were forcibly removed, and a freezing-cold fire hose turned on me. I was then led naked to a cell and the door was closed. There were no blankets in the room, and it was cold. I think I could hear air conditioning equipment running in the background. It must have been hours before anyone came.

I was asked in educated English if I was ready to confess.

"Confess to what?"

He chuckled as he walked away, "I'm sure you will think of something."

The guy must be crazy.

I noticed that my room wasn't as cold as it was before. Now it was getting uncomfortably warm. After a while, it was downright hot. At least I didn't have any clothes on.

Soon it got hotter. I was dehydrated as there was no water available. I needed a drink badly.

My new "friend" came back and stood there. Another guard came with him. The guard had a small table on which there was a pitcher of ice water. My friend poured a glass and stood there drinking it.

He looked at me and said, "Oh, I'm sorry would you like a glass?"

"Yes, please."

Some manners never went away, no matter the situation.

"Are you ready to confess?"

"I have nothing to confess to."

"Such a shame," as he upended the water on the floor. He and the other guy turned and left.

When they were gone, I was able to reach through the bars of my cell and get my fingers wet. I licked them off and went for more. As I went for the third time the guard came back in with a mop and cleaned up the spill. He turned to leave but then he spit on the floor.

In broken English, he told me I would drink that when things got bad.

Chapter 17

The rest of the day the cell alternated between hot and cold, the only comfortable time was when it was changing. Even that wasn't as great as it could be because every time it was changing from hot to cold, I was blasted with cold water from a fire hose. When it was cold, I was miserable.

I wondered if it would go on all night. It did. I tried to get some sleep, but when I lay down, bright lights came on. They were blindingly bright. When I finally started to doze off in one of the heat cycles, which appeared to be about an hour long, loud music started. Someone had a wicked sense of humor. It was "Rock and Roll Cowboy". I just thought I hated that song.

This continued for all the night hours. In the morning, my "friend" showed up dressed up in a suit as though he were an office worker.

"Are you ready to confess?"

"Confess what?"

"Whatever you need to. I hear it is good for the soul if you believe in such."

Then cruelty of cruelties, we went through the glass of water scene again. I had learned one lesson and that was to get as much off the floor as I could before the uniformed guard mopped it up. He ran true to form and ended the session by spitting on the floor.

Then a pleasant surprise happened. Breakfast was brought in. I was so hungry I wolfed the sausage and potatoes down. Only when I had finished did I realize how salty it was. My thirst was magnified.

The next time the fire hose was brought out I drank as much water as I could. It probably saved my life, at least from dehydration. Midway through the morning, I was taken to another room. My "friend" was there.

Once more he asked, "Are you ready to confess?"

This time I just shook my head no. He turned and left the cell. As he was exiting two more guards came into the room. They wore black leather gloves. I quickly found out that was to protect their hands as they beat me.

It was a professional beating. I was black and blue everywhere but my face. I tried to twist and turn away from the blows, but my chains prevented much movement.

I soon realized that it was better to hold still and let them hit their target or they would miss and damage parts of me that had been hit previously. When they were done, one of them talked to me.

"You learn quickly. Most fight us until they are hurt badly."

So nice to know that I met the thug's approval.

I was taken back to my cell where the loud music continued along with the bright lights plus the alternating temperatures.

I was so tired that I finally collapsed. I had no idea how long I had been awake. It seemed like days. They must have been watching because I was rousted out of my unconsciousness and hit with the fire hose once more.

The only good thing was that they had changed the music. "Rock and Roll Cowboy" must have been too much for them.

Finally, I collapsed into true unconsciousness. I have no idea how long I was out. At least when I woke up, I didn't feel like I was about to die. Only like death warmed over as Mum would say.

I was starting to hallucinate; I thought the guard brought me a cold glass of water and allowed me to drink. When I reached for the glass, he poured it on the floor. Maybe I wasn't hallucinating after all.

Once more my "friend" came to the cell.

"Are you ready to confess?"

"Confess to what?"

"Ah, progress."

At that, he turned and walked away.

The music stopped, the lights went off, and I finally could sleep.

I was woken sometime later by the guard. He handed me a paper that had my confession written on it. I read it and realized that I was heading for a show trial. I would be confessing that I worked for the CIA and was trying to cause problems between North and South Vietnam and blame it on the Soviets.

That was so stupid I tore it up.

Immediately thereafter, the lights came back on, and the music resumed. I think it may have been "The Flight of the Valkyrie" at about 100 decibels. It was loud. At least I didn't have to listen to it long as I was taken back to the room where I had been beaten.

There was no surprise when the two thugs returned and beat me all over again. I hadn't time to heal so the bruising was spectacular. It also hurt like hell. I wasn't sure which was worse, no sleep, being beaten, or the thirst.

They kept this cycle up for several years, or at least a while.

Finally, a day, or a week, or even a month later my "friend" asked me if I was ready to confess.

"Yes, bring the paper here. I will sign it."

It felt like another person was speaking. I didn't want to do this, but I had to stop this while I was still alive.

The paper was brought. It had the same words as before, so I signed it.

My life changed from that moment. I was given a glass of water. Real food was provided. I could sleep with no lights or music.

They allowed me a week of rest. I healed enough that I could move without feeling like an old man.

One morning my "friend" came in. "Tomorrow is your trial. You will read out loud the paper that you signed, confessing to working for the CIA, then plead guilty."

The court will find you guilty and you will be sentenced to twenty years of hard labor in Siberia. You will stay there until your government trades you for one of our brave agents who they caught.

Do you understand that if you do not do as I have said, this will start all over?

I nodded my head; I was beaten down.

"I must hear you say it."

"I will read the paper as written."

"Good, you almost set a record for holding out. The woman who set the record died, unfortunately."

It went as he said. They gave me a cheap suit and tie and took me to a courtroom. It was packed with reporters, mostly Russian but some from the free world. There were TV cameras.

I was numb to all of this. I just sat there as the court was brought to order. It was all in Russian, so I think that was what was happening. Everyone stood up when a fat man in black robes entered the room. I was forced to my feet.

The entire trial took about an hour and a half.

The guy at my side who in the US would have been my lawyer made a speech in English about how I was young and misguided by my evil masters in the CIA. He even named my master, a Rip Robertson. I laughed out loud at this, which turned out to be a major faux pas in a Russian court. I was immediately gagged and bound.

The only time the gag came off was when I read my confession. As I read it, I did the only thing that I could. I blinked my eyes in Morse code, SOS, tortured. I was able to repeat this twice while reading slowly. I was then asked for my plea.

"Guilty."

There would be no "Your Honor" from me.

The judge slammed his gavel down and sentenced me to twenty years of hard labor in a Siberian gulag.

I was taken from the room, my suit removed, and I had to put on a grey jumpsuit. I was then taken down the hall and outdoors. It was a closed courtyard still within the Lubyanka building. I was taken over to a wall and chained to a post. A white piece of paper was pinned to my chest.

Five guards with rifles came out and lined up facing me. I was being executed!

There was nothing I could do, so I stood as tall as I could. Give them a good target and die like a man.

The commands came.

"Ready!'

"Aim!"

It seemed like the last command took a million years, but it came.

"Fire!"

The rifles crashed. I had closed my eyes at the last moment. I stood there. What happened? Did they all miss?

My "friend" from my torture came out.

"Good joke, heh?"

Someday, somehow, I will joke him to death.

I was unchained from the post and taken to another windowless unmarked van. It still reminded me of a Black Maria. From there I was taken to a train station.

Chapter 18

My chains and shackles were removed, and I was shoved into a windowless railcar. I later learned these were called *stolypin*. They were used for transporting prisoners to Siberia.

It was small, maybe ten feet by ten feet inside. There were eight other prisoners there already.

It was going to be an uncomfortable crowded trip.

I was no sooner inside than a big guy came towards me like he was going to kill me. As he took a step forward several of the other prisoners started yelling at him.

He stopped and backed up. I swear he got pale.

He stammered in broken English, "I sorry, did not know you English CIA killer."

Sometimes a reputation can be a good thing, earned or otherwise.

The trip was long and boring. We had to sleep on the floor. There was barely room for us to all lie down at once. The train made frequent stops and we were allowed out to use the facilities. We were given bread, water, and hard sausages to eat. I don't think I will ever eat sausage again if I get out of this.

I learned a few Russian words during the trip, most of them nasty. I did find out that we were not all going to the same camp. They would be dropping off prisoners on the way. We thought this would give us more room in our car.

Not so. It seems they transfer prisoners from camp to camp. Usually, it was one off and one on; once it was one off and three on. That was a miserable two days.

I wondered why prisoners didn't run for it at the rail stops. Upon asking, I learned the locals were paid a bounty if they caught a prisoner off the train platform. I learned to be careful not to stand close to the edge while waiting for the restroom.

Locals were known to push prisoners off the edge of the platform and then capture them for the reward. The prisoner would have a year added to their sentence each time they were caught.

I thought about running for it, but it seemed high risk. I would wait for a better situation. In the meantime, maybe I will get lucky and be included in a prisoner exchange.

I found out that there were different levels of prison camps. There were the official state prisons with cells. These were more like the American prisons except with no TV and forced labor.

The three levels of outside camps ranged from almost a country club to a forced labor concentration camp.

The best ones allowed weekend passes and family visits but importantly had food and health care. The worst was like the Nazi slave labor camps. They would work their prisoners to death knowing there would always be more.

I wasn't getting a country club; no weekend passes for me. At the same time, we were kept in a barracks rather than a cell. After our workday, if we had the energy, we could wander the camp.

There were no fences, a prisoner could just wander off. Except the camp kept well-trained tracking dogs. The few locals who were around were paid a bounty on prisoners captured.

That and the fact I would be five hundred miles into the wilderness with only a dirt track road leading to the camp. This road was well patrolled and never had a prisoner make it out using it. At least that is what I had been told.

Most of this information came from one guy who spoke fairly good English. He talked a lot to me and the other prisoners, sharing reasons why we shouldn't even think about escaping.

I began to think he was in the pay of the KGB or Gulag authorities to create a mindset.

It didn't matter what he told us; I was going to escape as soon as possible.

Everything must end and so did that train ride in that stinking crowded rail car. It didn't seem possible that I would be glad to be at that prison, but I was.

We weren't yet at the prison. Two other guys and I were dropped off at a rail siding. There was a truck with one prisoner in it who was pushed into the railcar.

The other guy and I were told, at least he was and I followed, to get into the truck. We were on the back of a flatbed truck and had to hang on so we wouldn't fall off. A few boxes and fifty-pound sacks were loaded from the train.

We moved these around to form a barrier from falling off and to serve as a windbreak. The guards up front didn't seem to care what we did.

My traveling companion pried several of the boxes open. They contained cold-weather pants, jackets, hats, socks, and boots. We both put on a complete set of them. I thought I would probably be needing them.

We then pounded the nails back down as best as we could.

After eight hours of bouncing around, we stopped for the night at a way camp. Nothing was said about our new clothes. None of them were new. They were more like clean rags, but they were better than nothing.

Late the next day we arrived at our camp in the middle of nowhere. The check-in was simple. We were taken to an office where they asked our names. They then checked us off against a list and told us our barracks and bunk numbers.

We were going to different barracks, so I seldom saw my traveling companion again.

It was late in the day, so we separated to go to our respective barracks. No guard accompanied us. It appeared that we were free to rove about the camp after hours.

When I entered the barracks, an older man approached me.

In English, he told me, "I am Joseph. It is my job to see that you are settled in and to assign you a job and give you the tools."

"You are a big guy so you're going to be an axman. Tomorrow morning see me for your ax, gloves, and a sharpening stone."

Just like that, I was absorbed into the working life of the Gulag. I had a top bunk as the new guy. I was told as the lower ones opened, I could get one.

I made the mistake of asking how they opened.

"Men die here."

"Accidents?"

"Some. More from disease and many from starvation."

"They starve us to death?"

"Not on purpose. When the weather is bad, food can't get through. They never store any on-site. They are afraid we will steal it and run away. They bring enough food for a week at a time. When the weather is bad, we may not get any food in a month. Men die."

"Then there is tuberculosis. It is always here, but when we have no food, it gets worse. Many men die."

"Oh."

That was all I could say. What sort of place had I been sent to? I thought they had sent me here as a place to keep me until they could exchange me for their people.

Now it seems they don't care if I live or die. Welcome to the USSR.

"How did you know to speak to me in English?"

"Your haircut and how you hold yourself. It is easy to see you are not Russian. Your hair is cut differently like an Englishman would wear."

I was impressed with his observation skills.

"Plus, every day we get a form talking about any new people. If you spoke German, Pavel would have welcomed you."

He showed me my bunk and watched as I made my bed with the provided sheets. They were course material that felt like sandpaper. Thousand thread count, they weren't.

The next morning, I followed the other men, first to the stinking outhouse, and then to breakfast. Have I mentioned that I hate sausage?

I saw Joseph signaling me, so I went to him. He had a threadbare pair of gloves, an ax, and a sharpening stone.

"You chop down marked trees. Do many so we meet quota; if we miss quota, no food for a week."

I made a vow to myself to never miss a quota.

The men were filing out of the camp into the woods, so I followed.

This was not an environmentally friendly place. The forest was being clear-cut. It looked like a disaster zone. There were stumps everywhere and piles of limbs that were too small to bother with.

We went to the far edge of the cleared forest and started chopping down trees.

I had never done this before, so I had a lot of wasted motion. I was lucky to not cut a leg off.

When my first tree was falling, I yelled, "Timber!"

This must work in all languages as men looked at the falling tree and got out of the way.

I sharpened my ax and moved on. My shoulders were burning, and blisters had formed on my hands, but I was working for my life.

An older man carried a water bucket around with us all day long. There were no official breaks, but I saw men resting between trees, so I followed suit. There was no noon meal.

At the end of the day, my hands were bloody, and I was as tired as I had ever been in my life.

Chapter 19

When I got back to the barracks, I was given a nasty-smelling salve to put on my hands. It did remove a lot of the pain. He also had a better pair of gloves.

"You worked well today; the committee has decided to give you decent gear. If you had not done well, we would have let you die."

That made the inmate rules clear, produce to help the whole or die.

I wandered around the camp and saw men doing varied tasks. Many were playing chess. I watched a few games and realized that Grandmaster in New Orleans was wrong about my playing at an expert level, or these guys were all great.

I suspect the guy had been blowing smoke trying to get me into another game.

Guys were carving small figurines, some of them nice pieces. Mostly animals, but some of the better ones were people. One of them caught my eye and spoke to me in fairly good English. "So, you're the duke that they caught for spying?"

"I was kidnapped off a golf course and have never been in the USSR before. How could I be a spy?"

"They say you a spy, you're a spy."

"I'm glad we got that cleared up. Just call me Bond, James Bond."

"Where is your pretty girl?"

"At home."

"Then you not James Bond. He would have been in bed with Natasha the cook here at the camp."

"Natasha being a pretty girl?"

"No, she is ugly as fence post, has a big wart on nose, very fat, also only woman in camp. It is said that when she starts to look good, you have been here too long."

"I have been here twenty-seven years, and she still not look good. Though to be fair, she only came here twenty years ago."

I had to escape this place. The thought of Natasha looking good was too much.

"What do you do with these pieces you are carving?"

"We trade them to the guards for more food or little things."

"So, there is trading going on in camp?"

"Yes, you can get anything but weapons, women, or a way out."

"Why don't people walk away?"

"They do. Most are crazy and die in the woods. Some serious attempts are made, but the dogs track them down, or the locals turn them in for the reward."

"So, when I run for it, I have to make sure the dogs can't track me and that I don't get near any locals?"

"That's it. As the Americans say, easy peasy."

I knew it would be anything but.

A bell rang, which turned out to be the dinner bell. I got in line with the other men and was given a tin cup and plate. Dinner was a dished-up stew of some kind.

It was the sort of meal you didn't ask about; you just ate it. There was a barrel full of water which we all dipped our cups in. Sanitation wasn't high on the list here.

I was tired so was in bed early. There was a lights-out curfew in the camp at around ten o'clock, but I didn't make it that long.

The next day was more of the same. It took two weeks before my hands toughened up enough that they weren't bleeding by the end of the day. In another four weeks, I could tell I had put on muscle from all the ax work.

During this time, I was wandering around the camp in the evenings picking up what information I could. I was learning a few Russian phrases and numbers, but it wasn't much.

I did hear one word that I thought I recognized. I thought I heard "yew," but when I listened it was pronounced *tu*. Since they were talking about wood, I double-checked.

Fortunately, one of them had a little English. It was surprising how many of them did. Then again, it shouldn't be surprising as this camp seemed to be where they sent the intelligent residents.

The one who spoke English was called Dr. Z by the rest of them. He told me that it was yew, the same wood that the English made their bows out of.

Suddenly my chances of a successful escape rose.

I didn't know what a yew tree looked like, so I asked them. Once they showed me a branch, I realized that I had chopped many of them down.

The next day I deliberately picked a sixty-foot-tall yew to chop down. Once I felled it, I limbed half a dozen branches. They all were at least eight feet long, four inches in diameter, and straight.

I took them with me from tree to tree during the day. Maybe I should have waited for the last tree of the day.

Now all I needed was a knife to carve a bow stave.

I went back to Dr. Z and asked him how I could get a knife. He told me he would provide if I kept him in a supply of yew for his figures. That was a deal.

I had never carved anything, much less a bow. I had seen my archery instructor, Rod Bell, do that, so I had a vague idea.

It took me two weeks and four destroyed staves before I had anything that resembled a bow. I had to go back out into the woods to do my carving so no one would know what I was up to.

That meant I only had a few hours of light to work with. It was now September, and the light was fading. I wondered if Popeye became a member of the Royal Order of the Purple Porpoise.

I felt lonely that night, but I was determined to get through all of this. I had no idea what was going on in the outside world and couldn't count on help.

I knew a lot of people cared and governments would be putting pressure on the Soviets, but I don't think anyone would go to war over me.

The bow I had carved looked good, but I knew that was an illusion. It was greenwood that would warp as it dried. I had maybe two or three weeks' use out of it.

I carved another one and crawled under my barracks one night. I placed it on the cross beams that ran under one of the stoves that heated the place. I hoped that would dry the wood out without it warping too badly.

I had been collecting sticks to make arrows out of. They had to be straight and at least a yard long. They were as big around as my finger.

When I cut a tree down, I would check for birds' nests and feathers that I could use on the arrows. I never found any of the correct sizes. One evening I saw a guy set up feathers for sale of all sizes.

I asked him what they would cost me. The Soviets were paying me ten roubles a week, which was practically nothing, but since I had nothing to spend it on, I had fifty roubles.

For my fifty, I was able to get enough feathers for one hundred arrows. When I walked away, I thought that this was one of those deals where each party thought they had made out best.

Glue was common in camp; it had many uses. Inmates boiled hoofs down to make the glue. I never asked where the hoofs came from. I suspected they may have been dinner some nights but didn't want to know.

Now all I needed for my arrows were points. I set that thought aside for the moment and worked on making a bowstring.

There was plenty of hemp rope around the camp. I unwound a good length of that, and reverse wove half a dozen bowstrings. My Boy Scout knotwork had taught me how to make an eye splice at the ends.

My arrowhead problem took care of itself. Joseph approached me one evening.

"Rick, we have been watching you make your bow and arrows. What are your plans?"

"Immediately to help our barrack's food supply; long term to get out of here."

"I'm glad you are thinking of food; it is almost fall now; we have had several touches of frost. The game will be getting scarce. Anything you can bring in will help.

"Many of our people put out snares but they were having to go further afield every day. That leaves us with fewer people to cut trees.

"This, in turn, causes us to miss quotas which reduces the amount of food we are given. By the middle of the winter, there will be no game and we will have many deaths by starvation. One year many years ago there was cannibalism in this camp.

"If you can get me arrowheads, I will be able to provide deer or elk."

"That is a deal."

Within two days he gave one hundred arrowheads hand cut out of sheet metal. I placed them in the nocks of the arrows and whipped the nock closed with strands of hemp.

I practiced with my green bow, the good one was still drying. I had rough cut the stave so that when there was some warping when it dried, I could carve it out.

I was adequate with the green bow. It had good poundage, and the arrows flew straight. I would never win the Robin Hood contest in Sherwood Forrest with this setup, but I could hit a deer.

Chapter 20

The day of the hunt, as I thought of it, no snares had been set out. Five men were setting out snares. That day, two went with me, and the other three chopped trees to replace me. I didn't realize that I was contributing so much to the day's quota.

I shouldn't have been surprised as I was large, young, and still in good health. I could outwork any two of them.

The two guys and I headed deeper into the woods. With their setting small game snares, they had learned the woods. They knew where deer were most likely to be found.

They led me right to a small herd. We had come in downwind quietly, so they didn't know we were there. We were only one hundred yards away from them, so I had a good shot. I stuck two arrows in the ground to get them quickly and nocked a third.

Taking a deep breath and holding it, then gently exhaling, I let fly. Before the first arrow arrived, I had a second ready to go. You could hear the solid thunk of the first arrow as I released the second. Again, I went for the third arrow and another shot, but the herd was moving by then, and I didn't have a chance.

I had brought down two deer. They were small, called musk deer. They still had enough meat to make it worthwhile.

As I retrieved my arrows, the two guys started field-dressing the deer. They were fast. We headed back to camp with almost a hundred pounds of meat.

When we neared our tree-cutting area, we hid the meat and walked on in. Joseph saw us coming and came to meet us.

"You weren't gone long. Problems?"

"Success. Two musk deer, almost a hundred pounds of meat."

"Fantastic."

This was all spoken in Russian. I only picked up every other word or so but caught the gist.

"Can you go back out? The day is still young."

That had to be translated for me, but I nodded yes. Our second trip of the day yielded three more deer from two different herds.

It was all we could do to haul the meat back. When we got back to the day's worksite there were some happy people to see the results of our hunt.

I hope they didn't expect this every day. Deer weren't stupid. They never had been hunted before, but they would get skittish fast. Then it would become like deer hunting in the states, requiring patience.

I could be wrong. Siberia is a large place and has a lot of deer.

Joseph was excited. There was enough meat here to feed the whole barracks for three days. He went off in rhapsodies. He envisioned enough extra meat to trade with the guards for medicines and other necessities.

He thought the days of famine were over. There was the little problem that we were one of ten barracks. The others might have a say about all this extra meat.

Joseph wasn't clueless. He immediately made plans for hidden smoking facilities and a meat locker. These were to be deep in our sector of the woods and only attended by a trusted few.

I was given the duty of chief hunter, but also chief bowyer. I was to provide as many bows as possible and train selected men on using them.

This was the closest I had seen the camp to be festive. That night, men were able to eat their fill for the first time in a long time. Probably the first time since they came to the Gulag.

The next three days we went in different directions away from the camp to hunt different herds of deer. The worst day only had two kills, the best five.

We could have done better by starting earlier in the morning, but we had to be present for the morning headcount. There was a large open field where we assembled.

We had to line up fifty men across and twenty rows deep. We had to be five feet apart from the front, side, and back. Each of us was assigned a position according to our convict number. I was 33573. They may have had a rhyme or reason for the numbers at one time. Now they all seemed random.

It would be obvious if someone was missing, as there would be a gap somewhere in the formation. There were always gaps. Almost every night someone died for some reason.

It could have been violence, an accident, disease, or even suicide. No matter the reason, there were always deaths. If there were ten gaps, there better be ten bodies stacked in the field.

If someone was missing, the dogs would be taken to their bunk area to get the scent and then to the perimeter of the camp and turned loose.

I had seen it happen twice as men couldn't take it anymore and just wandered away from camp. The dogs tracked them both down. One man stopped when they came up to him.

The dogs left him alone and the guards bound him and took him back to camp.

The other man ran from the dogs. They chased him down and tore him to bloody shreds. I knew this because I was one of those sent out to collect the body.

I don't think I was chosen deliberately, just the luck of the draw.

About ten days into the hunt, we came across a herd of moose. There were over a hundred of them. When I put an arrow into the first one it went to its knees and was coughing blood. I thought the herd would run off. They ignored the dying one.

I managed to shoot four more of them before the herd got nervous and moved. We sent a runner back to the camp to get help.

We got busy field-dressing the moose and building travois to haul the meat. Field dressing ended up at nine hundred pounds per moose. After butchering it would be four hundred and fifty pounds of useful meat.

We had to drag back forty-five hundred pounds of meat. It was hard work and required twenty of us. We would miss our work quota for the day but knew we could trade meat for logs with other barracks.

I had carved five more bow staves from greenwood, along with twenty arrows per bow and two strings each. That took every waking minute. At least I didn't have to chop any more wood.

While doing my carving, I was teaching other men how to do it so I wouldn't be the sole source. I didn't tell them I was doing this so they wouldn't be left without bows and bowmen when I escaped.

How I was going to do that I didn't know yet, but the first steps had been taken, I had a source of food for my journey in the wilds of Siberia.

I also was training prospective archers. Some of the candidates didn't get it, some did, and one guy was William Tell reborn.

Even though they had little to do, the camp had an escape committee. I had the best chance of escaping of anyone ever imprisoned there.

Since my Russian was extremely limited, they drew me up a sample identity card.

My name would be Ivan Popov, a quite common name, from Vladivostok. What they had given me had to be copied onto official paper. They had little advice on how to get it, other than it would be at an NKVD office.

I still had to memorize the Russian alphabet and the sentences in that language that I would need to use to fill in my travel pass and school papers, but with my acting experience memorizing a few lines wasn't all that hard, even though they were in an unfamiliar language.

I would have to have better clothing. I was told how to bribe clerks to get into the backroom where what I needed might be available. This would cost a lot of money. They had no idea how I could get it. I did; I grew up on Westerns.

Then there was how I would hide in Moscow. If I could come up with the money, I could buy my way into the university. It turned out that there was a whole network of dissidents known by fellow camp inmates who might help me, starting with a fake transcript and recommendation papers.

I was given places and names where I could obtain both, and once again, my experience in memorizing lines paid off.

My escape method came about almost by accident. I had to find a way to leave no scent for the dogs.

It was a barter session one night when I saw a man sitting with a pile of parachute silk. He was cutting small pieces and selling or trading them.

I don't know where the silk came from, but I remembered a couple of the stuntmen back in Hollywood talking about a new sport called hang gliding.

It was simple in principle and had been done since the 1890s. It was a one-man glider with no shell, just a wing that the person would hang suspended under.

They had talked about a wing design called Rogallo. Rogallo must have been the inventor. It only needed about twenty square feet of fabric, and the parachute had much more than that.

I had the parachute reserved for me until I delivered one hundred pounds of deer meat. It took me two days to collect that. My co-workers weren't wild about me taking the meat personally as they thought it all belonged to the collective, but they finally yielded when they realized their dependence on me.

Someone must have known that I was receiving parachute silk for it, but no one brought it up.

This is where my aeronautical knowledge was important. I knew the wing shape I needed. I could calculate the lift provided by each square foot of wing, thus telling me how much weight I could fly with.

Sunday was our one day of rest in the camp. We didn't even have to hunt. Things, in general, were looking up in our barracks as the men were getting a regular source of protein in their diets. Healthier men could chop more wood. Quotas made earned more food in the form of greens.

I didn't feel like I was abandoning my workmates. It is strange how you can identify with a group. Anyway, two Sundays in a row I went off by myself and built a hang glider using one-inch diameter branches as the mainframe and some sort of long thin branches to keep the wing shape. I think they were a willow, but not a weeping willow.

Siberia is a large flat plain, but not perfectly flat. There are some cliffs and valleys. On one of my hunting trips, we came across a one-hundred-foot-high cliff that opened on a valley that dropped another couple hundred feet. The best part was that the prevailing wind blew from the west to the east. It would be a perfect launch spot.

When I finished the glider, I carried it to the cliff. I then went back and retrieved my bow stave which I had curing under the barracks.

As I crawled from under the barracks, Joseph was there. I thought he would try to stop me. Just the opposite.

"It is time that you go. The weather will be too bad soon. Here is something that might help. It only has three shells, so be careful."

He handed me a pistol. Later I was able to read Nagant Model 1895 on the barrel.

I thanked him, then on impulse hugged the man and walked away without looking back.

With a backpack loaded with twenty pounds of meat and five pounds of cabbage and my bow and arrows, while wearing my cold-weather gear, I ran and went over the edge of the cliff.

Chapter 21

Was I scared? Yes, I was. However, I was determined to escape from this prison. I had a life to live and a country to teach a lesson to. I didn't know what I was going to do but the lesson would be, don't mess with Richard Edward Jackson.

I fell forward and dropped until I felt the air expand the wings. The hang glider didn't fall apart, so I was okay for now.

The ground was coming up fast but when I felt lift, I brought my feet up and the glider started to climb. The further I got from the cliff the greater the lift. I seemed to be moving faster as I went.

This was confirmed as I watched the forest dwindle below me and pass at an ever-increasing rate. I was climbing higher. I flew on for another fifteen minutes and I realized that it was getting colder. My cold-weather gear was protecting my body, but I had nothing over my face.

I finally leveled my flight off. If I had to guess, I was between six and seven thousand feet in the air. I had no way of knowing how many miles I had traveled, but no dogs would be able to track me now.

I decided to glide as far as I could. I was going almost due east towards the Pacific Ocean. It was almost eight hundred miles away so I would never make that, but still, the farther I got from that camp the better.

Also, I had to worry about human contact. The closer to the camp, the more likely I would be caught and turned in for the reward.

I slanted my flight to the south as much as I could. I planned to get as far as I could and then head south until I ran across the trans-Siberian Railway. I couldn't miss it as it ran across all the Soviet Union.

Hanging in the air took a toll. I was getting hungry, had to go to the bathroom, and was freezing! The last reason was the one that made me decide to land. I had rough straps to hold me to the glider, but if I fell unconscious there was no guarantee of a safe landing.

During the three hours or so that I had been aloft, I hadn't seen one light nor sign of human habitation. This truly was a wilderness.

The first daylight was appearing over the horizon as I started to descend. I had gotten up safely; now, could I get down?

The farther I descended the more doubts I had. I was descending faster than the earth was rotating so I was going from light to impenetrable dark. I could never find a safe place to land.

This stark fact jolted me into a more wide-awake awareness. I hadn't realized that I was falling asleep. I leveled my flight up and continued.

Like the soap opera title, the world turned. Sunlight touched the ground and the lakes! Yes, it glinted off bodies of water of all sizes. I now knew how to make a safe landing.

Not in the water but on the shore parallel to my flight, if the shore was wide enough. I dropped my altitude so that I was now about fifty feet above the tallest trees.

I had spotted one large lake in the distance; it was the most likely spot to land. When I sailed out over the edge of the water, I was thrilled to see that there was a long stretch of grass running alongside the water.

Dropping my altitude, I flew directly over the long straight stretch of grass. The lower I went, the slower I flew as the wind died, cut off by the trees. I came within a few feet of the land at a running speed. I lowered my legs, touched the ground, and started running. At the same time, I pulled the homemade cords to collapse the wing.

The wing did collapse, and I took a tumble with the lack of support the wings had been giving me. It didn't matter as I was down without any injury.

I was well over a hundred miles from the Gulag, maybe two hundred. It didn't matter; I was out.

Taking my glider, I went into the woods. It had a lot of undergrowth, so I was able to disappear in short order. Not that I had seen anything to disappear from.

I only went in a hundred yards or so and came across a rock outcrop. I was able to nestle down between two boulders, cover myself with the parachute silk, and fall asleep.

When I woke the sun was going down. I had to go to the bathroom like crazy. Taking care of business, I started to set up a better camp. I improved my sleeping arrangement by making a roof over the boulders. By tripling the large nylon sheet over, I thought it would be waterproof if it rained. It was late enough in the year that it might even snow.

To keep warm, I collected downed firewood and started the fire with the flint and steel fire starter from the survival kit I had assembled in the camp.

Calling it a survival kit may have been a bit much. It contained a small compass about the size of a dime, the fire starter, and several bandages which I had boiled and wrapped in wax paper stolen from the kitchen.

I also had a small hand hatchet I took from the felling crew. Then there was that pistol Joseph had handed me.

This was what I had to get out of Siberia.

I ate well from the dried meat I had brought along and even choked down some of the cabbage. I hadn't ever liked cabbage but now it was a necessity for my diet.

I rested for two days. I didn't realize how much the escape had taken out of me. On the third day, I woke and felt great, so I rolled up the parachute silk. Why do they call it silk when it is nylon?

There was no sign of human activity so far. The first day walked many miles as I followed the lakeshore. It must have been twenty miles.

I had no idea how far I would have to walk before I ran into the rail line. Each night I would dry my socks out by my small fire. I would wash my feet in the lake. If I had foot problems, I was dead.

The days turned into weeks or at least two of them. I estimated that I had gone almost two hundred miles, give or take fifty.

One day late in the afternoon I saw my first sign of human habitation. It was smoke curling up into the sky. I cautiously approached the area where it was coming from. I'm glad I did. It was a small outpost of Russian soldiers.

Why they were stationed out here was beyond me. I was about to pass them by when I realized they were a mounted group. They rode horses!

I made a wide circle around the camp until I saw the small barn and corral. There must have been fifty horses in four corrals. Two soldiers were watering the horses. They made no effort to bed the horses in the barn. It wouldn't have held them all anyway.

I backed away several miles and set up a hidden cold camp. The next morning, I was out at daybreak and had the corrals under surveillance.

Five soldiers came out and selected horses from the nearest corral, saddled them, and went out on a patrol.

In a little while, two guys came out and brought bales of hay out of the barn for the horses, provided water, and left them.

I got my nerve up and crept closer to the building the soldiers were staying in. They had set up a firepit outside of their barracks and were cooking their breakfast. I about threw up at the smell of sausage.

I watched them for the rest of the morning. There were ten of them. That made a total of fifteen counting the guys on patrol. I wondered why they had so many horses.

I had enough Russian now to know they were bored. They played chess, tossed horseshoes, and griped about this duty. At the same time, they all agreed that this was a good duty. Watching illegal fur trappers was easy. Especially when you weren't expected to catch any.

An officer would come by once a week. He had been here two days ago, so I had some time. I repeated my surveillance the next day. It was the same routine. Late in the day, the patrol came out and another would leave in the morning.

I found a good use for that cabbage. I befriended one of the better-looking horses in the back corral. He was the only one who wandered up to me when I approached the corral from the back.

Chapter 22

That afternoon when the soldiers were either playing games or taking a nap I snuck into the barn. I found treasure. Not only were there extra tack and saddles, there were spare uniforms in their original cartons.

Trying not to disturb them, I found one the closest to my size. The arms and legs stuck out a little but not much. They were probably for a guy six foot three inches.

The best thing was that there were underwear and socks. I couldn't wait to get out of my clothes into these. There were even heavy coats and hats made for the Siberian winter. Taking what I needed, I carefully closed all the boxes and moved them to the bottom of the pile.

It took two of the Russian army backpacks to hold the gear. I cautiously crept out of the barn with my trophies. After stashing them back in the woods, I crept back for a saddle blanket, tack, and saddle.

When I had these, I moved away from the corrals. I anxiously awaited the evening routine when they watered the horses. It went off with no problems. They didn't notice anything missing.

After waiting an hour to make certain no one was coming back out, I removed logs from the corral. The uprights had holes in them where the crossbars fit. I slid them out and gently shooed the horses out.

All except my new friend. I slipped a bit into his mouth and a bridle over his head. He was well broken in and took it well. He didn't even fill his stomach with air when I tightened the cinch.

I led him to my other gear, saddled him, placed the backpacks on his rump, one to a side, and mounted.

I turned him south in a gentle turn and let him amble away.

I had to laugh a little. I had a six-shooter and had just stolen a horse. This was as good as any of my movies. The horse was fresh in that he was rested from doing nothing all day. Riding him was like being in a rocking chair. Easy rider.

We ambled south through the night. It was coming up to daybreak, so I found a secluded spot and set up a cold camp. After unsaddling and caring for my horse which I had yet to name, I ate some jerky and fell asleep.

When I woke it was late afternoon. I broke camp, saddled up the horse, and went on our way. We crossed a stream early on where I let him drink his fill. I also filled the canteen I had found in the Russian storage shed.

I had two hopes. One was that they thought the horses had pushed the fence over and wandered away on their own and that they would figure this horse had wandered farther than the others. The second hope was they wouldn't notice the empty boxes at the bottom of their supplies.

If those hopes made it, I would have a long head start. They would have just found the corral with its fence down at daybreak when they fed and watered the horses, so I had a rather good lead.

It was nice not having to walk. I made a few more miles a day but the big benefit was the lack of wear and tear on my feet and legs. My butt paid for it, but I was getting used to riding again.

All went well for the next several days, but I saw that Horse, not much of a name, but that was it, was about to lose a shoe.

I had to walk but at least the horse carried the backpacks. I came upon a trail. I thought about going into the woods and walking parallel until I knew what was going on.

I followed it for about fifty yards and rounded a bend into another Soviet Army camp. This one was much larger.

Several soldiers looked up from what they were doing, exactly what I couldn't tell, but they went back to it, ignoring me.

One guy, a sergeant came up to me and pointed over his shoulder. In Russian, he told me, "The farrier is over there. He will take care of you."

I just nodded and led Horse towards the farrier. It must have been a slow day in the horseshoeing business because the farrier took over Horse and reshod him. Not only the loose one but all four. He trimmed the hooves and did as good a job as I had seen done on the movie sets.

He finished up and grunted at me, which I took as a sign to move on. I did. I continued south through the camp and kept moving. No one questioned me. My clothes were from the army, but I couldn't believe what had just happened.

Anyway, I remounted Horse and continued south.

As soon as I was out of sight of the camp, I left the trail and headed out at a right angle. Someone might wake up back there.

After heading east for an hour, I turned south again through the monotonous woods. This section was more like a park. There wasn't much undergrowth.

I made another cold camp. I was reluctant to light a fire this close to the army. The next day I felt a little safer. I saw several herds of deer. My food supply was getting low, so I tied Horse and stalked the herd.

Great hunter, I'm not, but these deer weren't afraid of predators. They must not have been hunted much. I got close enough that it was an easy kill with my longbow.

That evening, I continued the train of thought I had all day long. After I found the Siberian railroad, which direction should I go? West towards Moscow, or east towards the Pacific then south through Manchuria to Beijing?

Beijing made the most sense, but Moscow had its attractions. The Soviets owed me for all this grief and that seemed like a good place to collect.

Another problem I faced was that I had no money. It didn't matter right now out in the woods, but when I got near civilization, it would become a necessity. I couldn't go to a bank and make a withdrawal. Or could I?

That would take some thought.

One thing I had been worried about was wolves. I thought Siberia would be full of them.

I hadn't seen or heard any, that is, until this night. They were howling all over the place. I felt like they were all saying, "Hey, Ricky Jackson is over here. Let's get him."

I was short on sleep the next morning and Horse wasn't so spry.

We continued south.

That night I lit a fire. I would take my chances on soldiers being around. It was the wolves that scared me.

It worked; well, at least there were no wolves around last night. About noon the next day, I came upon something I was beginning to think was a legend. The Siberian Railway.

At this section of the railway, there were two sets of tracks, so trains could go in both directions. That wasn't true of the entire length.

The problem was that I didn't know where I was on the rail line. By my best reckoning, it could be anywhere from eight hundred to twelve hundred miles from the Pacific Ocean and lord knows how many miles from Moscow.

Which direction should I go?

I decided to watch the trains go by to see if I could pick up any clues.

I got comfortable back behind the tree line so no one could spot me from a train. Trains went by about every hour, one in each direction. They didn't tell me a thing.

If I had a coin, I would have flipped it. I decided to head west in the morning after a night's sleep. Either direction had a chance of getting to a small village. I had no idea how far that small village might be.

It turned out that small village was a hundred miles down the track. If I had gone east, it would have been ten miles.

When I realized that there was a village up ahead, I got off the dirt track that ran parallel to the rails. Moving several miles north of the village, I searched for a vantage point to check things out. I couldn't just ride into town, though it had worked at the army camp.

Calling it a village was kind. There was the rail station, consisting of an open platform. About ten cottages, a general store, and two bars were the whole town. I would stick out like a sore thumb if I went there.

I was tired from my kidnapping, torture, time in the Gulag, and the journey to this point. I was out of ideas. What was I going to do?

One thing it wasn't going to be was give up.

Chapter 23

I decided to take a closer look at the town. I mounted Horse and rode in as if I belonged there. I tied him at a hitching post in front of one of the bars.

I thought I would look inside to see what I could learn. As I started to open the door, two men staggered out. They were dressed like train crew.

One was in better shape than the other. As I started to brush past them the one in worse shape threw up and promptly fell dead drunk to the world.

His buddy asked me in Russian, "You help?"

Having nothing better to do, I helped him pick up the drunk guy.

"Go to train?"

I didn't answer, I put the drunk guy over the horse's back, sorry Horse, and started towards the train platform. It was only a hundred yards or so.

The walking drunk guy asked, "You shovel coal?"

The fact that I understood him made me realize that I had learned some Russian.

"Da."

We took the drunk guy and poured him into the engine cab. That was a chore. The engine was tall. I had to climb a ladder built into the side of the engine and drop him on the floor.

I went back down to the other guy, who I figured out was the train engineer. He tried to push me back up the ladder. I came on down and told him, "Not give up horse."

A light bulb seemed to come on, and he started towards the rear of the train, I followed leading my horse. We came to an open car which turned out to be a stock car. He kicked an attendant awake and had the horse taken aboard.

I got Horse settled, making certain his gear and saddle were put up. There was grain in a bin and water. It was the best food he had seen in days, and he was right at home.

The engineer and I went back up front. The whole time I was thinking, this is no way to run a railroad.

We climbed back up into the locomotive cab. It had the smell of cinders and steam. I was surprised when I saw a nameplate for the engine. It was a 2-10-0 made by the Baldwin Locomotive Works, Eddystone, PA.

It didn't take much to figure out that I had to shovel coal into the firebox. The engineer showed me the footplate I had to step on to open the door. Even at a reduced fire, it was like looking into Hell itself.

I made a vow not to get too close when I shoveled coal in. I was lucky they had a fresh load of coal, so I didn't have to go too far to get it. When the coal car started to empty, it would be real work.

I shoveled coal until the engineer said to stop.

On the platform, a guy who we would call a conductor waved a lantern. That was our go-ahead signal. We were heading towards the west—Moscow here I come.

The engineer pulled back on his throttle lever, and nothing seemed to happen. Then the engine started to huff and puff with escaping steam.

Like a glacier, the train started to move. The train was a short one of only about fifty cars. They were all boxcars or the several stock cars, so I had no idea what we were hauling.

At one point I stepped on the hand of the drunk guy passed out on the deck. I checked he was still alive.

We picked up speed. We must have been doing forty or fifty miles an hour, which didn't seem like much, but it was more than Horse and I could do.

About three hours into our journey the drunk fireman started to show signs of life. Not much, a lot of moaning and groaning.

He finally managed to stand up, pee over the side of the moving train, and promptly lay down and went back to sleep.

It was a good thing that I had been using an ax and doing physical labor because this was hard work.

Another two hours and we pulled into another station. The fireman stood up and looked around. The engineer pushed him up against the side of the cab and took his wallet. He emptied a fistful of roubles and handed them to me.

"*Spasibo*."

I took it that my temporary employment was over. I climbed down and went back to the stock car and retrieved Horse and all my gear. I thought most would be missing but it appeared to be all there.

I gave the stockman, a kid of about twelve, twenty roubles. I had been given two hundred and fifty, so it didn't seem much. I had no idea what they would be worth.

I soon found out, as the train platform had a small café. That is if you counted two sawhorses with a door and four chairs as a café.

There was no menu. You sat down, and they served what they had. There was a sign stating ten roubles. I placed a ten down and I ate like I was starving, which I was. Have I mentioned that I hate sausage?

I had tied Horse to a post which I could see from my seat. No one approached him, but I saw several people slow and look as they walked by.

Not wanting to tempt fate or any thieves who might try to steal my stolen horse, I finished up and headed out along the tracks going east. I got out of sight of the town, left the track, and moved into the forest.

It was easy going once I was out of sight of the tracks. I went another ten miles or so on Horse, then started looking for a campsite.

There was a nice one, sheltered from the wind, which was getting a bit nasty at this time of year, and had a water supply. There was also good grazing for Horse.

After my day of physical labor, I was tired. I made a small fire and set up the two-man tent I had taken from the outpost barn. My fire was up against a boulder that acted as a reflector, so I was warm.

The Russian army issued good cold-weather sleeping bags, so I was set for the night. The horse was hobbled; I was warm; life was good, kinda.

The next day I continued my journey west. I had no idea if anyone was looking for me now. Well, they knew I was gone from the camp, so they knew I had run for it. The dogs would have tracked me to that cliff.

Would they think of a hang glider? Would they put it together with a missing horse at a remote outpost? Who knew? I think the odds were in my favor.

They were at least for now. As I got closer to true civilization, they would drop dramatically. I needed funds and identity papers. How was I going to get them?

My first thought was if I could get money, I could buy papers. Then I realized that I would be dealing with the underworld and that there had to be a reward for me. I would be turned in, in a heartbeat.

I still needed money, but that wouldn't take care of the identity paper issue.

Where do you even get real identity papers? I had been told the NKVD office, but I wanted to confirm that.

I decided I needed to get an answer to this question.

After two days of travel, I came across another small train stop. These stops served small farms and logging camps in the interior. I was more than ready for a bath, clean clothes, and a good meal, anything but sausage.

The whistle-stop town had what I needed. There wasn't a hotel, but enough trappers, farmers, and loggers came into town searching for a bath that there was a public bath. It only cost me fifty kopeks, which was a deal.

Clean with a freshly trimmed beard, I got dressed in my second set of clothes. My first set, which was a reeking mess, I had given to a washerwoman to see what she could salvage.

While she worked on those I went to a small restaurant. They had a menu. There was ham, rabbit, and sausage. I chose the rabbit. I hadn't had time to hunt any game, so it had been a while since I had any.

The restaurant was a bar/restaurant combination, and a guy was sitting there nursing a beer. He nursed it the whole time I was eating.

When I finished my meal, I joined him. My waitress understood my waving two fingers and brought us a beer each.

The guy looked at me like I was his savior.

I opened with, "Where does one get their lost identity papers replaced around here?"

I didn't want to give the impression that my Russian was anything near fluent, but it was getting better. At least he understood my question.

"The NKVD office."

"I know that; where is it?"

"Oh, I wondered why you didn't know NKVD issued. Their building is two streets down; turn left, and you can't miss it."

"*Spasibo.*"

I rode Horse out of town, passing the People's Commissariat of Internal Affairs. I rode five miles out and made a cold camp. I had no sooner got off my horse than I realized I had forgotten to pick up my laundry.

I rode the five miles back and collected it. I didn't want to make too many waves in town so that people would remember me. I was planning something that should take care of both my problems.

I tipped the washerwoman a full rouble. She had done a wonderful job.

Chapter 24

I lay down and rested for several hours and waited until early evening. Rested enough, I saddled the horse and rode back into town. I left him tied in the woods, as close to the NKVD building as I could get. Next, I walked around the area. As normal in a small town like this, there was no one around.

I even walked up and down the alleys that bisected the block the NKVD building was on. The building was a red brick, two-story-tall building. It wasn't that large, as would be expected in a small town this far out.

At the rear of the building, as I walked down the alley, I found a fire escape. It was nothing fancy, just iron-grated stairs that went from the second floor clear to the ground. There was no gate preventing someone from walking up. Removing my boots. I walked up the steps as silently as I could.

At the top of the stairs, there was a wooden door. Beside it was a window. Just for luck, I tried the door to see if it was unlocked. It wasn't. I tried the window. It also was either locked or jammed shut from years of disuse. I tried to look through the window but could see nothing, as the window looked as though it had never been washed.

Not having any fancy cutting tools, nor knowing how to pick the locks on the door, I chose the simplest method. I took my shirt off and placed it against the glass and broke it with the handle of the six-shooter which I had with me.

It shattered the glass and sounded like the world had exploded. I stood still waiting for action. Nothing happened; nobody stirred. Not even a dog barked. Clearing the broken glass around the window, I then felt for a latch. It was there, but it was frozen shut from years of disuse.

I carefully tapped the rest of the glass out of the frame of the window, making certain that I got it all so that I wouldn't cut myself when I stepped through.

After I had removed the fragments, I stepped through into a dark room. There was a little light from the outside, shining through the now nonexistent window. It lit up the room just enough that I could see a door across the way.

The room was empty, so I crossed to the door and quietly tried it. I cautiously turned the knob, trying not to create any sounds. It opened easily as though it was often used.

I opened the door into a dark hallway. Again, I listened carefully and could hear nothing that indicated the building was occupied. It looked like everyone had gone home for the day.

Some stairs came up the center of the floor creating a short hallway on each side of the steps. There were three other doors on this floor. I tried each of them, and they opened.

Two of them opened into one single large room, which looked like a document room. The last door opened into a workroom. Looking at the materials, I saw this is where documents were created.

I had to go this route because there was no way that I could walk in and say, oh, I've lost my documentation. Could I ask for some more? I would have been held until they confirmed my identity. Then it would be back to a Gulag for twenty or more years.

I checked around the room and found a basket. It had several completed identity cards, so I knew what my finished one had to look like. It also confirmed what I was given in the camp by the escape committee. I had kept the paper they had given me under my clothes. Finding blank cards, I practiced the signature that was used on the cards in the basket several times before I signed the blank card.

It wasn't a card as such. It was like an American passport with a green cover. My signing looked a little shaky, but it wasn't that far off. A quick look would make one think that it was the correct signature.

The stamps were not sitting out. I had to open several drawers and found a locked box. I knocked the lock off the box and found out it contained the proper stamps. I stamped my passport. Now the only thing that was missing was a photograph.

Fortunately, I had paid enough attention to Denny's photographic business that I could take a picture and develop it. Equipment to do so was over in a corner and it was like what Denny used.

Not as fancy, but it worked the same way. Since the room was closed, I had no problem having the lights on. There was no window for it to shine outside. Setting the camera up and getting the lights on the reflectors took just a moment.

I took several headshots, as that was what was required on the identity card. Then came the tricky part.

I had to develop the film. They had all the chemicals neatly labeled. It was a shame they were in Russian, and I couldn't read what they were.

I resorted to sniffing the bottles to identify the chemicals in them. I filled a developing tray with what I thought were the correct chemicals and tried my luck.

It took me four different tries, each time having to take new pictures, and then developing them before I had a set that would work. It also took additional time for the photos to dry.

I took my time. If someone was going to stumble in and catch me, I had nowhere to run. At this point, it was more important that I get this job done right.

I had the age and my description along with the photograph. I took the liberty of describing myself as an engineering student. I was to be traveling to Moscow to go to school at the University of Moscow. This would give me a certain prestige if I were questioned.

I then wrote myself and stamped a travel pass. This allowed me to travel to Moscow. All of this took the better part of the night.

As it approached dawn. I took all the photograph chemicals and spilled them around the area, then moved to the document room. There I threw paper files everywhere. Then using my fire starter, I lit the documents.

Picking up some burning paper, I took it over and tossed it into the workroom with the photo chemicals. They went up in a flash. I had to run for the window to escape. I retreated to the tree line and watched the building burn.

It was fully engulfed before anyone showed up. There wasn't a chance of the fire being put out. I now had documents to allow me to travel freely in Russia.

What I didn't have was money to facilitate that travel. I think it was time for me to make a bank withdrawal.

The next morning, I mounted Horse and rode farther west. I traveled for two days before I arrived at the next rail stop. This was another small town, too small for my needs, so I continued.

Four days later I arrived at a town that had a bank. I spent two days scouting out the area. I had to know the operation of the bank, if they had any guards, and how many. And how I could get away? But also, it would help to know if they had any money.

Fortunately, I had a 100-rouble bill left. So, I was able to go into the bank and get change. There were no guards. The best view that I could have of the clerk's cash drawer made me think that they would have several 1000 roubles on hand.

The bank vault looked like it was from another day and age. It had a combination lock. It was turned by hand, not a time lock. This gave me an idea of how I would escape.

I watched the bank and found that its closing time was around four o'clock in the afternoon. Locals all seem to know that and quit coming to the bank at three.

The next day, I waited until 3 p.m. and walked into the bank. I had pulled a bandana over my face like an Old West bandit.

Then I pulled out my Nagant six-shooter and said in my best Russian, "This is a holdup."

The three employees promptly raised their hands in the air.

Waving the gun, I signaled them back into the vault. I had a surprise when I investigated the vault. There were stacks of money. I pointed the pistol at some bags lying on the floor and the money. That was all the hint they needed. They loaded the bags, four of them.

I backed out of the vault with the bags in hand, locking the door behind me. It didn't dawn on me until much later that they might suffocate.

Not wanting to be greedy or stupid, I left the money in the bank teller trays.

Looking around the bank, I saw an old satchel of the style that was called a Gladstone bag. I dumped its contents, someone's laundry, on the floor, and then put the four money bags in it. I had to stuff them in but did get it closed.

I then calmly walked to the bank door, turned the sign from open to closed, and left town. I spent the next week on the trail bypassing two other towns. I had to laugh. This was getting almost funny. On a stolen horse with a six-shooter, I had just robbed a bank. Where could I find a black Stetson?

In the third town, which was larger than the others, I bought new clothes. These were a better fit. And they were civilian rather than the Red Army style.

I stopped at a stable and left Horse there, telling them that I would be back in two days. I patted Horse goodbye, knowing that I would never see him again. But at least I had left him in a safe place.

They would seize him for nonpayment, and he would end up with a new home.

From there I walked to the train station. I bought a first-class westbound ticket. I had to show my new identity papers to purchase the ticket, but they were accepted with no comment.

Chapter 25

I was able to afford first-class because that bank had two million roubles on hand, over fifty thousand US dollars. Why, I had no idea, but I was glad I chose that bank for my withdrawal.

I had several hours before the train left for Moscow, so I went shopping. I bribed the clerks, as suggested by the escape committee. It worked, as I was let into the backrooms of the luggage and clothing stores.

I had to buy luggage so that I would not look conspicuous. They were even able to put my new monogram on it. IP for Ivan Popov. I chose it for its commonness.

And I needed almost all new clothes. I had to buy ready-made and the fits were far from perfect, but they looked good for my supposed station in life.

It also included shaving gear and personal items. I bought only the best as I was traveling as an upper-middle-class student.

After I tried on my new clothes, I left on the last outfit. My Russian army uniforms I put in a bag, which I placed in an empty drum on the way to the train station.

I looked over my shoulder. I had no sooner thrown the uniforms in the drum than someone was digging through the drum and retrieving the clothes. That was good. The less I had connecting me to my recent trial, the better.

When the train came chugging into town, I was waiting. To board I had a redcap, a roughly dressed peasant, carry my bags onto the train.

I was directed to the compartment in my car by a conductor. When the door to the compartment opened, I had a moment of disorientation. It was as fine a room as I had been in months. It was decorated in a very ornate style. Probably from the time of the tsars.

I tipped the man. Probably over-tipped him from the way he thanked me. I settled in for a long ride to Moscow. The train left on time. Well only half an hour late, but that was good for the Siberian Railway.

A conductor came through the car checking my ticket. He tipped his hat. I didn't know if I was supposed to give him a tip, so I erred on the side of caution.

That was a correct action and my choice of five roubles was a good one. Whenever we came to a stop he was always there to see if I needed anything.

I didn't get off the train at any station, even to stretch my legs. I didn't want to take the chance of being recognized.

I realized it was dinnertime when the conductor came walking through the car ringing chimes on a portable xylophone. It was a pleasant sound that reminded me of better times.

Since I was in the last car on the train, I knew I had to move forward to the dining car. It was only the next car, so it wasn't hard to find. There were only three tables occupied out of the eight.

Two of them were families. At one of them sat an extremely attractive young lady. About my age, she was very well dressed and upper class. If this were the time of the tsars, I would say that she was nobility.

Today she would probably be the daughter of a Soviet commissar. It didn't matter. We wouldn't be talking.

At least I didn't think we would be talking. But when I entered the car, she looked up and signaled to the conductor, and he led me to her table.

This was uncomfortable as my Russian wasn't good enough to fool anyone that I was a native. Thinking quickly when I sat down, I asked her, "Do you mind if we speak English? I need to practice it."

In almost flawless English, she replied. "Let's do. I could always use practice myself."

We introduced ourselves, me as Ivan Popov and her as, Karen Romana from Vladivostok. This took me aback for a moment as I thought of Anna Romanov the actress. This girl could be a younger version of her.

I had another problem. I did not have a back story created. If she asked where I was from, I had no answer. Any personal questions would get me in trouble. How was I going to handle this?

"Karen, I do not know how to tell you this. Part of my education is being funded by the KGB. As such, I have been sworn not to tell anyone about my background. During my schooling, I will be given a new background. They are preparing to send me to America as a deep-cover agent."

She gave me a disgusted look.

"I've heard this type of story from many boys. They all want to make themselves look better than they are. You are going on a dangerous mission, and it is my job to send you off with good memories. Go away, you bore me."

I fled her table. And found my way back to my original one, feeling like I had played that well. The waiter came over to me. He asked me if I had struck out. I replied that I had. He laughed and said that is the way it happens.

There was no menu for dinner, they just served it. Fortunately, it was not sausage. It was lamb chops. I'm not a great fan. But it was certainly better than sausage.

After dinner. I sat with a cup of tea from the large samovar in the corner. I've seen several of these before, but this was the biggest one that I had ever seen. It had more valves, bells, and whistles than I could count.

Maybe not bells and whistles. But it had a lot of different controls. It did make a good cup of tea. As I ate my meal, I looked around the dining room.

I was having a dissonant moment. There was fine china, silverware, and decor. It differed so much from what I had seen the last few months that it seemed unreal.

It appeared as if I had come into a different world.

When a tray came about, I turned down the dessert. I had eaten enough dinner and was afraid that I would get ill because I had not had a regular diet.

I returned to my compartment and turned in for the night. I woke briefly once, as we had stopped to take on some coal and water. I turned over and went right back to sleep.

This was the most comfortable night's rest I had in a long time.

The next morning after washing up and putting on fresh clothes, I went for breakfast. The meal was eggs over easy, bacon, and fried tomatoes. If they had hash browns, I would have been in heaven.

In mid-morning, we came to a larger town. It had a longer stop than usual. I think they were changing train crews. Some men in uniform came through the cars, which I figured out were NKVD.

When they came through my car and looked at my papers, mine didn't rate a second look. He rifled through them, handed them back, nodded his head, and moved on.

That was a relief. Now I had to think of a back story because I would not be able to get away with what I had told Karen again.

Speaking of Karen, I had not seen her since I left her table. I wondered if she had gotten off the train. I hoped so. It would make things easier.

There was a Russian newspaper available at each table. I asked for a cup of tea and worked my way through it laboriously. My Russian was getting better. But there was no way that I would be able to get by as a student.

The paper had nothing but good news, except for two stories about an NKVD building burning to the ground due to faulty wiring, and a bank robbery, straight out of the Old West. It seems there was a whole gang of them, at least four and maybe more.

I read the financial numbers; all was not well in the USSR. They were hemorrhaging money like crazy. They wouldn't be able to keep up their social and military funding for much longer. The country would collapse.

I wondered how I could help this along. I thought about it for a while, but nothing came to me. I would keep working at it as I did want to get some revenge on the people who had done this to me.

If that required taking the entire system down, I was more than willing to try. I had to laugh at myself, as this was certainly an egotistical thought. Rick Jackson against the Soviet Union. No way.

Maybe I couldn't take the country down. But I could embarrass it. I had a thought, a joking thought, some time ago. It involved Lenin's tomb and flaming arrows. I wondered if it was possible. I will have to investigate it in Moscow.

If that didn't embarrass the Soviets, nothing would. If nothing else, it would show the USSR wasn't invincible. Now, if I could do something real like hurt their nuclear or space programs, that would damage their credibility.

Since they were cash-strapped, they would have a hard time settling down their satellite countries. If those countries could be given a reason to think that the Soviets could be overcome, they might revolt. I had to give this some serious thought.

Chapter 26

My trip to Moscow was going to take the better part of three weeks. I decided to spend the time as wisely as I could. I bought an English-to-Russian dictionary to help me learn the language. I also read the newspaper and listened to every conversation I could.

Even doing this for three weeks would not gain me a lot of proficiency in the language, but it was a step in the right direction.

Whenever possible, I engaged other passengers in conversations. My criteria were that they were younger children so that they wouldn't question my lack of fluency. I explained to them I was a foreign exchange student and was trying to learn Russian. Since they were children, they were naive enough to buy this.

At the same time I was practicing the language, I was trying to catch up on current events and personalities in Russia.

I already knew his name, but I had to be able to recognize a picture of Yuri Gagarin and other famous Russian cosmonauts.

I also found that it was important to know who were the best chess players and their ratings. There's no question the soccer team I would be following was the Moscow Dynamo. I had to learn their schedule and their roster. Who were the star players and their statistics?

At first, I had trouble getting the mindset to do this studying. I finally decided that I had an acting role and that was of an exchange student in Russia trying to fit in. I had to use my best acting abilities and adapt to another personality.

Instead of for the box office, this would be for survival. It made the game much more interesting. Not that it was a game.

I also had a Russian history book. It covered the last several hundred years back to Catherine the Great. She couldn't have had the sexual appetites they portrayed, could she?

I found the sections on the revolution. They were quite revealing. They lied about almost everything.

I also had read enough books to know that what I had learned in my Western textbooks may not all be true. But when you compare the accounts, it was obvious which ones were more accurate.

The textbooks glorified the leaders of the revolution. They did not talk about all the bodies they left around them or the betrayals that they made on their rise to power.

What I found amazing was they skipped over all the millions that Stalin had killed. Even today, they continued their five-year plans, which were resulting in crop failures and starvation.

At least the West could ship grain to make up some of the shortfalls.

One thing that I picked up from observing the people around me daily, most Russians were religious.

Their communist masters were antireligious and did everything they could to suppress religion. The normal citizen religiously lived their life.

They didn't have a lot of symbols and emblems. But watching, you could see signs of respect for the Eastern Orthodox Church.

Each time the train crew changed I made certain to tip the outgoing and incoming conductor. I had bought several engineering textbooks and let them know I was studying for entrance exams. I would keep these books open at the table during mealtime.

The conductors would make sure that the student wouldn't be interrupted. At the same time. I was able to listen to conversations around me. I think I learned more about Russia from eavesdropping than anything that I had read.

The engineering books themselves were interesting. I had enough engineering education that I was able to tell what the books were about. A formula is a formula no matter the language surrounding it. When I recognized the formula, I could figure out what was being said.

This helped me in learning the language. If I kept it up at the rate I was going, I would be able to talk intelligently to a five-year-old.

If I kept it up, I would be at the same level of comprehension as I had of Chinese Mandarin. I had a concern about my Mandarin. I had not practiced it in four months. I was afraid that I would lose it.

I think the gods of luck were looking after me. Because soon after I had thought this, a Chinese gentleman sat down at the next table.

I greeted him in Mandarin and then helped him order his dinner, as he was having more trouble with his Russian than I was.

I was afraid at first that he might recognize me. But he didn't. Or wasn't expecting to find me in this situation, so didn't make the connection.

He and I chattered for several days. It was refreshing to know that I had remembered a lot of the Mandarin that I had learned. Speaking to him brought back many words. It was a shame they didn't have a Chinese newspaper available. I could have caught up on my reading of the language instead of just speaking it.

Relations between China and Russia were still strained. This gentleman was a salesman for rare earth. It seemed China had some of the largest, rare-earth reserves in the world. They just had to find a market for them.

I asked the gentleman how the new Empress Ping was being viewed. He told me the people loved her. They knew that she had them at the center of her heart. All her actions were taking care of the Chinese people.

She had shoved aside, imprisoned, or killed all their old communist masters. She was firmly in control of the country. Corruption had been reduced significantly. And the people's standard of living was rising.

Most importantly, there was less starvation. That was because of the deals that she was able to enter with the support of the rich American Richard Jackson, who was the Duke of Hong Kong.

When he told me this, I thought the game was up. That I would be recognized. I wasn't. I changed the line of conversation as I didn't want to take any more chances of being recognized.

Not that I wouldn't welcome a chance to get word outside of Russia of my situation, but I just did not know how shocked his reaction would be and what he would do.

I was asked for identity papers at every stop once we crossed the Ural Mountains into Russia proper. Looking more worn all the time from being handled, my papers had lost the new look, which was a good thing.

I only had one scare. An NKVD officer held my identity card in his hands and kept tapping it against the other. I didn't understand what he was trying to tell me.

He finally gave up on the stupid student and rubbed his two fingers together. Then it dawned on me he wanted a bribe.

This was so blatant that I didn't mess around. I reached into my pocket pulled out a 100 rouble note and handed it to him. He looked at it with distaste as though he expected more but took it and walked on.

There are a couple of fun things that happened on the trip that relieved the boredom. At one stage of my journey, two sisters were interested in me.

Without talking to each other very much, we flirted back and forth through eye contact and finger motions. Their parents were watching them like hawks so they didn't dare approach me, and I didn't think it would be wise to try to approach them.

It was still fun winking and blinking at them. At one point one of them even made a kissy face at me. Her sister looked scandalized and then started laughing. That caught their parents' attention and got them a scolding. That was the last of our flirting.

Still, it was human contact and different. I needed that. I had been alone for so long.

At another stage, two young men got on board. They sat at my table. They were also students. I thought I was in for a rough time trying to keep my identity secret and pretending to be a student.

It turned out to be ridiculously easy. They were more interested in bragging to me about the stunts they had pulled and the girls they had conquered. Either they were both Casanovas reincarnated or exaggerating. I think they were exaggerating.

All I had to do was listen. And make an exclamation occasionally like I believed everything they were telling me and thought they were the greatest thing since sliced bread.

After those interludes, the trip was long and boring. I did get a lot of studying done. I was feeling more comfortable in Russian all the time but was under no illusions that I was where I needed to be. All I could do was keep studying and hope to keep from having conversations.

Chapter 27

Arriving in Moscow was an event. I had been to Grand Central Station in New York, so I knew what a busy station would be like. Compared to Moscow, New York was a backward farmer's market.

There were people everywhere in every type of dress you could imagine. The various republics of the Soviet Union were diverse, to say the least. This could be a strength but also a major weakness. Other than military might, what was holding this all together?

In New York one heard a dozen languages; here it was more like fifty. That was an uneducated guess because they were all so strange.

I collected my belongings. Here a real uniformed attendant was glad to help me after I waved a hundred rouble note at him.

He put everything on a hand truck and led me to a waiting cab rank. He managed to get my bags in the cab. The hardest one was my bow, which was wrapped in canvas. He and the cab driver opened both rear windows on the car and stowed it that way.

I held onto it the entire trip. That bow had seen me through some interesting times, and I had plans for it.

I had been given the address to a youth hostel by the escape committee. They warned me that I couldn't trust anyone there because the KGB planted people there all the time to catch dissenters.

However, it was clean, and the price was right. For me, it was more than right since I had made my bank withdrawal. I could live here for several years on what I had taken.

My cab driver's biggest concern in life was how Dynamo Kyiv was winning the football championship. This threatened the very foundations of civilization!

All I had to do was say, "*Da*," occasionally. I handed him a normal tip and thanked him for his insights on the state of the world. He took my sarcasm as a true thanks, so I let it go.

Thankfully, the youth hostel, named appropriately, The Moscow Youth Hostel, had a room. It was small, but it was clean. That is what I had been promised. I paid the small charge for a week in advance.

I had to show my identity card and travel permissions, but they were accepted without comment.

I stowed my gear and locked the door. The door was so flimsy it could easily be kicked in, but I left it on faith. I kept the six-shooter shoved into the waistline of my pants at my back. I had to get a better arrangement.

I don't even want to think what would happen if I got caught with it. At the same time, I couldn't leave it in my room as there was a one hundred percent chance the room would be gone through. Maybe by more than one group.

I thought the bow and arrows would get by. I mean who could do major harm with them currently?

The escape committee had instructed me to go to a coffee house to contact people who would help me. The committee hadn't been wrong yet, but this was the acid test.

At the given address was a shop named with a sign "Coffee Shop." This must be the place. I could tell a lot of thought had gone into the names used in this area.

Inside I followed instructions. I found an unoccupied table. This wasn't hard as I counted ten tables and only four were occupied. Their occupants looked like they were pulling all-nighters, or in this case, all-dayers studying for final exams.

When the waitress took my order, I asked if they had a newspaper, *Komsomolskaya Pravda*, a tabloid aimed at Russian youth and students. It wasn't the same as the better-known newspaper which was simply known as *Pravda*. Of course, they did, as it was the largest student-oriented newspaper in the country. If I had asked for any other, I would have been looked at as a possible agent provocateur.

As per my instructions when it was handed to me, I folded it in half and set it aside. I left it there while I drank four cups of coffee. Whoever came up with these recognition signals had an iron bladder.

After finishing my last cup, I folded the newspaper in the opposite direction and left the building. I had to do this for three days in a row at approximately the same time. I assumed this gave them, whoever they might be, time to follow me and arrange for a search of my room.

I was glad my underwear was all clean.

On the third day, the waitress dropped a note on my table as she served my fourth cup of coffee. As usual, I left a generous tip with my bill, read the note, and left.

Following instructions, I walked across the street, obeying the traffic light. I don't think getting stopped for jaywalking or walking against a light was in my best interest right now.

As I crossed the street a guy came abreast of me, tersely instructing me to follow him. After walking a mile of twists and turns, he led me to an apartment building.

We walked up to the sixth floor. The elevator was out, like most elevators in Russian apartments. As I walked through the doorway of an apartment, I was seized from behind and searched. Of course, they found the pistol.

I thought that I was in trouble. Instead, I heard a voice behind me say, "It is the correct serial number; he is okay."

I was let go and the guy who had said I was okay answered my unasked question.

"We were sent a message from the Gulag. If you showed up there was a good chance you would have a pistol with this serial number."

I should have kept my mouth shut.

"How do you know I'm not KGB, and we captured the pistol?"

"Right, Duke of Hong Kong. How many six-foot-five members of the KGB are there? Besides, we have your picture. The pistol serial number was just another bit of confirmation. Congratulations on your making it this far."

"Thank you."

"We are working on your escape route. We should have you on your way within the week."

"I'm not ready to leave yet. I have some unpaid debts to settle."

"We don't have much money; how much do you need?"

"None. These aren't that sort of debts. I don't think you want to know what I have in mind. Also, I don't want to know who you are or anything about your group. All I need is some assistance in getting into the University of Moscow as an engineering student."

"It can be done, but it will take several thousand roubles."

"When do you need them?"

"As soon as you can. Also, a copy of your identity papers and travel permissions."

I had planned for this possibility and had five thousand roubles separate from my main stash in the satchel I was carrying.

By having only five thousand, I had enough for their needs but not enough to tempt them over much.

I had to sit and wait for them to take my papers somewhere and copy them. We sat silently waiting while the errand was being run. By unspoken mutual consent, we weren't gaining knowledge of each other.

When the guy came back, he was the opposite. He wanted to talk.

"Where did you get these papers? They looked like they were made in an NKVD office. Please tell me how you got these so we can do the same."

"They were made in an NKVD office. I made them using their paper, stamps, and photographic equipment. Did you read about an office burning down about a month ago?"

"That was you?"

"Yes, or *Da* as you say."

"Well, that won't work for us very often, but it is something to keep in mind."

"Why don't you have someone get a job as a clerk?"

From the uneasy looks that were exchanged, I had stepped my foot in it. I changed the subject.

"How long until I have admission papers to the university?"

"You will have to wait in the lines with everyone else. Ivan Popov's name will be on all the proper lists in two days."

I didn't question this, but thought they had to have someone in the admissions office. After retrieving my papers and pistol, I returned to the youth hostel.

I would spend the two days waiting to enroll in school learning how Moscow is laid out, particularly around the Kremlin and some other government buildings. Other than that, I hung out at the coffee shop. I drew the line at drinking four cups of coffee, stopping at two.

Neither my bladder nor my nerves would take anymore. I did take the time to read the newspaper thoroughly each day to keep up with local happenings. It wouldn't be good to have an escape route blocked by a parade route!

Chapter 28

Monday morning, I was in line early. At least I thought it was early. I was a block away from the entrance to the building. The Russians know all about lines and waiting so they were prepared for it. I think some of them camped overnight.

I saw several guys selling their place in line. It seemed normal to everyone, just a cost of doing business.

It took me two hours to get inside the building and another to get to the front of the line. It was set up like every school I had seen. My line was divided down to K through P. I almost got in the J line, which would have been embarrassing and possibly dangerous, but what saved me from that mistake was the alphabet was different. There is no J in Russian.

The students or prospective students in line seemed a happy bunch, just like any other group of students in the world. Flirtation was going on everywhere. I tried to mind my own business.

When I got to the head of my line I was asked and gave my name as Ivan Popov. The guy went down the list, checked my name off, and handed me a packet of papers.

"This has your class schedule, book lists, and room assignment. There is also a bill for your fees for food, room, and classes. These have to be paid before you will be admitted to any classes."

I thought about not paying the fees, as I had no intention of attending any of the classes but then thought better of it. Someone might realize I was staying in a room that I hadn't paid for. This kind of thing had to have happened before.

I also snarked a bit to myself about how this socialist society was operating its primary school on a capitalistic basis.

Mind made up, I went to stand in another line at the bursar's office. It was only a two-hour wait until I was able to pay my fees. The total for the year was equal to two hundred and fifty dollars a year for room, board, and classes. Maybe they weren't so capitalistic after all.

I wondered if my paying in cash would be a problem. It turned out that not paying in cash would have been a problem. Receipt in hand, I went on the hunt for my dorm room.

The packet handed to me had a campus map, which had my dorm on it. It was an easy walk to my room.

On the way, I passed a bookstore, so I went in, or at least tried to go in. Students were lining the entrance selling books. They were hawking their old textbooks so they could afford to buy the ones for their next set of classes.

Always wanting to help my fellow man and leaving as little footprint as possible, I attempted to buy my books. It turns out that my fellow students were a rapacious bunch. They wanted new book prices for some tattered stuff.

I didn't know what the pricing should be, but all I had to do was listen to the cries of outrage by my fellow purchasers. Some were reaching a deal, whereas most were going on into the store.

I was carrying a light load, only four classes this semester so only needed four books. I had to buy a cloth bag to carry them in as the store provided nothing. While I was at it, I picked up a couple of University of Moscow sweatshirts and a grey sweater. They were cool, and if I could get them home, neat souvenirs.

My dorm was like I imagined it would be. A Soviet-style concrete behemoth with no architectural grace at all. My third-floor room was not any better. The walls were painted battleship grey, and the floors were a grimy linoleum.

There was a single bed with a mattress that was scary-looking, and there was no bed linen to be had.

I went down to the ground floor with the idea of asking where I could buy a new mattress, sheets, and blankets.

I soon found out that they were being sold from a ground-floor office. It seems the building superintendent or whatever they called them had a nice sideline going.

It also explained why I had seen other students carrying bedding up the steps. The building had only six floors, so they hadn't bothered to include elevators. I sent a silent thanks to the person who had arranged my room.

One poor kid came in the front door with sheets and blankets he had brought from home. A couple of thugs took care of that. This was a monopoly. At least they only stole his stuff. They didn't beat him, at least not much.

Again, keeping a low profile, I bit the bullet and bought my bedding, then had to carry it up the steps. The mattress was single so it could have been worse.

On the way up the stairs, I wondered how the thugs could sell us bedding for the equivalent of twenty US dollars. It would cost them more than that. It dawned on me that the bedding cost them nothing. They were selling us the bedding that went with each room.

I thought at least they were industrious in carrying all that bedding down the steps to resell it to us. Being a little slow, it took me a minute to realize that the bedding hadn't been taken up the stairs at all.

The thugs were probably being paid to haul the stuff upstairs. Instead, they had us doing their job for them.

I thought about what I could do about it but realized that I had bigger battles to fight.

Shortly after I made my bed and hung up my clothes, my roommate showed up. I don't know where he was from, but I can tell you they don't speak Russian there. Maybe it was Tajik or Kyrgyz. I know they don't speak Russian there.

I tried Russian, Spanish, Mandarin, and English. Not even my little bits of French, Portuguese, German, or Italian helped.

We gave up trying to communicate. Maybe it was for the best. We managed to work out a few signs, like going to the bathroom or to eat and that was about it.

I kept my bow and arrows under my bed. Since I knew he would look as soon as I was out of the room, I showed them to him before placing them there. With no common language, I didn't have to come up with a story as to why I had them. I always kept the Nagant pistol with me.

It was hard to imagine that he hadn't got a glimpse of it, but he never made an issue of it.

That first day I walked around the campus getting to know the layout. It was a nice campus. The modern buildings on Sparrow Hill were ugly but functional. The best Soviet building designs were among the worst in the world.

The university had been established in 1755, but this campus was built in 1953. How do you build an old modern building that looks like it is going to fall until you look at the base structure and then you think it will outlast the pyramids? Unless shoddy cement was used in its construction.

It was kind of sad. The Russian government wanted a true university campus but didn't know how to go about it. I suspect the faculty and courses are the same. Not that I had ended up that impressed with Oxford. I suspect the US schools weren't that much better, buildings yes, faculty no.

There seemed to be a trend in the US that everyone should have a college degree and that working with your hands was to be looked down upon. I couldn't see that ending well.

All you had to do was look at China, Africa, or India. There everyone wanted a white-collar job and looked down on those that didn't have the education. That resulted in backwardness and corruption. I was an example of a person getting the education they needed, not one decreed by a remote bureaucrat, and being a success.

While I was thinking these high-minded thoughts, I also realized Russia has some of the prettiest girls in the world. Not that I would be unfaithful to Nina.

I wonder what she was up to these days, I had been gone now for almost five months. Was she waiting for me?

I found five possible escape routes from campus. Two by subway. One by train tracks or even hopping a freight car and two more by footpaths.

These would only be used if I had to flee the campus, probably having to abandon my gear. That made me think about having small stashes at various points, so I would have some money and a change of clothes, if nothing else.

After my afternoon out I tried out the dining hall. I was awfully glad that I wouldn't be here very long. I hate sausage.

Chapter 29

I hadn't slept in any sort of dorm situation for a long time. I had forgotten that some students were up at all hours and had no respect for others. It was a fitful night's sleep at best.

The next morning, I ate in the dining hall. They were serving scrambled eggs, hashed browned potatoes, and sausage. I skipped the sausage.

There was a coffee urn. After trying that I had a cup of tea. The tea was black as a witch's heart, sweet as a maiden's breath, and strong as a pig's odor. I didn't make that up; I read it somewhere.

Anyway, the tea was better than the coffee.

After taking care of my morning needs, I went to Red Square. I had the idea of destroying Lenin's tomb with fire arrows.

I would find a safe place to shoot them from and land a pattern on the roof as I had in the limo parking garage at the Soviet Embassy in London.

It would show the world that the Soviets weren't invincible, and the Soviets would know who had done it.

When I arrived at Red Square, I found one small miscalculation in my plan. Lenin's Tomb is made from red marble. My arrows wouldn't set that on fire. I doubted if they would even damage the marble.

So back to the drawing board. What could I destroy or damage that would hurt the Soviet government but not the Russian people?

Even if I managed to set someplace like the Winter Palace on fire, it would enrage the people, but not hurt the Soviet Commissars.

I decided to move on to my next target. I wanted to hurt the Red Army. There was no way that I could do that by force of arms. I had even thought about attacking the facilities where they made nuclear bombs.

There were two obstacles to that plan. The factories would be well defended, but the real plan killer was that I had no idea where those factories were.

I would hurt the Red Army in its pocketbook. I had talked with one of the dissidents and found out that the Red Army followed the Soviet model of top-down control.

A central point in the treasury would issue an order of payment to the banks who in turn would deposit money in each army command's account. The commands in turn would issue orders to transfer money to their unit's accounts. This would continue down until orders were issued that money would be given to the individual soldier, sailor, or airman.

My plan was simple, burn down the building that contained the records that started the whole process.

I was told which building in the State Treasury complex that was. I walked through the complex. There was free passage along the sidewalks. If you attempted to enter any of the buildings, you had to go through a security setup.

What they checked I had no idea and didn't care, as I had no intention of entering any of the buildings.

I just needed to find a good spot to shoot from. I could hit the roof of a building like the one in front of me from four hundred yards.

Next, I had to find a place within four hundred yards that I could not only shoot from but escape from.

I circled the area around the building, sticking to the sidewalks and looking both ways before crossing the street. Russian drivers are terrible. I don't think they ever looked at the road.

I wasn't the only one on foot in the area, but I was the only one not dressed as an office worker. While not sticking out like a sore thumb, I was different. Different enough that a police car pulled over beside me.

The cop riding shotgun signaled me to stop where I was. They got out of their cruiser and approached me. The way they did it told me they were professionals. I wouldn't have a chance against them, even if they didn't have guns.

I did the only thing I could, I played my role. My role was an innocent student out for a walk on a clear fall day.

"Papers, please."

At least it was, please. I wasn't in trouble yet.

"Certainly, officer," as I handed him my papers.

"Mr. Popov, or may I call you Ivan?"

"Ivan will do."

"Well Ivan, your papers say you are a student at Moscow University. Why are you walking around here? It is over five miles from your school."

"It is!? I have been walking for hours but have no idea how I got here. I was thinking of my girlfriend back home and lost track of everything."

"Where is home?"

"Vladivostok."

"You don't sound like you are from there."

"I grew up in Manchuria. My parents moved to Vladivostok several years ago, and I have had trouble picking up Russian."

The other officer surprised me by asking me in Mandarin if I understood him. I did barely because his accent was atrocious.

I replied in Mandarin, "I do understand you, but your Mandarin accent is like my Russian, not good."

He laughed at that.

"Why did your parents move?"

"They started a business there when relations between China and Russia were good. Dad thought he would get in early on a new marketplace. Then things went bad, and we had to leave. Our neighbors who had been friends stopped buying from our store and wrote bad things on the side of our house."

The officer who spoke a little Mandarin was shaking his head in agreement.

"I was in the army stationed there when it started to go bad. Your parents made a wise decision."

"Enjoy your walk and thinking of your girl."

"I will officers. I need to head back, or I will miss dinner."

"You don't want to do that; the chef there is famous for how many different ways he can prepare sausage."

"Then I had better get moving. I wouldn't want to miss that!"

They returned to their cruiser and pulled away.

I think I deserved an Oscar for that performance.

I had no choice now but to head back to school. If I continued to walk this area and they saw me again, I would be taken in for some serious questions. My cover wouldn't stand up to any inquiries to Vladivostok.

As I walked back toward the university, I saw the answer to my shooting location. It was five hundred yards from the building, but it was elevated.

Railroad tracks crossed the road ahead of me. There was a signal tower over the tracks. It was a huge metal framework crossing the tracks. It had a series of lights on it which acted as traffic lights for oncoming trains.

The beauty of these was that they were very tall as engines had to go under them and that they had steps built in so that the lights could be changed when they burnt out.

With the added height I could hit the roof of my target building. The rails weren't rusted, so I knew the tracks were in use.

I didn't stop walking as I looked around. Instead, I went back to my dorm. I ate at a little café on the way back. It was a shame I had to miss out on one of the chef's famous sausage recipes.

Once back in my room I was prepared to study one of the engineering handbooks so as not to arouse any suspicions in my roommate.

He wasn't there, so I read the newspaper to work on my Russian. He stumbled in drunk several hours later and went right to bed. I didn't think I had to worry about him.

The next morning, I didn't bother going to breakfast at school but stopped at a different restaurant that served breakfast. Bacon, eggs over easy, and hashed browns set me up for the day.

I know bacon and sausage come from the same animals, but what a difference. I also bought a bread and cheese sandwich for lunch. They also sold me a thermos of tea. I had given up on Russian coffee.

Back at the railroad tracks near the treasury complex, I settled in for a long day. I chose a spot that was out of sight of the road, but I could see passing trains.

It turned out the track must have been the mainline. I thought so as there were four sets of rails. There was a train at least every half hour. Since there were no crossing gates, I was able to see how reckless Russian drivers were.

They would speed up if they saw a train coming. Not once did I see a driver deliberately give the train the right of way. One guy had the train clip his rear bumper but not enough to spin him out. These guys were crazy.

Now, these tracks were on an uphill grade, so the trains were moving slowly as they reached this point. This gave me a better idea of how to escape after I took my shots.

Chapter 30

That evening I walked back to the train crossing. If nothing else, I was getting exercise. Maybe not the running I used to do, but certainly in distance covered.

It was dusk when I got back to the crossing. I was relieved that the train traffic had remained the same. It was almost like clockwork.

Growing up in a railroading family in Bellefontaine, I knew how to hop a freight train. Waiting for the right moment, I ran alongside a boxcar and grabbed the ladder on its side.

I swung in the air for a minute but was able to catch my feet on a lower rung. Then it was just a climb to the top of the car.

I sat cross-legged on top of the car as it moved slowly along. The night of my attack I would drop down from the signal bar to a boxcar. It was only a three-foot drop, almost a long step, so easy to do.

The brakemen at BN yard would do that in the winter as it was safer than running alongside a car coated in ice trying to jump up to the ladder when your hands could slip at any moment.

Jumping from the signal bar was considered a safety violation, but no one was ever called on it.

I was looking for a get-off spot that was far enough away from the treasury building that if I was seen, I wouldn't be connected with it.

What I found was much better. The train rolled into a huge marshaling yard. This is where trains were made up by switching the boxcars around so those that heading for a common destination were hooked together.

I was going to head west towards Poland, then on through East Germany. If I could figure out where the westbound trains were assembled, I could go directly from the treasury hit to my Russian escape.

I had to escape from the treasury hit, a "friend" hit, and a Soviet hit. Then I had to escape from Russia to friendly territory.

As the last chance, I would go to the American, British, or even Chinese Embassies. The only problem was that I would be seen going in and would not be able to get back out.

Now all I had to do was scout out my "friend", and find something to destroy that would be perceived as a hit on the Soviet Union and not the Russian people.

I got off the boxcar by climbing down the ladder and lowering myself. When I felt my feet touch the ground, I took off running in the direction the cars were rolling.

I was able to clear the track bed and tumble down the side. Not the most elegant dismount, but it worked as I didn't get injured.

My dad could make it look like he was taking a simple step, never losing his balance, or awkwardly changing his speed. Of course, he had done it many times.

When I got off the train, I saw the ground was littered with white cards. They were about four inches by eight inches. I got a big smile as I knew what they were for.

A switchman, a guy who is qualified to make up a train by switching cars around, is given a list by the yardmaster as to what cars by serial number are to be hooked together to make up a train.

The best part is that at the top of the card was the train number, track number, and destination. Now all I had to do was learn the track numbering system, and which direction the common destinations were in.

Since trains were being made up constantly, I watched a switchman make up a train. When he was finished, he tossed his card on the ground. By seeing where he had the brakemen put the cars, it was easy to learn the yard layout.

It was getting late or early, depending on how you looked at it. I decided I had better head back to school and get some sleep.

Since I didn't know where I was relative to the school, I simply waited for the next train that was heading back the way I came.

Stepping off the car at my original crossing worked better this time. From there it was a long but easy walk back to my dorm. I kept an eye out for police cars, but none were around.

The sun was just rising when I climbed into bed.

I woke up to my roommate returning from class. He was noisy as all get out. He didn't say a word to me as he threw his books on his bed and left. I suspect heading to the nearest bar.

I was wrong as I saw him in the commons room as I was leaving to find some food. He had a bottle of beer in hand so at least I had that part right.

After eating a dinner of borscht and golubsty, I headed on my next mission. That was to find out how to ambush my "friend" who had tormented me in prison and faked my execution. He would pay for his funny joke.

I took a cab to Lubyanka Square where my target worked. I would watch the front door at quitting time, which was soon, and see if he would come out that way.

There was a group of men playing chess in the immediate area surrounding the statue of Felix Dzerzhinsky, the founder of the Cheka, the forerunner of the KGB.

I would wander from a chess match to match, pretending I knew what going on. These guys played better than I ever would. I did learn several chess terms I hadn't heard before, fianchetto and en passant. I also learned Russian for son of a bitch, but I don't think that is restricted to chess.

Around five o'clock, play was suspended as the men all gathered to look at the main entrance. That was convenient for me as that is what I was here for.

I soon learned why they were watching the front door. A young woman came out. She was stunning. I heard the guys talking about her. They couldn't figure out how a beautiful person like Katya Mayorova could work in such an ugly place.

There were many theories given but no knowledge displayed, so I would probably never know. All I knew was that she was a classic beauty who would give Helen of Troy a run for her money.

I was so wrapped in the girl that I almost missed my "friend" as he exited the building. I managed to recover and start after him. He beat me to a corner where a bus was getting ready to leave. I had to watch him get on it and ride away.

I took careful note of the bus route and was on that bus when he boarded the next day. When he got off at his stop, I stayed on.

One more day, and I was waiting at a distance when he got off the bus. I followed him for two blocks until he turned into an apartment complex.

The next day I was in place to see him push an elevator button for the sixth floor. The day after, I was at the end of the hallway on the sixth floor and saw him put a key into the door of unit 604.

Thank you, Mum, for your lessons in spycraft. This was front-tailing at its best. It had taken me a week, but he never saw me or suspected that he was being followed.

Now I had to know if he lived alone or had a family there. Unlike some buildings I had heard of, there were no old women on each floor watching the comings and goings of the tenants and ready to report anything suspicious.

That didn't mean there weren't old men sitting in the lobby, either talking or playing chess. Did you know chess is a favorite pastime in Russia?

I sat down next to a group of men who were just talking. At a break in the conversation, I asked.

"Do any of you know that clown who lives in 604?"

One of the guys said. "I do, why do you ask?"

"He just kicked a dog when he was coming in, and I wondered if he was like that with his wife and children."

"No, he is single, and I'm not surprised that he kicked a dog. He works for the KGB, and none of them are nice people."

"I'm not surprised to hear that; it is good to know that he isn't married."

One of the guys laughed, "He has a woman come to his place at seven o'clock every Saturday night. Who knows what he does with her?"

I didn't want to know but that gave me the information I needed. I sat back quietly and after a while wandered off.

Chapter 31

I still hadn't figured out what I could damage or destroy that was identified with the Soviet Union and not the people of Russia.

As I made my way back to my dorm, I saw one of the secret police prison vans, a Black Maria. I wasn't the only one. I was on a crowded street, and I saw people making the sign of the cross, Eastern Orthodox style. That is touching their right shoulder first then the left, Roman Catholics do it left shoulder first. I have no idea why the difference.

That was what I needed. If ever there was a sign of the Soviets, hated by all, it was the Black Maria. Now I had to find out where they were kept.

It took me three days and some discreet questioning, but I found the home depot of the prison vans. It was in a warehouse district about five miles from the center of town.

They were kept running twenty-four hours a day, which said something about the police state. The building is a large brick building built before the nineteenth century so there was an excellent chance that the internal framework was wood.

I could tell its age from the huge numerals at the top front of the building, 1886.

The entire lot was surrounded by a chain-link fence with barbed wire coiled on top. There would be no climbing over that. The only break in the fencing was a manned gate. All vehicles entering were checked; some guards even had a device with mirrors on it and slid it under the vehicle to see if anything was attached to the bottom.

That was fine with me, I had no intention of getting that close. Instead, I walked the area around the warehouse. I stayed at least one block away from it at all times and didn't go on any of the streets immediately adjoining the depot.

I was looking for a place to shoot from. I thought I had a good candidate when I found a dilapidated warehouse with an iron fire escape going up its side. I carefully ascended the fire escape and found that people were living on the roof.

They had built shacks from scrounged materials and had a small community. They even had a garden. I backed away from them as quietly and quickly as I could. I didn't think I would be welcome there no matter what they thought of the Soviet Union.

I had to go to the other side of the van depot before I found another likely candidate. It truly was abandoned, and the fire escape was shaky, to say the least.

The warehouse I was on stood five stories tall, and the van depot was only four. Since it was the middle of the afternoon, I got a good look at the area.

Of particular note was the roof of the depot. It was tarred and was probably wood underneath. That was perfect.

Another plus was that they had a fuel farm. There were large tanks for gasoline and several sheds where I saw workers take out what looked like five-gallon cans of lubricants. Russia was on a variation of the metric system, so I don't know how much they defined as being on-site. By the Ricky Jackson system, it was a bunch.

I now had my targets and the start of a plan. I returned to my room at school. I wished I hadn't. My roommate had allowed our room to be taken over for a floor party. He had a large bowl of grape juice filled with vodka and any other alcohol that could be found.

That my side of the room was now a disaster area was one thing; what followed was worse. My drunken roommate insisted on introducing me to everyone there, one at a time.

I had managed to avoid all of them as there was bound to be someone from Vladivostok who would know I had never been there.

After the round of introductions, one boy approached me with a big smile, "It is nice to meet someone from home."

Oh boy. Thinking quickly, I took him aside in the hallway.

"Yes, it is wonderful. Let's have a drink together."

He grinned and said, "My pleasure."

"Let me get them."

I went back and found a vodka bottle still half full and a grape juice bottle. He got a double shot of vodka with his juice. Mine was straight juice.

I handed him his drink and before he could ask me a question, I asked him which schools he attended. He named several and I shook my head.

"I didn't attend any of them."

"Which ones?"

I leaned in close as if to share a secret and whispered, "I went to a church school."

His eyes got big.

"I thought they were only rumors."

"They are real."

"Your secret is safe with me; how did you get transcripts to allow you to enter here?"

I rubbed my fingers together in the universal sign of money and bribery. He had finished his drink, so I got him another glass. A triple shot this time.

He kept asking me questions which I managed to dodge, but you could see even in his drunkenness he was wondering.

My timeline had been moved up, or I needed another place to stay. That would only work for a few days as I would be reported as missing from school. When they started checking, they would find that while I had slept in the dorm, I hadn't attended any classes.

Even the worst students attended some of them.

My new friend from Vladivostok passed out after his eleventh shot of vodka. I had to admire his alcohol tolerance. I doubt I could have been awake after five shots. I didn't intend to ever find out.

I left him asleep in the hallway. He was one of several. I waited until the party died a natural death, gathered all my gear, and went down one floor. I knew of an empty room that I could use. I had to sleep on the floor, but it was better than trying to find a place in the middle of the night.

I woke at first light. After using the restroom, I left the dorm for the last time and headed out. I had my backpack with several changes of clothes, my bow and arrows, and my money.

Before I did anything, I had to have caffeine. I found one of the many small coffee houses and spent the morning thinking while I drank cup after cup of coffee.

It was good coffee, better than anything else I had found in Russia. They charged almost double per cup, but it was worth it. A lot of other people thought so, as there was a continuous stream through their door.

I asked my waitress what brand. She leaned over and whispered, "Maxwell House."

It was a good thing I didn't have any in my mouth as it would have gone everywhere.

It was Friday, and if I wanted my plan to work, I had to proceed tomorrow evening. There were several things I had to do first.

I had passed a garage that was working on motorcycles and scooters. For five hundred roubles I bought a scooter which looked like it was good for a few more miles, and I mean just a few.

Russia has many shortages; hemp rope isn't one of them. I bought a hundred feet of quarter-inch hemp.

I had to wait until after dark for my next step.

Looking like a pack mule with my backpack, wrapped bow, and rope draped over the rear of the scooter, I went to the warehouse next to the prison van depot. I crossed my fingers the whole trip when I found out that the headlight didn't work.

At the warehouse, I parked the scooter in an alley, hoping that no one would steal it in the short time I would be gone. I took the hemp rope up the fire escape, along with my bow and backpack. Those were items that I didn't dare lose. That and the six-shooter in my jacket pocket.

Finding a stout pipe that I pulled on as hard as I could to check the sturdiness of its connection, I tied off the rope. I then suspended my weight over the edge to make certain the pipe wouldn't break. It didn't, so I cut a length of rope long enough that I could rappel down the side of the building. When it was time to leave the scene, I wanted to be gone.

I hid the rope and my bow and arrows under an old water tank on the roof.

My scooter was still there, so I went to my next stop. That was the marshaling yard where they made up trains. I hid my backpack under a stack of railway ties that looked like they had been there for a long time.

I didn't do it until I observed the surroundings for over an hour to make certain no one was around. Not only were my clothes there but the balance of my money. I hoped to make it useless shortly but wanted to hang onto it until then.

The weather had turned cold, so I took a chance and returned to the dorm and my room. My roommate was sound asleep when I got in, so I didn't disturb him. He was gone when I woke in the morning.

My backpack hadn't had room for all the clothes I accumulated, so I was able to take a shower and put on clean clothes I kept with me. This was my big day when I was going to let the Soviets know that messing with Ricky Jackson was not a good idea.

Chapter 32

I had a large breakfast at one of the cafes in the university area. While I was drinking my tea, the coffee was terrible, a couple of NKVD police came in and went from table to table demanding to see identity cards.

One unfortunate guy told them he had forgotten his in his dorm. They handcuffed him and took him away. Life in the USSR.

I went over my plans in my head trying to visualize each step of the way. When I got to the part with my "friend" answering his apartment door, I realized that what I had assumed might not be true.

I spent the next few hours taking care of that. It only required another few feet of rope from the hardware store and an eyehook. I took the only eyehook on the shelf, so I was lucky to find one.

There were constant shortages of everything in Russia. I wondered how much longer the people would put up with it.

I had read enough in *Pravda* to know that they had a huge disinformation program going, telling people that Russians had it good, that Americans were starving in the streets as their capitalist masters lived like royalty.

I was careful to obey all traffic rules on my scooter. It had a license plate on it from the people I had bought the scooter from. For all I knew, the scooter was stolen so I couldn't afford to be pulled over.

The one thing for certain, if I were pulled over it would be for pollution and not speeding. The scooter was a white Italian Vespa which was immensely popular with a bunch of them on the road, just not in Russia.

It didn't stick out like a sore thumb, but it was different from the few Russian scooters I saw. If mine hadn't had many thousands of miles on it, it would have been worth a lot of money here.

I liked the ease of handling of the scooter. It was more like a toy than a motorcycle, but it was a toy that would go places. It was a shame that I couldn't take it with me. I would have to see about buying one for the 707 when I got home.

I had a late lunch at a small family restaurant near my "friend's" apartment. Across the street was a small park. Though a little chilly, people were picnicking.

After lunch, the men would take a nap on their blankets while the children would play while being watched by their mums. Some things were universal.

It gave me an idea. I rented a blanket from the owners of the restaurant. I paid five roubles for the afternoon. I wanted to take a nap!

Since the ratty old blanket they handed me wasn't worth a rouble, they were getting a good deal even if I didn't return it. The blanket smelled like it was the dog's blanket. This was confirmed when the family pet came up to me and whined while pawing his blanket.

I would be certain to get it back to him. Life was hard without losing your bedding. I knew from experience.

I did manage to doze off and catch a couple of hours of sleep. I needed this as I wouldn't get much tonight.

At six-thirty, I was in place at my "friend's" apartment. I had debated where to wait. I decided on the end of the hallway on the sixth floor. There was a small vestibule there with a chair.

I didn't know what the woman visitor would look like and didn't want to approach the wrong one. This left me with the tradeoff of being conspicuous by sitting in the vestibule or talking to the wrong person. I decided to take my chances with the vestibule.

I was lucky as only one man got out of the elevator and went to his apartment. He did glance up at me but ignored me as he went into his apartment.

At almost seven on the dot, a middle-aged woman got off the elevator and started towards unit 604.

If I had waited downstairs for her, I would have let her pass. I had an American Hollywood prostitute in mind, one that would work the strip in Vegas.

She and I reached the door at the same time. I was ready for her. As she reached to knock on the heavy metal door, I held out my hand.

I held five thousand roubles. Even high notes made a thick wad. "Go home."

She looked at the money and then grabbed it as she left. I waited for her to get on the elevator and then knocked on the door. I pulled my six-shooter out.

When my "friend," answered the door I was glad I had visualized the events. He was wearing a bathrobe with no pants on.

I shoved the pistol in his face, backing him into the room. I forced him to his knees, then using a small length of my hemp, tied his hands behind him. I tapped his head with the gun barrel. Not hard enough to knock him out, but enough to disorient him. At least that was my goal.

He fell forward. I used the opportunity to circle his waist with the length of rope that I had fixed up in the morning. Then I clipped the eyehook onto the other end of my original rope.

Then the piece de resistance, a hangman's noose around his neck. I forced him to get up. He couldn't see the noose because I had draped it over his back.

One thing you could say about these apartment buildings was that they were sturdy. I tied the other end of the rope off on a chandelier. I was careful with my measurements so that I had the exact length of rope.

I didn't want to kick him off the chair and land on the floor. He had to dangle in the air. The fall wouldn't be more than a few inches so he wouldn't break his neck.

At gunpoint, I had my dazed "friend" climb up on a kitchen chair. I tightened the noose and pulled the rope, so he was standing on his tiptoes. I tied it off and went to his bedroom where I found a hand mirror. I took it out and showed him that his head was in a noose.

He peed himself. That was great.

"Remember me?" I asked him.

He stammered, "Yes, please don't do this."

At that, I kicked the chair out from under him and he fell.

The rope around his waist, which was attached by the eyehook to the main rope, stopped his fall before the noose could pull tight. My time on the sets in Hollywood had not been wasted.

I then said the words I had been waiting to say for months.

"Good joke, heh?"

I left him dangling.

Returning to my scooter, I headed to the van depot.

Parking my scooter in the same back alley as I had before, I climbed the fire escape for what I hoped would be the last time.

The first thing I did when I reached the top was to retrieve the rope I had set up for rappelling down the side of the building.

Then I restrung my bow. I physically checked all my arrows to make certain none were warped or had missing feathers. They were all good and usable.

In my backpack, I had also stashed a can holding a mixture of gasoline and styrofoam that one of the stuntmen had taught me. He called it napalm.

I had stuffed toilet paper in the cardboard rolls that it came wrapped around. I had collected them for over a week in the men's dorm. Russian toilet paper was good for this if nothing else. It was rough.

I then poured the napalm mixture into the center of each of the tubes, which I fitted over my arrows.

Without lighting it, I shot one away from my target building. I hadn't had a chance to see how much the flight characteristics would be affected.

They weren't, at least not enough to worry about.

I lit a candle and then used the candle to light my arrows quickly. I launched them onto the roof of the van depot.

The place burst into flames. The wood in that building was dry. Within ten minutes the roof had collapsed into the next floor. People came pouring out of the depot.

Within five minutes no more people were coming out, so I shot my last arrows into their fuel farm. At first, I thought nothing was happening, but then it exploded.

I wanted to burn the place down, but this was much better. The explosion took out the side of the building and within a few more minutes the building collapsed into a pile of burning rubble.

Taking my bow and arrows, I rappelled down the side of the building to my scooter and headed for my next target. The Black Marias would be off the streets of Moscow for a while. I didn't doubt they would be back, but the people would know that the Soviets weren't invincible. Maybe it would embolden the dissidents.

Chapter 33

I rode my scooter over to the railroad tracks near the treasury building. I had gotten fond of the little scooter, but we now had to part company.

I parked it on a side street and left the key in it. It wouldn't sit there very long.

Taking my bow and arrows, I walked to the signal tower. Climbing to the top, I waited for a slow freight train to come into sight.

It was only a fifteen-minute wait, and one was coming slowly up the grade. I lay down on the walkway on top of the tower. I didn't want the train crew to see me.

When the steam engine chugged past, I stood up and lit my candle. From there I shot five arrows at the roof of the treasury building. One drifted off course due to an errant breeze, so I nocked and loosed one more.

When I saw it hit the roof of the building, I unstrung the bow and stepped off the tower onto the top of a boxcar. As the train trundled out of sight, I saw the building was engulfed in flames. These old buildings were fire traps. I hoped no one was inside and couldn't get out.

There were no cars in the parking lot and the buses didn't run in this area after dark, so I thought there would be a cleaning crew at the most.

I rode on top of the car until we came in sight of the marshaling yards. There I stepped off the car in a slow jog. I had done it enough times now that I wasn't falling anymore.

I retrieved my backpack from under the pile of railroad ties. It hadn't been disturbed. I then worked my way around the yard to where the switchmen were working.

I watched as a train was made up and the switchman tossed his white card with the train makeup. Litterbugs!

I had to wait for the third train to be made up until I recognized a destination in the direction I wanted to go. It was through freight to Kyiv. That was better than I could hope for.

I climbed on top of a boxcar. I had debated trying to ride inside an open car but if I were unlucky, someone would shut the door and lock me in.

On top of the car, I wrapped myself in a blanket I had taken from my dorm. A good sleeping bag would have been better, but I hadn't found one.

Using my backpack as a pillow, I dozed off. It had been a stressful few hours, and I had better get some sleep while I could. I wasn't looking forward to being on top of the train when it started moving.

I had been asleep for maybe an hour, and I was awakened by the engine hooking onto the train of cars. It bumped the car it was coupling with, and the jolt rippled down the line of cars.

Peeking over the edge of the car, I saw a signalman give the all-clear to the engineer, and the train started its slow movement.

My escape had entered a new phase. It was called get out of the Soviet Union and its satellite countries.

I thought back to the guy I had left dangling in his apartment. He probably would hang there for several days until someone missed him at work. He might even work himself free.

I worried about his health and safety as much as he worried about mine. Not at all.

The train moved slowly through the yards. Switchmen were throwing the switches to move the train onto the mainline going west. I couldn't be happier.

After half an hour we moved on to the mainline. The signal tower had all green blocks of light, so we were clear to go. The engine began to pick up speed.

It was a good thing I had brought the last of the hemp rope with me. I tied the rope to the top of the ladders at each end of the boxcar. This gave me a safety rope. I tied my backpack to it and crawled under the rope until it was in my middle.

Then I tried to go back to sleep.

Who was I kidding? Every time the train hit a sleeper that was out of alignment I was bounced around. At least I wasn't freezing to death as I had my head towards the front of the car, so my backpack was acting as a windbreak.

Wrapped in my blanket, I was comfortable.

It was a long night as the train traversed the Russian countryside. It started to snow lightly at dawn, so I was starting to get wet. This wasn't fun by any stretch of the imagination.

Dawn brought another problem to light. There were other people on top of the boxcars. I wasn't the only one riding the rails.

I could see three other guys, two were together and one by himself. The two guys were farther back. They started working their way forward until they were on top of the car with the third guy.

It happened fast. One of them hit the third guy, knocking him down. The other guy jumped on top of the guy that had been knocked down and was going through his clothes.

As I realized they were robbing him, they tossed him off the train! It was some pretty rough country at this point, so I doubted he would survive the fall.

They were two cars behind me and started towards me. The previous night I had debated leaving my bow and three remaining arrows behind. I was glad I didn't.

Standing up, I restrung the bow as quickly as I could. They were one car away when I was able to nock an arrow.

They stopped coming at me. I shouted, "Jump!" This didn't have the effect I wanted as they started working their way forward again.

I waited until they were ready to jump onto my car and let an arrow fly.

It was at point-blank range for me, and my arrow hit the one I was aiming at center mass. He fell between the cars. No way would he survive that.

The other guy stopped trying to move forward. I yelled, "Jump," as I nocked another arrow. He had to be stupid as he kept coming, jumping onto my car. I was at the other end of the car.

I let fly with the arrow just as the train hit a misaligned sleeper, my shot missed. I quickly loaded my last arrow and shot him in the chest. He fell from the train.

That was more excitement than I had bargained for. Why they kept coming, I will never know. They must have been very desperate.

We pulled onto a siding mid-morning next to a water tower. They filled the engine tanks, and off we went again. I had dried beef with me to eat but not enough to get me to safety.

I would have to find food somewhere along the line.

That evening we pulled into a small town and the train slowed as it moved to a siding. There was a coal dock. The train stopped with the coal car under the dock and a chute was opened, allowing coal to pour into the car.

I could see lights ahead from the town. I took a chance and got off the train. I rescued my rope that was tied to the boxcar. Once on the ground, I stashed my backpack and bow in some underbrush away from the tracks.

There was an access road next to the tracks, so I followed it into the town. There was a small train station, so I used their facilities and cleaned up the best I could. I wasn't looking like a bum yet but would soon.

There was a small diner-type place across from the station, so I went in and ordered a large meal. I had to pay in advance. I didn't blame them.

After eating, I went back to my stuff. The train had moved on so I would have to wait for the next one that stopped for coal.

Wrapped in my blanket, I slept for a few hours until I heard another train coming in for coal. It was now downright cold, and the snow was coming down heavier than it did the night before. I was in a race with the Russian winter. I thought of Napoleon's retreat and the German army and shivered.

I wished I could have bought a passenger train ticket, but my travel papers didn't permit me to go to Kyiv. Only from Vladivostok to Moscow.

As it got colder, I even put on both of my University of Moscow sweatshirts. That night was one of the most miserable I have ever spent. The next two days weren't much better.

I ate meals twice in the next three days. I would get off a train while it was taking on coal and water. Each time I went into a restaurant, advance payment was demanded.

On the third day at dinner, I went in with a fistful of roubles showing to save everyone the trouble. Even then they made me sit in the kitchen so I wouldn't bother other customers.

I didn't mind it at all as it was nice and warm there. I lingered as long as I could until the manager started giving me the evil eye.

Chapter 34

I had misjudged the manager. He stood next to me but facing away. It was like he was talking to the wall.

"If I were a student dissident from Moscow on the run, I would break into one of the *dachas* by the lake. The commissars who use them are never there during the week. If one broke in now on Monday, they could stay until Thursday without being disturbed. It would give the student time to rest, eat, and clean up."

He never looked at me, instead, he went back out front. I'm so glad I had my University of Moscow sweatshirt on. I would have to consider donating to their alumni fund; that is, if that were a thing in the USSR.

As to that restaurant manager, I don't know how I will ever repay him, but I will do my best.

Gathering my gear, I left by the kitchen backdoor. From the exit, you could see the lake. I worked my way around to the far side. The lake wasn't that big, several hundred acres at the most, but it had twenty or more *dachas* surrounding it.

Getting to the far side of the lake, I could see no sign of human occupation, but one thing I had learned was patience, so I sat for the next two hours waiting for full darkness. It didn't take long as winter was coming on. By six o'clock by my stolen watch, there were no lights inside any of the *dachas*, so I thought it safe to break into one.

I chose the largest. Breaking in was a simple matter of smashing a windowpane in the kitchen door at the back of the house and opening the door.

They hadn't even turned off the electricity at the mains as the lights came on at the turn of a switch.

The large oven in the kitchen even had warm coals. I searched through the kitchen drawers and found a flashlight. I turned the kitchen lights out and used the flashlight to find my way around. It would be less noticeable.

There was a large bedroom with a fireplace. There was a wood supply in a box, so I built a fire, using coals from the kitchen oven.

The room had heavy drapes, so I closed them tightly. I turned on the electric lights and went outside to check. Nothing was leaking through the curtains. They were like the blackout curtains Mum described from the war.

Full of dinner at the restaurant, my next action was to take a bath. There was hot water. It was wonderful. I was able to get clean for the first time in what seemed like forever.

I poured water over my head, and using their shampoo, I washed my hair. Wonderful! I even shaved and brushed my teeth. Thankfully, one of the few things I had brought with me was my toothbrush.

Next, I had to do something about my clothes. There weren't an electric washer and dryer like at home. They did have a washtub with one of the old, corrugated metal washboards. I scrubbed every item of clothing I owned. There was a wooden clothes rack, so I was able to hang everything on it.

I was wearing a man's house robe which fit me in the shoulders but was too short in the arms. It reached my knees.

I searched every room in the house but couldn't find anything that fit me.

Being clean and warm for the first time in days, I went to bed after making certain there were no lights on. I banked the fire in the fireplace. I didn't want any sparks in the middle of the night.

After a night's sleep in a good bed, I felt great. I still was weary from my train riding, but several days here would do me a world of good.

There was plenty of food in the refrigerator, so I didn't have to go back to the restaurant.

After dressing and repacking my now dry clothes I went to a room I had only glanced in. An office.

From the papers lying on the desk, I was able to confirm the owner was a high-party official, an undersecretary of some sort.

What was most interesting was the old iron safe in the corner. It was locked, but a search of the desk found the combination written on the bottom of a large calendar on the desk.

Opening the safe, I found a stack of roubles and better yet, gold coins. There were ten of them with a picture of Tsar Nicholas II on one side and a double-headed eagle on the other. They were small and weighed about a quarter ounce each. Still, they were a great find.

I relaxed all day long doing nothing but eating and taking naps. I took another bath late in the day. It felt great to be clean again.

After dark, I started breaking into other *dachas* around the lake. I had two objectives, finding warm clothes in my size, and opening as many safes as I could.

Over the next three nights, I broke into fifteen different houses. I was able to find my size clothes in one house. I carefully packed a suitcase with a suit and several shirts and ties. I refused to take any of the underwear even if I washed them.

The reason I packed a suitcase was that I was going to be traveling in style. I hit the jackpot at one *dacha*. There was a motorcar in the garage. It was in good shape and started immediately. The fuel gauge showed full and there were several ten-liter full gas cans. I knew they were ten liters because they were labeled as such. They didn't look the same as what I was used to but who cares?

I put the cans in the boot of the car, not the best safety practice, but as Mum would say, "Needs must when the devil drives."

I think the devil drove her a lot.

The real treasure was the blank pad of travel permissions which were all pre-stamped and signed. All you had to do was put in your destination.

This *dacha* was occupied by a high NKVD official.

The *dachas* were used by a mixed bag of people. There were several families with children. I left their things alone, not even breaking into their safes.

Of the fifteen *dachas* I robbed, I left three family safes alone and another because I couldn't find the combination anywhere.

The rest had them written down near their safes.

I weighed the gold coins I found. It came to almost ten pounds. It was a mixed lot of Russian roubles, American eagles, South African Krugerrands, and British sovereigns. There were even a couple from India.

The contents of one safe were sickening. Whoever lived there was a pedophile. There was a stack of pictures that turned my stomach.

They showed a man who I assumed was the owner of this *dacha* with children as young as three. I found several pictures on the mantle place that confirmed it was him.

I made up three packets of obscene pictures that clearly showed the man. I left them in a sealed envelope in the offices of the family-occupied *dachas*.

I didn't think even the communists would put up with this.

Thursday morning, dressed casually, I went over to the restaurant. This time I didn't have to show roubles in advance. I wasn't even made to sit in the kitchen, though I wouldn't have minded it.

The owner came over and stood near my table with his back turned to me.

Speaking to the wall, I said, "After I leave, check outside your back door."

After breakfast, I left by the front door and followed the path to the lake. It took me right by the kitchen's back door where I left a bag full of roubles and five pounds of gold. The man had probably saved my life.

From there I walked back to my motorcar. Ivan Popov had the papers allowing him to travel to Kyiv and a blank pad for the next legs.

There was a map in the glove box, so I had no problems following the route. It was really strange after the desperation of riding the rails.

There weren't a lot of towns along the way and no petrol stations. I wondered how they gassed up. I soon after found out.

I came to a checkpoint. I was treated with respect. I think it was because of an emblem on the front of the car. I knew the name of the commissar, so I was able to tell them that Uncle Yevgeny was having me deliver his car to Kyiv, where he wanted it in place for a tour of the area.

He was being transferred there and wanted a head start on learning the area. They bought it; my Russian was getting better, enough that I could get by on a day-to-day basis.

I didn't even have to ask about fuel. A captain, I think, told me that the NKVD depot in town had just received a load of fuel. He would be pleased to call ahead and tell them to fill my tank.

Brown noser.

Chapter 35

Since at this point, it would be suspicious if I didn't take the chance to fuel the car, I followed the directions I was given to the NKVD vehicle depot.

A guard at the gate had it open for me when I pulled up and saluted me as I passed. I guess Uncle Yevgeny is an important person. I know he will be pleased when they tell him how they helped me.

I drove until after dark. I had made two hundred and fifty miles in a day without freezing to death. I pulled over in a car park, slept for several hours, and got back on the road.

It was now Friday morning, so my time in this car was limited. Someone would have noticed all the *dachas* that had been broken into and the word would be out. This car would be the subject of an intense search.

By the map, I was only twenty miles outside of Kyiv, so I chanced it and drove on into the city. Once there I went downtown and parked it on a side street with the keys in the ignition. It wouldn't stay there long.

I left the bow and suitcase full of good clothes in the car. I had heavy warm clothes, a blanket, a sleeping bag, and some camping gear in a backpack.

I had to disappear quickly. Uncle Yevgeny would be looking for Ivan Popov. There was a good chance that Popov would be connected to Richard Jackson. My only hope was to keep moving.

I had also exchanged my six-shooter for a Makarov 9mm handgun along with two full clips and a box of fifty shells. If I needed all fifty, I would be in deep trouble, but I couldn't let myself go short.

I took a taxi to the train station. There I found a coffee shop that catered to train crews. It didn't take much listening to find out that only passenger trains came into the station.

There was no way that I would get on a passenger train at this point. I would be trapped when they came through looking at identity cards.

What I needed to find were the marshaling yards where they made up freight trains. This proved easier than I thought it would. The café had a map on the wall showing all the tracks and yards around the city.

The yard I was looking for was on the southern edge of the city. It was a three-mile walk from where I was. I chose to walk it as I didn't have a drop-off point nearby, and the taxi driver might report dropping me off at the yards. That would give my hunters a lead.

It wasn't a bad walk because I had a good pair of boots and was in good shape.

Once the yard came into sight, I had to find a way to get off the sidewalk I was on and disappear into the yards.

A stream passed under the road I was walking along. It had a deep stream bed so once in it I wouldn't be seen from the road.

Looking around for people and other traffic, I took the chance and slid down the bank to the stream bed. The stream had running water in it and plenty of ice.

I managed to stoop enough to get through the tunnel under the road and onto the railyard grounds. I followed the stream bed until I was certain I would be out of sight of the road when I climbed out.

It was mid-afternoon and was already starting to get dark. In a way, this helped because I could see the lanterns of the working trainmen.

It became the same drill as the Moscow marshaling yards. Find the train makeup cards as they were discarded to understand what trains were going where.

I was hunting for a train heading towards Warsaw. It was only five hundred miles. That was easy to say, given that it had taken me almost three weeks to go the five hundred miles from Moscow to Kyiv.

It took until after midnight before I identified a train of cars that would be hooked to an engine going to Warsaw.

I climbed up on top of a boxcar towards what would be the rear of the train. Something I had heard in the restaurant was worth checking out.

The engine with its tender which carried the water and coal backed into the line of boxcars I was on. This made the usual accordion of cars bumping together. What I was watching for was when they hooked up the guard car, what we called the caboose.

If there were to be any switches thrown on the journey or cars set off on sidings, the switchmen would ride in there with the train conductor. This conductor was a supervisor, unlike the ticket collectors on passenger trains.

They hooked up the guard car, but no one got on board. I had read the cards right and what I heard in the restaurant was correct. They had stopped putting a conductor on through freights which didn't require a switchman on board.

If this were the US, the railway workers' union would be screaming bloody blue murder. For me, it looked like a warm ride. This train would be going straight through to Warsaw with no stops. They must have had an exceptionally large tender along with an oversized water tank.

I waited until the train was on its way before I worked my way back to the guard car and went down the ladder to the car.

Inside, it was out of the wind. There was a potbellied stove without a fire. There was coal and kindling to burn. There were even fuzees to light the fire with. It didn't take long, and I had the car toasty warm.

I unrolled my sleeping bag and curled up for a good night's sleep.

I woke up to the sounds of the train changing. The train was coming to a stop in a yard. I hoped it was Warsaw. I quickly bundled everything up and jumped off the slowly moving train. There was no one in sight so I walked to the edge of the yard.

I worked my way around the edge of the marshaling yard until I was at a side with a vehicle road. I could see more buildings to the west than the east which made sense, so I headed that way.

After several miles I was in a residential area, then an area with small shops. I went into a restaurant open for breakfast. I confirmed that I wasn't in Russia or Ukraine anymore as I could tell they were speaking Polish. I still didn't know if I was in Warsaw or not, but at least I had made Poland.

It was open seating, so I sat at a table. When a harried waitress came over to me, I pointed at the meal the guy at the next table was having. Over easy eggs, bacon, and hash browns plus coffee.

She asked me several questions, at which I shrugged. The guy at the next table asked me if I spoke Russian or German, he had both. I told him about my order in Russian, and he relayed it to my waitress.

I took a little chance and asked him if roubles were accepted here. He told me they were. He also gave me a funny look like why I didn't know that.

I smiled at him and in Mandarin asked him if he spoke any Chinese. Now he did have a funny look. I told him in my not-fluent but getting-better Russian that I grew up in Manchuria and that this was the furthest west I had ever been.

He asked me what I was doing here in Warsaw. That was the first I knew that I was actually in Warsaw. I took a wild chance and told him that I was fleeing to the West.

He got a huge laugh out of that. Others around him wanted to know what was so funny. He told them I was fleeing the Soviets. That didn't seem to bother them at all. I did notice one guy make a hasty exit.

That was my cue to get out of the area. He probably was going to turn me in, hoping for a reward.

Taking the last drink of my coffee, I handed the waitress a hundred roubles and left. From her thanks, it was an extremely large tip, but I couldn't wait for change.

As I walked out the door, there were many shouts. They sounded like shouts of encouragement. At least I hoped so. I wondered how I would get to my next waypoint on my journey, which was Berlin.

If I could get there, I would be almost home free. All I had to do was get over the wall. That made it sound so easy. People had died trying to do that.

Chapter 36

I started walking towards downtown Warsaw when a car pulled up beside me. At first, I thought it was the police. It was the guy who had translated for me at the restaurant.

"Get in, and hurry."

He and his friends could have detained me at the restaurant, so I took a chance and got in his car.

"That guy who left quickly is an informer, so we have to get you on your way."

"Thanks, I appreciate this."

"We all have hopes of getting out from under the Russians one of these days. It may be sooner than we thought."

"Why is that?"

"The Russians are losing control in Moscow. The resistance there burned the prison van depot. That encouraged other groups to attack places. Troops have been called in. The last I have heard, dissidents hold the mayor's office and the troops are refusing to attack them.

"Also, Russian troops in the field aren't getting paid. It has been almost a month since they paid any troops. The troops are selling their weapons so they can feed themselves and their families. Rumor has it that some groups are selling tanks and cannons. It is getting insane."

I had to ask, "Who is controlling the nuclear weapons?"

"No one knows. For all we know, they may be for sale."

It sounded like I had pulled a scab off the rotten Soviet Union and pus was pouring out. It could get ugly.

We passed a small airport on our way into the city.

"It would be nice to be able to fly out of here."

"Are you a pilot?"

"Twin engine, instrument-rated. I have some hours on a 707."

This got me a sharp look.

"Who are you?"

I can't believe I had just outed myself like that. In for a penny in for a pound.

"Richard Jackson. I escaped from a Gulag, and I'm trying to get home."

My driver got a pensive look.

"If you had an airplane, where would you fly to?"

"I have studied the maps. Originally, I was going to fly to Berlin, which is 321 air miles, but the East German air defense would be dangerous. Instead, I would fly to Ronne, Denmark. It is 324 miles, mostly over water, and avoids East Germany altogether."

"That makes sense. From there it is an easy jump to Copenhagen."

"The only problem is that I don't have an airplane."

"That airport we just passed has a flying club. I'm a member. The Soviet Commissar for Warsaw keeps his plane there. It is a Cessna 310. Could you fly that?"

"I have over two thousand hours in a Cessna 320."

"Then all you have to do is steal the airplane."

"How well is it guarded?"

"It isn't. There is a guard at the airport gate but nothing at the hanger."

"So, if I can get on the airfield, I could take the plane."

"I believe so."

"What is the best way for me to get on the airfield?"

"In the trunk of this car."

"Won't they know later that you smuggled me onto the field?"

"Yes. That is why I'm going with you. I have no family or other ties here. If I help you, will you help me get started in the West?"

"What is your occupation?"

"I'm a welder at the railroad yards."

Thinking of my factories in Pittsburgh, I told him I would get him asylum and a job.

"When do you want to do this?"

"How about right now?"

"Why not? Let's go."

My new best friend, Boris Badenov, turned onto a little-used side road and pulled over. He opened the trunk, and I crawled in. His car wasn't that big, and I had to double up.

When he slammed the trunk closed, my doubts started. Had he just captured me so he could turn me in for a reward? It was a little late to think of that.

My fears proved groundless as the car slowed, and he talked to a man at the airport gate. I could hear him tell the guard that he was there to do some maintenance on the flying club's airplane.

This seemed to be all in order as I could hear a gate swing open. It sounded like an old farm pasture gate.

We drove for another five minutes, and the car stopped. Boris opened the trunk and let me out.

We were behind a T-hanger. The rear door to the hangar wasn't even locked. The commissar must feel pretty secure.

Inside was a beautiful Cessna 310. Before opening the hangar door, I performed the flight pre-check. Inside the aircraft, there was a set of maps in a leather pocket in the door.

There were several of them, including the one I needed most. Bornholm Island and the airport at Ronne are also known as Bornholm Airport.

We had a full tank of gas, so we could make Ronne with no problem. I spent time plotting the course. Using a grease marker that was with the maps, I wrote the compass headings we needed to use on the side window.

This was easier than trying to use the map. I usually did this with radio frequencies, but this time I had to write only one down, Bornholm Airport itself. I had no intention of talking to anyone else.

Boris opened the hangar door as I started the engines. This aircraft was well maintained. He joined me in the cabin, and I taxied out of the hangar and stopped the plane.

We then waited as various aircraft went around. At one point there was no one taking off or landing that I could see. I revved up the engines, and using the taxiway, took off. It was more than long enough for the Cessna.

By doing this, I would catch the control tower staff off their guard. No one did this: it was considered insane, immoral, unethical, dangerous, and probably a few other things I hadn't thought of.

Most importantly, it had me flying towards Germany. I wanted to leave a false trail if I could.

Without climbing to more than fifty feet off the ground, I flew out of sight of the airport. Only then did I let it climb to one hundred feet, still dangerously low. I then performed a gentle turn to line my compass up with a flight to Bornholm Island, Denmark.

This aircraft had a cruising speed of 183 knots at 7500 feet. We reached that speed and never went above a hundred feet.

It was nerve-wracking, but I kept the pedal to the floor for the one hour and forty-five-minute flight. We were low enough that we wouldn't appear on radar. My real fear was hitting an ocean-going freighter.

The only ships we saw were in the distance. When we made landfall over Bornholm, I brought us up to five thousand feet and made my first radio call of the flight.

Not that we hadn't received any calls. For the first fifteen minutes of the flight, the tower made all sorts of threatening broadcasts. What I loved about them was they called us, "East German-bound aircraft."

They could sortie all the MiGs they wanted in that direction.

As we descended towards the Bornholm Airport, I identified myself as an inbound flight from Poland wanting to know if VFR was in effect, knowing full well they weren't.

They informed me to get my head out of my posterior and treat them like a real airport. I apologized and followed their directions to land.

I did this on purpose to make them think I was stupid, so any small mistakes in the next few minutes wouldn't cause alarm. I was going to alarm them enough with the big red star on my tail.

The landing went smoothly, and I was almost to the transient apron before the coin dropped that they had an unauthorized visitor.

Boris and I were out of the plane before we were surrounded by about ten cops, all with sidearms drawn.

We raised our hands without being told to.

Since I spoke no Danish, I asked in English if anyone there spoke English. That stopped them a little. One of them had particularly good English.

"I'm Richard Jackson, Duke of Hong Kong. I have just escaped from the Soviet Union."

"And that's a camel I won't swallow."

He turned and told this to the other cops in Danish. One of them looked at me and then started talking quickly to the others.

The one that spoke English told me, "You look a lot like him. How do we know that you are not an imposter?"

"Toss it upstairs. Let your boss sort it out."

This must have been the right thing to say as he told Boris and me to follow him. We went into the flight center where the policeman called his boss.

I was put on a second phone as the boss didn't speak English. The boss, a captain, asked the same question. I gave the same answer, "Toss it upstairs to your boss."

Again, this was the right thing to say. Our translator was told to hold us there while he made some phone calls.

It took an hour but finally, they had a police superintendent on the line in Copenhagen. Again, I was asked the same question. This time I told him that it would be easy to confirm. All he had to do was get the British ambassador on the line.

Being no dummy, the superintendent saw a chance to dump me into the laps of the British and maybe get me out of Denmark. That or he could ship me back to Poland as an airplane thief.

Boris and I were held there for another three hours.

The phone rang and when it was sorted out, I was talking to Mr. Norman. A few questions, and he confirmed to the Danes my identity, and could England have me back? I was free. Unless the Soviets captured me again.

Chapter 37

The Danes were only too glad to let me refuel the Cessna and fly with Boris on to Copenhagen. To show how badly they wanted us to leave, they didn't even ask for payment for the fuel.

Once there, we abandoned the airplane on the visitor's apron and took our gear to a waiting car from the British Embassy. Arriving at the embassy, I was given a welcome. They wanted to know where Boris came into the picture.

When I explained how he had helped me in my escape, they relaxed a bit, especially when I told them I was going to help him in America. I had learned my lesson well. The thing that a bureaucrat likes to hear the most is that the problem belongs to someone else.

I was foolish in thinking that all I had to do was call the American Embassy and that they would give Boris a temporary asylum visa. No one wanted to upset the all-powerful Soviet Union.

Now they tell me.

I had one more card to play. I sent a long telegram to the Governor of Hong Kong asking for his help.

Boris was allowed to stay with me at the embassy so he wouldn't be snatched off the streets.

It didn't take long for the Soviets to figure out who had stolen their Cessna. I suspect it tipped them off when the Danes called the Soviet Embassy and asked what they wanted to be done with the aircraft.

It seems that pictures were taken of us as we got out of the Cessna in Bornholm. The pictures were taken by a Soviet agent or sold to one who in turn sent them to the KGB. It only took the KGB and NKVD two days to sort out my trail across the Soviet Union.

A demand was sent to the British Embassy that I, an escaped felon, and Boris Badenov, a wanted felon, be returned to their custody.

I had to sit in a meeting where some assistants suggested that they do just that to gain favor with the Soviets. No one had thought that I might be armed or needed disarming so there was dead silence in the conference room when I laid the Makarov down on the table.

"We're not going back."

I must have sounded sincere because the ambassador turned to the junior and asked him to leave the room. I left the pistol on the table as a reminder. I had enough of this nonsense.

The next day I received a telegram from Hong Kong telling me that asylum had been granted to Boris and paperwork would follow.

In the meantime, I had been on the phone with my parents to let them know I was out of Russia. They had already heard. I guess the way I had left had the newspapers spinning.

By burning down the prison van depot, I had demonstrated that the Soviet Union wasn't as all-powerful as people thought. The Black Maria was a symbol of fear and repression. They still weren't back on the streets in Moscow.

There had been no knocks on the door in the middle of the night for over a week.

The burning of the treasury building was blamed on me by *Pravda*. Not the smartest story they ever published. It had disrupted the military pay for a week.

That doesn't sound like much, but the average Soviet soldier, sailor, or airman lived week to week at the best. Miss one week's pay and no food that week.

Units occupying East Germany had resorted to stealing food from the local population who were already on short rations. Discipline was breaking down rapidly.

Dissidents had seized city hall in Moscow, demanding Lubyanka be emptied of its prisoners. Red Army units were called in to quell the dissidents but refused to fire on them.

The Soviet Union was in trouble.

After talking it over with my parents, my 707 was dispatched to Copenhagen to pick Boris and me up.

In the morning, a temporary passport from Hong Kong arrived for Boris. My plane landed later in the day.

We had no evidence that the Soviets had the embassy under more than their usual surveillance. Taking no chances, Boris and I rode out in the back of a bakery van that was making a routine delivery.

We changed vehicles in a gated lot as the van would have been noticed going into the airport. It might have been too late for the KGB to do anything at that point, but no sense in taking a chance.

The limo we were in turned into the airport and drove directly to my plane. I realized the flaw in the plan when I saw the Jackson Enterprises logo on the side of the 707 sitting there. Maybe we should have taken an ad out in the *Copenhagen Post*.

Since the car had pulled up to the base of the wheeled stairs leading to the plane, we moved quickly out of the car and up the steps.

No one took a shot at us. As soon as we entered the airliner, the door was slammed shut, and we taxied to the runway.

Boris and I grabbed the first seats we came to; these were the first-class ones in the front cabin. We took off while still being buckled in by the head stewardess.

After we were safely in the air, I showed Boris how the other half lived by giving him a tour of the airplane. To say he was impressed is putting it mildly.

"You live like a tsar."

"Not really, maybe a minor prince."

"A not so minor prince!"

Taking the polar route, we landed at the Ontario airport nine hours later. From there, it was in my Cessna 320 to the Forestry Service station. And a Jeep ride home.

I noticed that the hotel that I wanted had been completed and now was in use. This station once considered a hardship station was now one of the better ones to be at.

I hoped the smoke jumpers had full use of the facility because they had inspired it. I would follow up later to see how things had worked out.

At Jackson House, it was a joyous reunion.

After the greetings, there was some serious conversation.

My mum started with, "Rick, you have changed. A young boy was here last. You now look like a hard man."

I knew my body had changed from the hard work in the Gulag. What I hadn't given any thought to was my face. Any softness in my features was gone. There were fine lines around my eyes and overall, I would call the look grim.

"That's what being in Siberia will do for you."

"Tell us about your escape."

"My escape started on day one in the Gulag."

From there I told the whole family about my adventure. It is now an adventure, though at the time it was mostly terrifying.

How I made a bow and arrows to collect food, then a hang glider to get clear of the camp and the dogs.

Then there was the army outpost where I became a horse thief. The boys loved that part. That and the part where I robbed a bank.

I glossed over my time in Moscow and the guys who tried to rob me on top of the boxcar. Dad could tell I was holding back, but I told him I would tell him more tomorrow.

I introduced Boris to the family. He was well-received. He had been looking around Jackson House the whole time I had been telling my story. We were in the dining room, but he could see other rooms.

No one else understood when he said, "Like the crown prince."

He was given a guest suite to stay in. Dad and I would take him out tomorrow to buy him a wardrobe. We also had to get his statehood status straightened out.

I was having second thoughts about his working as a welder in Pittsburgh. He might have to live in Hong Kong since I had influence there.

My little sister Mary informed me that she had learned how to play gin rummy and asked if I would like to play the next day. I knew she was up to something, but I didn't know what.

I didn't get a chance to play cards with her the next day as I spent most of it on the phone with JFK, the queen, and the empress. All wanted to know how I was. And if I was done punishing the Soviet Union.

Later on, in the news, we learned that the Soviet Army was pulling out of East Germany as its troops were starving. With no Red Army support, the East German army was proving to be a paper tiger. There were so many desertions there were no combat-capable units left. Because of this, the Berlin Wall was being torn down by citizens.

Already the Soviet satellite countries were declaring themselves independent. There was a real concern about the Soviet nuclear arsenal. It had to be contained before bombs went on the market.

Chapter 38

I called England and let Mr. Norman know that I had flown directly home. I couldn't wait to see my family. He understood.

"MI6 would like to debrief you on your escape. They think you can give them some valuable hints on what to do. They want to incorporate it into their training program."

"I'm willing to share what I had to do but don't want to be treated as though it is a hostile interrogation. I have had enough of those."

"Her Majesty has been made aware of their request and has put her conditions on the debriefing. I don't think you will have any problems."

"For some reason, I don't have much trust in anyone's secret services."

"Ah, you have learned."

"I'll do it but with the understanding I can walk away at any time."

"When will you be available?"

"I'm not sure yet. I have to talk to some other people. Mostly I need to see how my family is doing, catch up with Nina, then my businesses, and after that, probably JFK and the empress."

"Your plate is full, that is for certain. Give me a call when you can head this way."

"Will do, Mr. Norman."

Next on my agenda was lunch with Nina. We hadn't rushed into each other's arms immediately. I think we both were concerned with our five-month separation. I know I was.

I picked her up in my T-bird with the top down. I had feared that I would never be able to enjoy this life again.

She was waiting on the front steps of her parents' home when I drove through the gates.

I jumped out of the car ready to run to her and grab her into a hug. I slowed down as I realized she was hesitant in approaching me. What was going on?

"What's wrong, Nina?"

"Nothing and everything, Rick, I had almost given up on seeing you again. Now you're here, and I don't know what to think."

We were close enough for me to reach and hug her. She clung to me like she was drowning. She was shaking; I realized that she was crying. I just held her and let her sob herself out.

Finally, she looked up at me.

"I must look a mess. Let me go in and wash my face. You can talk to my parents while I do that."

Mr. and Mrs. Monroe were welcoming, but I could see a reserve in their words. It appeared they were afraid of me.

"Rick, we saw that show trial on television and then nothing for months. Your blinking out the word "tortured" caught the whole world. We didn't know if you would live. Do you care to tell us about what happened?"

Nina came back just then, so I told them the complete story. It would all come out at some time, so I might as well get it over with.

While I was relating my tale, I noticed that Nina was clutching her mother's hands until both of them turned white.

The part about the fake execution had her in tears again. My stealing a horse and then robbing a bank was cause for laughter. We all wondered what would happen to that pedophile in the *dachas*.

Setting fire to the prison van depot and then the treasury building had them jumping up and down. My fake hanging of my "friend" was considered fair retribution.

The robbery attempt on top of the boxcars and the result was grim.

Mrs. Monroe stated it looked like I had destroyed the Soviet Union on my way out.

I demurred, telling her that it was rotten, and any catalyst would have set it off.

Nina then said something that concerned me.

"Rick, if I remember right, a catalyst starts a reaction, but it isn't changed. You have changed."

"How do you mean?"

"Your looks, for one, but more importantly you act like a mature confident adult."

I thought I had been a mature confident adult for some time now, so didn't know how to take that. I let it go at the time.

Mr. Monroe asked me what my near-term plans were. I told him that I had yet to talk to Empress Ping to see how this affected me in China. I don't think it will be anything bad, but you never know.

We finished dinner and I could tell that it was time for me to go. Nothing was said. I just felt it. Maybe it was me.

Nina walked me to my car. I hugged her and drew her into a kiss which she returned. However, when we drew back from each other, I saw a look on her face that I had come to know. She was looking at me with fear.

I had a lot to think about on the way home. Had I changed that much? A lot had happened, and I had to react to it. Was I no longer a civilized person?

At home having late coffee with Mum and Dad, I found out that Popeye and Aunt Sybil had both become members of the Royal Order of Purple Porpoises. Good for them. Popeye had earned this several times over.

It made him one of the senior seamen of the world. He had been interviewed by the *Maritime News*, so the word was out where it counted for him.

A copy had been saved for me of the interview. The list of places that Popeye had been to was mind-boggling. Even in this day of jet planes, it would take a long time to match the feat.

I stayed up late so I could call China. The empress wasn't available to take my call, but she wanted me to come to China as soon as possible. I wondered what that was about.

As I was about to go to bed, I got a late-night call from the White House. Would I please make myself available at ten o'clock tomorrow for a call from the president?

Since I had no plans, I told them yes. Who was I kidding? I would be here for that phone call bar violent circumstances.

Thinking of violence, I tuned the short wave to BBC Overseas to see what the latest on Russia was.

It was not good. Nikita Khrushchev had stepped down from the leadership of the Soviet Union. At this time, no one knew who would replace him. While there was no outright fighting, there had been several deaths of high-ranking party members.

The UN had passed a resolution that if the Soviet Union collapsed, a peacekeeping force would be sent in to seize the nuclear weapons. Who would lead the peacekeeping force had not been decided. Several countries wanted leadership with someone else's troops. In other words, the glory but not the cost.

At exactly ten o'clock the next morning, the phone at our house rang. I picked up the phone and it was the White House switchboard as expected. They asked me to hold for the president.

He came on quickly. I immediately informed him that I had him on speakerphone with my parents present. No one else. That wasn't entirely true, as I saw Mary's head peeking around the corner of a couch, but what harm could she cause?

"Richard, I hope you are recovering from your adventure."

"I'm in good shape, Mr. President."

"That's more than the Russians can say."

"I suppose so. Can you share any thoughts on where this is all going?"

"That was going to be my question to you. You've been there and seen a lot more of it than any of our agencies. The CIA is beside itself over this. They didn't have any information that the collapse was this imminent. They have no predictions as to the result.

"Rick, what do you see as the result?"

"The creation of a whole bunch of new countries and many of them will have civil wars to decide who ends up in power."

"What do you think the US should do?"

"That is way beyond my pay grade, Mr. President."

"Let me rephrase that. What would you like the US to do?"

"Stay out of it. This meets and exceeds the old saying, stay out of a land war in Asia. You can't win."

"I agree with that thought. What about the nuclear bombs?"

"I don't even know where they keep them, or I would have gone after them."

"Should the US military?"

"No! That would be seen as a power grab. You would be better off supporting someone like the French. Everyone knows they don't have the power to invade Russia. However, they could send in troops to support inspectors."

"Who should the UN appoint as a leader?"

"Again, keep the world powers out of it. Someone that the French, Russians, and the UN would accept."

"Who would that be?"

"I have no idea. That is just the criteria I would suggest. Maybe a Dutch or Argentine general. That way the US's hands would be clean."

"That is food for thought. By the way, the CIA doesn't believe your story of how you got out of Russia."

"Who cares what they believe?"

"They think this demonstrates that you are an MI6 operative."

"Tell them they have it completely wrong. I work for the Ministry of State Security."

"What!"

"Just kidding. Remind them I won't be nineteen until this October. I doubt if anyone would hire me."

After I hung up, Mum told me that saying I worked for the Chinese MSS was a mistake, as it would twist the CIA in knots. I couldn't figure out what was bad about that.

Other than that, both Mum and Dad agreed with all my answers. We also discussed my going to China soon.

Chapter 39

Before I went to China, I went to England. My stated reason was to be debriefed by MI6. My real reason was to try to get some guidance in this crazy new world.

My 707-flight crew seemed genuinely glad to see me back. Beyond their jobs being at stake, I think they liked me and what they were doing. At times they spent long hours in the air but more than made up for it in downtime in interesting locations, sometimes vacations like Hawaii and other times places like Beijing. This trip was going home for most of them and that was the best place of all.

There was a limo waiting for me at the airport to take me to the Plaza. I had a good night's sleep on the plane. I needed the time to let my mind and body catch up with themselves. From Gulag to luxury, Russia to America to England was taxing on mind and body.

If this was tiring to me, I wondered how thirty-year-old people could handle it. Older than that, and they couldn't do it. I had to stop and laugh at myself. What I had gone through would be considered a walk in the park by World War II GIs of all ages.

I still felt like I had to take time to let my thinking catch up with my situation. What was I hoping to get from this trip?

Guidance, but guidance in what? I had set some things in motion that would have occurred sooner or later, so I wasn't a world mover and shaker.

Though some people might view me like that, it did give me some clout, but that could fall by the wayside with my first false step.

That made me ask myself a basic question. Did I want to be involved to that degree, and would I have any choice in the matter?

As I watched traffic up and down the Thames, I thought things through. If I didn't want to play the game on the world stage, I could go into seclusion. That would be easy. Fly home to Jackson House and ride George or play golf at the Forestry Service station.

At first, that sounded attractive, but the more I thought about it the more I realized I had set some things in motion. Now I could watch how they played out or try to influence where they went.

Thinking about it I realized there was one thing I wanted to happen. Dismantling the Soviet Union was one thing. I wanted to make certain that Russia couldn't become a world power again.

The only reason that Russia could play on the world stage was its access to raw materials. They hadn't a sophisticated manufacturing base like the US or even England and most of free Europe.

The US had an advantage over all the others in its wealth of raw materials. Put that with its manufacturing base and it was no wonder they were a world power.

Others like Canada, Australia or a good bit of South America couldn't. They didn't have the population or the political will, and in some cases, neither.

China and India were overpopulated, which caused them so many internal problems they couldn't emerge onto the world stage. China was changing and might be able to do that.

As these thoughts circled in my mind, a plan began to form. Thinking about it and pulling it off was another thing.

The next day at Buck House, I told Mr. Norman my grand plan to end the Soviet Union and make it impossible for Russia to become a threat to the world again.

Russia would be vulnerable to large actions without nuclear weapons. I would have China invade Siberia, and using the Trans-Siberian Railway, take all of the territories up to the Urals. To keep the UN out of it, it would be a civil war.

The Chinese would be fighting for the rightful tsar of Russia. As the entire Romanov family had been wiped out, you would have to go back to Queen Victoria and take it from there. Using that logic, Queen Elizabeth was the tsarina.

As a reward, she would grant all of Siberia to China, forever weakening Russia.

Mr. Norman was genuinely nice as he pointed out the many flaws in my plan, starting with: did Queen Elizabeth want to be tsarina? He went on for almost an hour.

I guess I won't be a mover and a shaker on the world stage after all. I'm glad I brought all this up with him, as I knew he would keep it confidential. Well, maybe he and the queen would have a good laugh, but that was it.

I didn't even want my parents to know of this cockamamie plan I had come up with.

He did tell me the one thing I had done right, which was to talk it over in confidence before I sent it out to the world.

I spent the next two days being debriefed by MI6. They were thorough. I had to go over everything at least three times. It didn't feel like an interrogation, so I went along with them. It was amazing the small details I remembered the third time through.

These details didn't change the basics, but they taught me why they had to be so in-depth in their questioning.

One thing that occurred to me as I described the trip was that I owed a great debt to my archery instructor, Rod Bell. Without his knowledge, I would still be chopping down trees in the Gulag.

After all the grilling, the MI6 grillers (which sounded like they worked at a hamburger joint), complimented me on my ingenuity on my escape.

I was told for the second time that anyone who made me mad had better watch out.

Mr. Norman called me at the Plaza that night. Would I be so kind as to stop by the palace tomorrow at ten o'clock sharp, and, by the way, wear your full-dress uniform?

Now that didn't sound suspicious at all.

On time and dressed as directed, I appeared at the palace gate. Once processed through I was led to a formal audience room. Waiting there was the brigadier in command of the Coldstream Guards, the queen, and my parents. Even the kids were present.

The queen herself read the description of my award. I was being awarded the George Cross! I was so stunned by what was happening that I heard only a few of the words.

One phrase stood out, "acts of the greatest heroism or for most conspicuous courage in circumstance of extreme danger."

Later I was told that my award was as much a political poke in the eye to the former Soviet Union as to my actions. Not that I didn't demonstrate bravery but that this was another nail in the USSR coffin.

I was all for nails in that coffin. Maybe they would leave me alone now. That seemed to be the case, as one of the first actions of the new government in Russia was to throw out all the political convictions of the USSR, which included mine.

For some reason, I didn't get all warm and fuzzy.

There was a press conference that was held under strict control by the palace. I wish I could take those people with me everywhere.

I gave a barebones description of my escape, leaving out the damage done as I left. I was asked about the major fires, bank robberies, and horse theft that occurred on my way out.

I told them that was all a coincidence. What would an American cowboy know about horse theft and bank robbery? As far as fires set with fire arrows, I had only placed third in the Robin Hood shootout in Sherwood Forest.

I don't think I convinced them that I wasn't involved with all that.

I did say that there were some very upstanding people in Russia to whom I had a debt of gratitude and that all Russians weren't hardcore communists who would kill anyone in their quest to equalize society. Equal like some pigs are more equal than others.

The flight home was pleasant. Mary roped me into a game of gin rummy. Playing for a penny a point, she took me for ten dollars. As rich as she is, you wouldn't think she would get as excited as she did.

She then tried to talk the stewardesses into playing, but they told her they had to work. I noticed their work was retiring to their quarters in the aircraft hold for a cup of coffee or even a nap.

Seems like they knew about my sister and her teacher, Mum.

The news on the TV when we got home was that the US would be leading the effort to contain the USSR nuclear stockpile from being sold.

A world mover and shaker I was not.

Chapter 40

When I got home, it was too late in the day to do anything but make some phone calls. I called Nina to see if she would like to go out to dinner tomorrow night. She didn't sound as enthusiastic as usual but agreed.

I was to choose the restaurant. I had one in mind not far from Nina's. It was a small place that had spaced seating so we could have an open conversation but private enough that there should be no scenes.

I didn't have a good feeling about where our relationship was going. I didn't think it had anything to do with another guy, Nina wasn't that dumb or malicious.

I was able to get a reservation so I called Nina back and let her know the time and place so she could be ready and dressed appropriately. It wasn't dress-up, dress-up, but it wasn't casual either.

She was okay with my selection and sounded a little more with it on my second call.

I had no idea what was happening with her or why she gave me a look of fear after the dinner with her parents, but it had to have something to do with it.

Next, I called Rod Bell at his home. I asked Rod where I could meet him the next day. I had a few things to discuss with him. He suggested that I come by his house. I wrote his address down and he invited me to lunch with him.

With those calls made, I turned in for the night. I didn't read anything. I wondered where my reading habit had gone. Instead of reading about life, I was now living it.

In the morning it felt good to get a real run in. My time in the Soviet Union had cost me some of my stamina for running but not as much as I feared.

It was in the weight room that I saw the difference. Being a lumberjack is good for bodybuilding. I had gained in every type of lift that I performed, and I don't mean marginally.

Five months of forced labor had been good to me. Maybe every teenager should have to do that. Not really.

I saw too many injuries and even deaths doing it; how I got through it is amazing. I put it down to my ability to accept things as they are and concentrate on my plan of action. There I had planned to survive and escape. Plan achieved.

After a hearty breakfast, I rode George. From the way he acted, I think he was miffed that I had been gone so long, but we settled in for a nice ride.

After that, I cleaned up and got ready to go over to Rod Bell's for lunch. Before I left the house the phone rang. The caller identified himself as working for the CIA at a place they called the Farm.

He gave me a code and told me to call the public CIA office in Virginia to confirm that he was who he said he was. I called information and they connected me to the CIA.

After holding and being shuffled around, the code was confirmed, and Tom Johnson was the head of the Farm. He would call me right back.

I no sooner hung up, and my phone rang again.

It was Johnson.

"How can I help you, Mr. Johnson?"

"Start with calling me Tom."

"Okay, Tom, how can I help you?"

"I've read the report on your escape from the Gulag you were in. I would like to discuss it with you and see what we can learn from it. I'm especially interested in your use of a longbow."

"I thought the CIA didn't believe the story of my escape."

"That's the clowns in suits in Langley. Out here at the Farm, we deal with the real world. This is the training center for active agents. We don't play the political games they do."

"I thought part of the CIA's mission was political."

"It is with foreign governments. I'm talking about the games they play with each other in-house."

"I've seen some of that."

"So could you come here and tell us more about your escape?"

"Yes, I can, but I'm about to have lunch with the man who taught me everything I know about the longbow. Could I invite him?"

"By all means. He sounds like the guy we need on our staff if this is as good as it sounds."

"I need to know where to come, and when."

He gave me a number to call after my conversation with Rod. I gave him Rod's full name and address so they could start the background check. No one went onto a CIA facility without such a check.

I was surprised by where Rod Bell lived. Most stunt people made rather good money. He lived in a dump, at least from the neighborhood and its surroundings. The building was from the 1930s and had a hard life.

I had to walk up to the third floor as the elevator was out of order. It probably had been out of order since 1945.

The stairwell stank. I shudder as to what his apartment might be like. What was going on?

Rod opened the door as soon as I knocked. He had been waiting for me.

His apartment was as neat as a pin as Mum would say. All was well cared for and in its place. There were bows and arrows everywhere but stacked and racked neatly. Where there would be a desk was a workbench for him to practice his craft.

"Rick, I bet you are wondering about the area I live in."

"It did surprise me; I would think you could do much better."

"I could, but I moved in here right after the war and got comfortable. As the neighborhood went down, so did the rents."

"Aren't you concerned about your neighbors?"

"You got it backward; they are concerned about me. We used to have a pigeon problem, but I went up on the roof and took them down in flight."

"The gangsters who live around here aren't afraid of guns, but a yard-long arrow scares the bejeezus out of them. Every six months or so I put on another show to remind them of what could happen. It is a peaceful neighborhood. I put the word out that the old people and young families were under my protection. It works, so now I don't want to leave."

"If you are happy here, it works for me. I stopped by to let you know the knowledge on bow work you gave me saved my life in Russia."

"How's that?"

As he prepared a simple lunch of ham, egg, and cheese sandwiches, I related my escape. How I had made my weapon and then used it.

He had a dozen questions on my making of the bow and arrows. He smiled a lot and then frowned as he realized I could have done something better.

"So, my escape worked, but you believe that I could improve on my bow, arrow, and string making?"

"Don't get me wrong. You did a wonderful job, but there are some things you were never shown that would have made a better weapon."

"Are you willing to share that knowledge?"

"Yes, I would love to. Bow-making and fletching are dying arts. I would love to carry them on."

"Good, we have an appointment in two days at the CIA training center in Virginia."

"You don't mess around. Fortunately, I'm free for the next while, as there are no movies on the horizon that will need me."

"Can I use your phone?"

"Be my guest."

I called Tom Johnson back and told him that Rod Bell and I would fly into Baltimore Friendship the day after tomorrow.

In turn, he told me there would be a light plane waiting for us to fly to the Farm.

Rod wanted to know what airline we would be flying. I told him the Ricky Jackson special out of Ontario Airport. Be there by eight o'clock.

"I will be early; I hate to miss flights."

"This one will wait for us. It is my airplane."

That is when I found out that not many people in Hollywood know about my 707.

Rod and I spent several hours chit-chatting about Hollywood, what was going on, and who was seeing whom or had fallen out. The more I heard, the less I wanted to go back to that world.

I finally had to take my leave so I could go get ready for my dinner with Nina. I was filled with dread about how this was going to go.

It was funny, I wasn't so worried about Nina breaking up with me, but how she would do it. From the way she had been acting, I knew we were done as a couple. I just didn't know why.

Would there be drama? I hated that sort of thing. As far as her leaving me, I was sort of ambivalent about it. I liked her a lot, but I think I had grown at a different rate than her.

We had been a perfect high school couple; this wasn't high school anymore.

Chapter 41

I picked up Nina on time and we rode to the restaurant. We had little to say. She had welcomed me with a peck on the cheek. Not the best of signs considering the scorching kisses I used to get.

After settling in at our table I suggested that we eat and then have a serious conversation about where we were in life. She agreed at once.

We both passed on appetizers and dessert. It was obvious that we wanted to get this over with.

"Nina, I can tell we both have serious questions about our relationship. What are your concerns?"

"Thanks, Rick, this will make it easier. I just graduated from high school. I'm starting college in the fall. I'm looking forward to a summer at the beach and trips to an amusement park. Maybe a picnic or two.

"When I start school in the fall, I would like to join a sorority and live in their house. I'm looking forward to football games and dances. A hayride in the fall would be nice followed by bobbing for apples. Skiing at Christmas break, and then getting a tan on Spring break.

"Even classes can be more fun. There is the panic of pulling all-nighters before final exams. I'm looking forward to all those experiences.

"I see you flying around the world on your jet plane seeing kings, queens, and presidents. Making business deals in the millions of dollars.

"I can't do both, and I don't feel up to your world or even know what place I would have in it. There is no other boy or man for that matter.

"That's another point. I'm up to dating a boy and finding out what a relationship is, but you are a man, and I'm not ready for you."

At that, she paused and waited for my reply.

"I hadn't looked at it from your viewpoint, but it makes sense. My life is different, and I don't see it changing soon."

"There is also the danger you always seem to be in. Do you think it will go away now that the Soviet Union has collapsed?"

"No, I don't."

"I just can't handle it. I like you a lot—I thought I loved you at one time, but I realized I loved the glamour of your life as much as you, and now I realize that the glamour isn't so great and that it would prevent me from living the life I want."

"Nina, I would never expect you to give up your life to be with me. I think we both realize that we can always be friends and go our separate ways in life."

"I would like that, the friends part I mean. I know it is trite for the girl to say she wants to be friends, but I would like that. Our directions are too different for anything else."

"Friends, then."

"Friends."

I paid the bill and took Nina home. I walked her to her door and kissed her lightly on her lips.

"Goodnight, and it was fun while it lasted."

"Yes, it was."

As I was driving away, I saw that her mother had met her at the door and was starting to question her.

I pulled over in a small park and thought about what had transpired. I wasn't upset. I had similar thoughts about her situation but not from her point of view. The life I was living didn't fit her dreams at all.

While she hadn't said it, I think that after college she was dreaming of getting married, buying a house with a white picket fence, and having two children.

Any house I bought would probably have a ten-foot wall around it with glass embedded in the top.

When I got home, Mum was waiting up for me.

"How did it go, Rick?"

"Nina and I broke up."

"I knew that was going to happen. How was the breakup?"

"Calm and friendly."

"That bad?"

"Yes, Mum. I understand why she doesn't want to be with me, but the rejection still hurts."

"Did she reject you or your path in life?"

"My path in life."

"Are you ready to change your path to be with her?"

"No."

"Then you have your answer. You weren't rejected; you rejected each other's directions in life. That happens. It is better that you found out now rather than later."

I said goodnight and headed to bed. Walking down the hall I ran into Dad.

"Rick, it will always hurt a little, but time does heal."

I guess everyone saw this breakup coming. One thing for sure, I didn't want to make any movies at the studio, soon, or maybe ever again. I couldn't face Nina's dad on the lot. Not very adult of me but I wasn't feeling like an adult at the moment.

I thought I would have trouble falling asleep, but I slept like a log. That said something. I'm not sure what, but it was something.

Rod Bell and I flew to Baltimore on the 707. Most of the flight was spent giving him a tour of the jet.

It freaked him out when he realized I had a valet accompany me on my trips and that a copy of all my clothes was in the cargo hold. By the time we got to the Bentley, I think he was in a state of shock.

At the Baltimore Airport, we were met by a casually dressed man who escorted us over to an old Beechcraft Model 18. It was configured for eight seats. He was our pilot.

We were asked to sit in the back where the windows were blacked out. I guess we weren't to know where the Farm was located.

It was only one hour of flying time to our destination. We were met by a tall gentleman who looked like he lived outdoors. He introduced himself as Tom Johnson.

I introduced myself and Rod. They took to each other immediately. I was treated well, but they were two of a kind.

At Tom's request, we both brought a small overnight bag. He got us settled into a guest cottage for our two-day stay. We didn't go directly to work, at least anything physical.

We had dinner in a cafeteria. The food was exceptionally good. The CIA knew how to treat its people. Of course, once they were in the field it was a different story.

There were twenty other men and women there. Without any names, they were introduced as the training staff.

After a fine dinner, I was asked to relate my experience from the time I was kidnapped to the time I landed in the US.

They were an attentive audience and took a lot of notes without interrupting my narrative. When I finished, the questions started. From how I learned to make a bow to how I figured out how to use the cloth strips that the Soviets used rather than socks.

We finished dinner around 6:30. The questions and answers lasted until 1:30 a.m. It was a friendly experience for me. No one challenged my story. They just wanted to know how I addressed the issues.

Rod had sat quietly throughout the whole talk. In the end, I threw him to the wolves.

"Many of your questions centered on how I knew how to carve a bow and arrows, glue the feathers, what feathers to use, how to weave the bowstring. My friend Rod Bell, a professional stuntman and archer, taught me all. He will demonstrate tomorrow to all that want to learn."

I just thought I threw him to the wolves; it was a case of please don't throw me into that briar patch.

After breakfast, Rod took center stage. Considering he hadn't time to prep for a course on making bows and arrows, he did fine.

First, he took his five students out to the woods to show them what to look for in a bow stave and limbs for arrows.

After that, a trip around a local pond gave up feathers for his arrows. At the same time, he was able to collect enough thin reeds to weave a bowstring. He cheated on the glue because of time.

He recommended hoofs melted down as the most available material in a wilderness situation. The larger the better but small claws would work; it would just take more.

That took up the morning. He then carved a bow stave for a rough longbow and made several arrows. After winding the string, he demonstrated that he had made a bow that would kill. Even with no points on his arrows, they penetrated a can of tomatoes used as the target. Red was everywhere, which was the purpose of the demonstration.

While all this was going on, I was given a tour of the Farm. I got caught up in a class on lockpicking. It seemed to be a handy skill to have.

I didn't pick a lock, but I learned the principles involved. I thought I could set up a practice area in my workshop at Jackson House. It would be a way to unwind at times.

Chapter 42

On the way back to LA, Rod was elated. He had been offered a contract to be a part-time instructor at the Farm. The CIA had been impressed with how he could teach their people to make a field-expedient powerful weapon.

They knew about the longbow in theory. My use in the Soviet Union had confirmed the theory, and Rod was just the person to make it a tool in their arsenal.

I wonder if James Bond will ever use a longbow. I doubt it. He doesn't live in the real world as I do.

On the flight home, I told Rod that I owed him a great debt, and if he ever needed help of any kind, he was to call me. I would be there for him.

After landing and putting away the plane, on my drive back to the house I realized I had never given any thought to Nina. This was so different than when she had cheated on me. Then I was in continuous misery. Now I accepted our new status.

I thought about that for a minute, then shrugged, and moved on to thinking about a trip to China.

I needed to do that soon to explain what had been going on with me and to check on all my investments and other commitments over there.

Boris had already flown over to Hong Kong and was settling in at Jackson House East. I kept changing the name I used for it. One day it was Jackson House Asia, the next Jackson House Hong Kong.

I had to settle on something soon since stationery and business cards needed to be printed.

One of my first acts the next morning was to contact Jim Williamson. I had woken up in the middle of the night realizing that my practice of sending cards and congratulatory notes was more than five months in arrears. There was no way I could sign my name that many times.

I drove over to our Hollywood office to see what was going on. Once he calmed me down, he explained that I wasn't behind. It was now standard practice to sign my name by machine.

There were a dozen or so personal notes that I should hand sign but that was it. He presented them to me for my signature. I see that the daughter of one of our workers in Pittsburgh had won the national spelling bee.

I remembered thinking that I wanted to attend if possible. The Russians got in my way. I wrote her a note and told Jim to ensure that she had a scholarship to attend any school that she could gain admittance to.

Another was to the son of a worker in Australia who had saved a person in the water from a shark attack. Now that was a brave kid. He had got off with no injuries. I asked Jim to make inquiries about what would be a good reward. We needed more heroes in our world.

I checked with my aviation service to see if the 707 could be flown to Hong Kong in two days. It could. Next, I called the governor of Hong Kong to let him know that I was returning.

He made certain that he knew exactly when I would arrive and wanted to know how long I planned to stay.

I asked him why all the questions.

"So, we can plan and put on all the parties."

"Why parties?"

"The Duke of Hong Kong escaping from the Soviet Union and bringing about its downfall on his way out is a big deal here."

"Why?"

"The Soviets had political tensions here on a knife-edge. We never knew if a war would break out in the Vietnams, and also it disrupted China. All that is settling down now that they are out of the picture. You are a hero here!"

"I never looked at it that way, I was just trying to get home. I was tired of cutting down trees.

"May I quote you on that?"

"Uh, no. That is too flippant."

"Rick, I thought you weren't political."

"I'm not. I just don't want to sound like a smart aleck."

"If that's what you want to believe."

"Forget it."

"Yes, Your Grace."

"Arrgh!"

The wretch laughed at me and wished me a good day before he hung up.

I had a quiet day with the family before leaving on my trip. I evaded Mary's request to play gin rummy. I knew her for what she was now.

Mum and Dad and I had several talks about my future. The bottom line was that we didn't know. I had a business to run and was acting as a high-level emissary for China. I also had obligations to England, though I was behind on my robbing dogs.

While I thought of this as a joke, it might take a serious turn as I had to be seen performing duties for the queen if I were to retain my position in the Coldstream Guards.

Of course, the question was, did I need to do that? Also, my being a Queen's Messenger was now an open question. I thought my whole life right then was an open question.

We had dinner one night at the Brown Derby. In the past when I was there, I would be approached for my autograph or by people I had appeared with in the past.

Now it was as if I had a leper sign on me. No one approached our table. Even Mr. Sinatra only nodded at me as he walked by.

I asked my parents if they had noticed this, and they had. Dad thought it had to do with my being involved with national affairs.

Being a movie star was one thing, bringing down a country was another.

I no longer considered myself a movie star, as I thought I was done with them. Unless I was asked to play a role in a James Bond film. Some dreams never die.

The next morning, I boarded my 707 for the long trip to Hong Kong. Since we left in the early morning hours, I went back to sleep after we took off.

I woke when we landed in Alaska to refuel. I even took a walk along the runway while the jet was serviced. It was snowing with a wind blowing, but after Siberia, it was uncomfortable but bearable.

The long flight down the Russian coast of Kamchatka past the line of extinct volcanoes was awe-inspiring as usual. I think I counted forty-four on this trip.

Flying along the coast of Russia was always a dicey thing. One never knew when they would take it in their minds to shoot you down.

I thought that was going to happen when two MiGs came up close. They could see my coat of arms and read my name on the tail of the plane. I thought they would shoot us down for my recent deeds.

Instead, they waggled their wings in greetings and let us proceed. We landed in Tokyo for fuel. It was a quick stop. Since we were in transit immigration left us alone.

I slept once more on the way to Hong Kong. We landed in the middle of the morning. The governor had a limo waiting for me to take me to Jackson House Asia. I had finally decided on that name.

Harold rode with me to the residence. He was looking forward to checking out the wardrobe stored there to ensure all was in order. We all have our passions.

Boris had been warned of my arrival and was waiting in the driveway. He had decided he was to be the butler and was dressed appropriately. I didn't have the heart to tell him that butlers never wore brown shoes.

I wondered if there was a butler school where he could learn the art of butling. I made a mental note to make inquiries. If he was going to do the job, he was going to do it right.

I did ask him how things had been going. He told me very well. The local tradesmen were fighting over our business. They all wanted to be known as being provisioners to the Duke of Hong Kong.

My word.

He also let me know that he had made some discoveries about Jackson House that I would find interesting.

At this point, I was more interested in dinner. It was breakfast for them but dinnertime for me.

The governor called me after my meal of a T-bone steak, and French fries. He thought that I should take the day to rest up and come into the city for the festivities starting tomorrow. It appeared that they had something lined up every day for a week.

There would be a ball, a parade, and several dinners that I had to attend. I don't know what all the fuss was about, but I had to go along with it until I found out the real state of affairs.

Chapter 43

Between Harold and Boris, my morning started well. Harold selected a lightweight suit that fit perfectly. Of course, it did! Harold was in charge of my wardrobe.

Boris saw to it that a hearty breakfast was waiting. He took to heart my one stricture, no sausage. I complimented him on the meal, and he told me that I owed him nothing. The cook had taken care of everything.

I asked to be introduced to her so I could thank her. She turned out to be a majestic lady of large proportions. She wasn't fat or anything, just large. She was over six feet tall and looked like she could lift a two-door sedan.

I guessed her age around sixty. Her name was Alexandra. She told me she was of Russian descent and that her grandfather had been a grand duke. She thanked me for killing those godless communists.

Since the only ones I had killed were those thieves on the train, I wasn't certain I knew what she was talking about. I decided I didn't even want to know.

She started to wave a meat cleaver that she had hidden somewhere on her person. This was some household I had inherited, though I had to admit she could make a good omelet. I would keep her on. Any wandering Russians would have to take their chances.

Before I left the house Boris took me down to the basement and opened a hidden panel. He switched on the old electric lights and told me that the exit was a quarter mile down the hill. Whoever built this house was ready to run.

I didn't tell him that I knew more about the builder than I wanted to know. Also, there were probably more secrets to be discovered. In the coming week when things settled down, I wanted to examine where the tunnel exited and the rest of the house.

A driver was waiting with a limo out front to take me into the city. Boris had made certain that the latest editions of the Hong Kong newspapers were available.

After reading the lead stories, I had a better feel for what I was facing. It was a severe case of hero worship. From the stories, you would think I was the second coming.

I hadn't realized how much trouble the Soviets had caused in this part of the world. Ever since the days of the tsars, they had been trying to expand to warmer ports. Causing dissent in the area would give them openings to help one of the parties.

Like the camel, you didn't want its nose under your tent.

Arriving at the governor's mansion, I was immediately escorted to his excellency's presence.

"Your Grace, I'm so glad to see you looking rested after your ordeal."

"It has been several weeks now since my hardship. I'm doing fine, thank you."

"Now you must be wondering what all is in store for you."

"From what I read in the papers, it's probably over the top."

"Nonsense, my boy, nonsense. You have earned all the accolades we can give you. I see Her Majesty has awarded you the George's Cross for your deeds. Good show that."

"I don't feel like a hero. I was running scared for my life most of the time."

"That's what most heroes say, and I met a few during the war."

"Could you tell me what the plans for this week are?"

"There is a luncheon here today, invitation only. Followed by greetings to our government workers. Then a formal dinner tonight, again by invitation."

"How will I greet the government workers; won't they be on the job?"

"They have been given the afternoon off and will have a chance to shake your hand in the outdoor garden."

Hmm, if any workers were smart, they would really take the afternoon off. I didn't say anything. Somehow, I didn't think the governor would take kindly to this.

The governor and I spent the next hour talking about Hong Kong and how its manufacturing business was faring.

He told me that Dr. Deming was now considered a god in the industrial sector. What he was teaching worked. Their product quality was improving, production costs were down, and profits were up.

These improvements hadn't made much of a splash in the marketplace yet, but they would.

From my experience with my documentary on cargo containers, I knew that it was a powerful tool to bring something to the world's attention. I asked the governor if he would like something like that.

He waffled a bit; you could tell he had no idea what I was talking about. I then asked if he had a trade committee that could look into it. He grabbed it as though he were drowning, and it was a lifeline.

"I will have them look into it and present us with a report on the possibilities."

Another good bureaucrat saved by passing it on. I liked him, but he was so typical of the breed.

Shifting to more innocent topics, we chatted for half an hour until it was time to join the luncheon crowd.

It was a good thing I wore a suit today because it was a formal affair. I hoped I didn't slurp my soup or some other social faux pas.

Not to fear, I didn't spill anything at lunch. That is, I didn't spill any liquids or food. I did spill something that should have been kept quiet for my own good to a stranger at the table.

"Your Grace, how is the lovely Nina?"

"We are no longer together."

"I'm sorry to hear that."

He may have said sorry, but I had just given him a juicy *on dit*. Not only that. I had declared open season on the current most eligible bachelor in the world.

I knew this to be true because I read it in one of the scandal sheets. I think it was the *New York Times*.

I thought I would have until tonight's dinner before the daughters, nieces, cousins, and orphan waifs would be presented.

I was kidding about the orphan waifs.

Word spread up and down the table like wildfire. The governor glared at me for not letting him know first, so he could be the one sharing the news.

Thank goodness, none of the younger set had been included, or they would have been presented to me as the perfect match. Even some of the guys. Since it was well known that I liked girls, it was in poor taste.

Those guys must have been embarrassed. It wasn't for me to judge, and from being in the movies, I knew several and for the most part, they were good people. Then there were the idiots who had to act like spoiled two-year-olds. Those I had no time for.

I was able to escape the lunch crowd but was taken immediately outside where I was in a greeting line for all the government workers at the government house. There weren't many, and they rushed things along. They had the rest of the day off. I didn't blame them.

Then to the city park where a parade was assembling. The parade route would go from the park to the Hong Kong Cathedral for a thanksgiving mass for my safe return.

Hey, I had been involved in politics and sex so far today, why not religion? While it wasn't my strong suit, not at all, I was tolerant of people's beliefs. I made no comment public or private of my opinion of a mass for a nonbeliever.

I realized that my thoughts on politics, sex, and religion were to stay in my head, or I would be headed to an *auto de fe*.

The governor and I would be riding in an open carriage. These people had no idea how much this scared me. Recently the Soviet Union had been trying to kill me, and now they were making me an open target.

As our horses clip-clopped down the street, I used the royal wave. That silly motion that looked like you were washing a window. Silly looking it may be, but it works.

I'm so glad masses are in Latin. At least they sounded good. If I had to hear it in English, I bet it would be boring. It puzzled me that the Church of England held this mass in Latin. I found out that they did this once a month in Hong Kong, for people educated enough to understand Latin.

I don't pretend to understand religion.

After all that, we were taken back to the governor's mansion, where we took an hour's break. The governor expressed sorrow that Nina and I had broken up.

You could tell he was fishing for details. Since he had been so nice about things and helpful, I told him and his wife the terms we had left on.

They were surprisingly insightful on my story.

"That happens too often at our level in life. One partner rises above the other, and they grow separately. Neither did anything wrong, they just grew in different directions or at different speeds."

His wife added, "Now all the sharks will smell blood in the water. Be prepared to be attacked from all directions, and many tricks will be employed."

I told the story of finding an air hostess in my bed during a flight. They thought that was funny.

"Did you make her walk home?"

"I thought about it."

"I guess with your acting career, you have learned how to handle such things."

"I have, but it is never pleasant. I wonder how I will ever meet someone equal."

"You will. It takes time."

From the way she patted his arm, I knew they were equal.

Chapter 44

Tonight was a formal dinner. Harold had my dress uniform with all my decorations, pressed and good to go. He insisted on dressing me. That meant he adjusted my clothes as I donned them.

There is no way I could have as much lint as he swept off me. I must say I did look good in the uniform. My gauntness from my captivity was going away. He told me that I now had a lean and hungry look.

Julius Caesar would have loved me, at least Shakespeare's version. All I needed now was a Heidelberg dueling scar and I would fit all the stereotypes.

There was a formal receiving line, and it quickly became apparent that the word was out about my breakup with Nina. The governor told me they had to expand seating three times in the afternoon and rearrange it multiple times.

His staff was getting rich from the bribes paid to have a daughter seated near me. I asked who I would escort to dinner. Why am I not surprised that it was the governor's granddaughter?

He laughed when he saw the look on my face.

"She is twelve years old, Your Grace. She is your protection for the evening."

"I owe you big time."

"Never fear, I will collect."

The granddaughter Iris proved to be a delight. She had many questions for me, all about Mary's clothing line. She wanted to know what the new Princess spring line would be.

I could honestly tell her I had no idea, but that we could call the US tomorrow and ask Mary. That made me a friend for life. She was my friend for life, as she was as innocently rude as only a young lady could be as she fended off encroaching females.

Unfortunately, after dinner, there was a dance, and she could only dance with me once because it was her bedtime.

You know how mosquitoes come out after dark? Well, the young ladies of Hong Kong are like that, annoying as all get out. I found refuge in the library with some old soldiers.

Listening to their campaigns in World War II and in one case the Great War was worth it. Some of them were even interesting. It was more what was not said in many cases. These guys weren't bragging; they had been there and done that.

The evening came to an end, and I escaped. Not before the governor informed me that there would be a reception in my honor at the Chinese Embassy tomorrow night.

Other than that, I had the day off. That was so kind of him. I slept in until eight o'clock, which was late for me.

After my run and exercises, along with a large breakfast, it was almost eleven. I decided I would like to explore Jackson House Asia. Before I could start that, Boris had a couple of questions for me.

It was about housekeeping accounts. So far everything had been obtained on credit, but we really should pay those pesky tradesmen. Something about their children needing to eat.

With a build-up like that, I had no choice but to sign a bunch of authorizations he had obtained from the Bank of Hong Kong. Nothing was out of line. It just let him pay the staff and household bills and other odd expenses.

I signed without demurring. It would be interesting to see how honest he was going to be with me. He had room and board, the use of a vehicle, and a hefty salary, so I wouldn't cut him much slack.

He also informed me that I had a call from a young lady named Iris. It seemed I had made a promise of an introduction. She had left a number.

I took a chance and placed a call to the States. I was able to get through in a mere fifteen minutes, some sort of a record. It was after school, so Mary was available.

I told her about Iris and her inquiries about the latest Princess line. Would she please call her?

She would for a mere one-hundred-dollar consulting fee. I asked to be transferred to Mum. She reduced the fee to ice cream the next time I was home. That was reasonable.

Brat. I'm so proud of what she has already done in life.

I decided to take my life in hand and play a round of golf at Clearwater. When I called for a tee time, they about fell over themselves in accommodating me.

When asked if I wanted to play alone or with a pickup group, I chose alone. I remembered all too well the last pickup group that picked me up there.

When I got there, I was told that I would be in a twosome. I started to frown at that until I recognized my partner. He was one of the governor's guards.

Both caddies were familiar, so we proceeded. I did notice that we had a small gallery following us. They were all in the Royal Hong Kong Regiment known as the Volunteers. They all carried submachine guns. I thought I could concentrate on my golf game.

I didn't set any course records, but I didn't disgrace myself by scoring a 65. I made certain to thank all my escorts, including the gallery.

I ended up posing for pictures with them as a group and individually. It seemed like it was an Asian pastime.

At the Chinese Embassy, it was white tie and tails for me. Again, there was a receiving line with introductions to all the young ladies and hearing their praises sung. You would think I was in heaven with a choir of angels.

One young lady came through the line, and she was the most beautiful girl I had ever seen. She appeared to be of mixed parentage, Eastern and Western. She had the best features of each.

Somehow when she got to me in the line, I had turned away a little and she floated right by me without even making eye contact.

I looked for her the rest of the evening but didn't spot her. I was so focused on her beautiful face that I couldn't tell anyone the color of her dress, much less describe it.

There was one couple who were right before her in line, but they were of no help as they hadn't looked at her.

By the next morning, I had forgotten what she looked like, just that she was beautiful. I hoped that I would see her at one of the two dances scheduled this week or maybe one of four meals.

If nothing else, I was gaining my weight back.

Alas, finding her was not to be, and I gradually forgot about her. She became a memory of fleeting beauty glanced and gone. Most poetic of me.

I did see little Iris again. She thanked me so much for having Mary call her. She and Mary had exchanged contact information so they could stay in touch. My sister was becoming quite a networker.

Iris was being sent a secret edition of the catalog which normally went out to the princesses, so they could be ahead of fashion.

I didn't know princess tweeny fashion was so cutthroat.

I had one interesting call from the States. It was from my R&D division. It seems they had made a breakthrough in transistors. They had made a single crystal that contained the transistors, resistors, capacitors, and connecting wiring on what they called an integrated circuit chip.

They used two different materials, silicon, and germanium. They both worked and patents had been applied for both methods.

They weren't ready for commercial production yet as the yield was so low when forming the chips. Contaminants ruined over eighty percent of them.

During the phone call, I suggested they look into pharmaceutical cleanroom methods, as they had to fight bacteria as small as five microns. I authorized whatever funds they required since this appeared to be a big deal.

By putting everything on one crystal, they had significantly reduced costs and improved efficiencies.

I thought this would be a good addition to our core business line if the concepts involved worked on a commercial basis. I could think of dozens of uses for these chips. In the realm of space, they would be invaluable. Less weight, less waste heat, and faster calculations.

I didn't think of all those benefits myself. The R&D engineers had brought them up.

I set those thoughts aside and concentrated on what I had to do to improve the lives of Hong Kong's citizens.

I asked to speak to a consortium of jewelers who were experts in their field. The many wonderful pieces I had seen in store windows gave me this thought. I wanted to know what had to be done to make Hong Kong a destination to buy jewelry.

The response I got was to reduce taxes. They could then improve their level of service. I asked what they would do at the service level. It was everything from champagne for customers to personal showings at the customer's hotel or home.

The governor said it was possible to get a twenty percent tax reduction for one year as a test. This would make them competitive with all the other Asian countries. The next step was a publicity campaign, which I left in their hands.

I was hoping they would succeed, and other groups would follow. If sales went up enough, it would justify a permanent reduction of taxes.

Chapter 45

I had a private conversation with the Chinese ambassador. He had greetings from Empress Ping and congratulations on my escape. She wished to thank me in person for accelerating the downfall of the Soviet Union.

At least she didn't think I did it single-handedly.

The ambassador relayed her understanding that I had several other visits to make before I came to China, namely North and South Vietnam.

"I need to go to South Vietnam next to see if I still need to support their army. It has been over six months now. I hope that they have enough control over the country and tax income that they do not need outside support."

"I have wondered what you were going to do with your private army of over a hundred thousand troops."

"I have never thought of them that way, though if I had, I would have declared war on the Soviet Union to break me out of the Gulag I was in."

"I think that the way you did it was for the best."

"You're correct, but it will be fun to think about. In the meantime, I'm putting them on notice they have to be prepared to support themselves."

"Are you aware that the airport runways at Saigon have been lengthened and will now handle your aircraft?"

"Yes, my chief pilot notified me yesterday, and we are planning to leave early in the morning to be there right after lunch."

"I wish you well on your trip, and may all your dragons have five toes."

"Thank you. As long as they don't have ingrown toenails."

The ambassador laughed at that. "I will use that; it is good."

"Maybe it could become a Confucius saying."

"That borders on sacrilege, my friend."

"I meant no offense."

"I know, just your terrible Western humor."

"Ouch, are you sure you're my friend?"

"I would hope so."

"I suppose Confucius even has a saying about that."

"Have no friends not equal to yourself."

"In America, we would say you are known by the company you keep."

"Very close. I'm surprised at that. I didn't think you Western barbarians were so wise."

"We aren't. I think that saying was developed from our jury trials. If you hang around with bad people, you could end up hanged with bad people."

"And with that my friend, I have other appointments. Please give my regards to the empress when you see her."

"I will."

This conversation was very typical of those I was having with the Asians I met. They seemed to be trying to understand Western culture, as though the idea of dealing with us was new.

We were wheels up at o'dark thirty in the morning. I had lunch on the plane. It would save time, and you couldn't get pizza in Saigon yet.

Instead of riding in the decrepit limo they still had, I used the Bentley stored in the 707 hold. It had to be the most modern car in the country. One of the copilots was pressed into chauffeur duty. We even had a hat for him.

We drove directly to Independence Palace, or as it was known, the Dragon's Head Palace, where President Trần Văn Hương lived.

I needed to pay my respects at the American and British Embassies, but that would wait. It made me think of the reception I had at those two embassies in Buenos Aires.

That led me to thoughts of a girl and a swimming pool. Alas, that was never to be, but at the time it was the highlight of my life.

President Trân was expecting me, so I was admitted to his office in short order. From the looks of his office, he was a working president. Books and papers were stacked everywhere. I suspect he knew what was in every pile.

"Your Grace, it is good of you to come. My congratulations on your recent escape from Siberia."

"I thought that I should check up on how the port operations are proceeding and if you are being successful in rooting out corruption in the country."

"I'm pleased to report good progress on both fronts."

"Excellent."

"You will be pleased to hear that our revenues will now support our armed forces and that we will no longer need to rely on your generosity."

"That is good news for my wallet and your country. How is your relationship with the Australians?"

"They have become a strong trading partner with us and with the North Vietnamese. Our rubber and the North's metals have proven to be moneymakers for us. The Australians are also moving some industry here as our labor rates are attractive."

"This sounds like it is working, and the Australians are doing very well out of this."

"They are, but since we are benefiting also, we don't care. The officer cadre they lent us will be here for at least another five years at the field grade level, as we build up our corps of officers. Some of the young men have reached captain's rank and we hope to have some colonels within five years. That is young for such a rank, present company excepted, but we want to have an all-South Vietnamese army within twenty years."

"That seems like a long time."

"Think how long it takes a general to reach that rank and then to gain experience. It is ambitious of us. Our military academy is scheduled to graduate its first class in three years. I think we are doing well."

"Can you develop your roads and other infrastructure?"

"Since we have no war to fight, and you can only train so much, our troops are building the roads and buildings for schools and hospitals. I am proud to say that our country is finally becoming a country."

"My congratulations, Mr. President."

"Thank you, Your Grace. That reminds me, we are having a dinner in your honor this evening. Please wear your full-dress uniform."

After I left the palace, I went to our port construction offices. The president had told me all was going well. I wanted to hear what my people had to say. Trust and verify. I had heard some actor on the set say that.

The chief engineer on site confirmed that not only were things going well, but they were on schedule and under budget.

"These Vietnamese are some of the hardest workers I have ever worked with. Occasionally, one will start spouting communist nonsense. They disappear pretty quickly. I think a few are in the foundations."

"As long as there aren't so many. They weaken the base."

"I was kidding!"

"I wasn't."

Maybe the Gulag had changed me.

I stopped at the American Embassy first. I wasn't given the bums rush, but the ambassador didn't have time to speak with me. An attaché thanked me for stopping by. It wasn't until after I left, I realized they didn't know how to handle me. Should they treat me as an American, British, or Chinese citizen?

The British Embassy had no problems welcoming the Duke of Hong Kong. The ambassador and several senior staff members took the time to give me a third-party view of how things were proceeding.

It was all good. What was especially notable was the reduction in corruption. Anyone demanding a bribe these days was taking their life in their hands.

While the executions for corruption had declined in recent times, there were still three last week. At this rate, the country would be clean in no time.

I was pessimistic. In the best case, it would be kept down to a dull roar and not enough to damage the economy. If we could get it there, I would count it as a win.

Other news was that a leader of the Cambodian Communist Party by the name of Pol Pot had been captured when he attempted to flee into the jungle. He died in prison two days later. No cause of death was listed.

That evening, I returned to the Presidential Palace in my dress uniform. Harold had clucked over it all afternoon. He told me that I had worn it so many times that I would need a new one soon. I could only remember wearing it a half dozen times. Maybe I should ask him if the fabric was bought on the cheap. No, he didn't deserve that.

The dinner had a major surprise for me. I was made a Knight Grand Cross in the National Order of Vietnam. It was the highest level of the highest award in the country. It was for the help I had given in bringing stability to their country.

I was informed I was a national hero. Schools, hospitals, and babies were being named after me.

Poor kids.

During dinner, I sat next to the commanding general of the Australian officer cadre leading the South Vietnamese Army.

He told me that they were shaping up well and that he was proud to be helping these people. He hoped they wouldn't have to go to war with the North, but he was confident they would win.

I asked him how they were for heavy equipment like artillery and tanks.

"This isn't tank country. As far as artillery, we are now making heavy cannon, mortars, and machine guns in Australia."

"Do you think there will be any wars?"

"No, this army is a stabilizing influence in the area. No one can take them on and are afraid we might ally with an enemy. So, I think it is peace for some time to come, not that I want to be a Chamberlain. Our peace is through force like the US."

"We can only hope."

Chapter 46

My trip to the president's palace had gone unnoticed on the way. The next morning as the copilot chauffeured us to the airport was a different story.

Word had got out that I was in-country and what I was driving, or riding. As we drove down the main street, people lined the street and waved. It was like a one-vehicle parade. I gave up and started to do the royal wave. It still felt silly.

The ramps were in place to drive the car onboard, and I stayed with it. The crowd had even come onto the airport runway.

The police tried to clear the runway but there were too many people. I finally had them open the aircraft door so I could wave again to the crowd. This time it was an American full-on wave.

The crowd roared their approval. Without a sound system, there was no way that I could speak, and I didn't even know what to say unless it was, "Get off the runway, you damn fools."

I backed off, and the crew closed the door. The pilot revved the engines and all of a sudden, the runway was clear. Maybe they weren't damn fools after all.

The next step in our plan was simple. The 707 couldn't land in Hanoi so I needed a smaller plane. We taxied across the field where a mobile stair was pushed against the side of the aircraft. I ran down the steps and climbed into the waiting turboprop.

If I had gone straight to the turboprop, the crowd would never have let me take off, or worse yet, someone would have been killed by the props. The chief pilot had come up with this plan when he saw the crowds coming onto the airfield.

I felt like the Ricky Jackson Circus was on the road again. That would make a neat song, "On the Road Again".

After that, the flight to Hanoi was uneventful. The North Vietnamese were expecting us, so I was only mildly frightened by the old MiGs that escorted us in.

I wasn't frightened of being shot down; I was scared that one would fall out of the sky on top of us. For my personal safety, I may have to invest in the North Vietnamese Air Force.

This time I had to ride in their old limo. I would have thought that it died after my last trip, but it kept chugging along.

Maybe I could gift them a limo. How to do it without them losing face?

I was taken to the Presidential Palace, or the Yellow Palace as it was known. Every country but France had houses for their leadership. They had palaces. Maybe France would become a monarchy again one of these days. Would that boy that Mary liked become king?

I was given a grand welcome by the leaders. Unlike the South, the North kept its citizens under control, so there would be no impromptu parades.

They got right down to business. The port was going ahead nicely. Employment was up because of the port construction. This was leading to a level of happiness among the citizens. This was proof that communism worked.

To say I was flabbergasted would be an understatement. At that moment I was so glad that I had acted in movies where I had learned to keep a straight face.

They all looked at me for a reaction. I had to bite the inside of my cheek, but I didn't give them one.

"Impressive," said the chairman. "I didn't think you'd keep from reacting upon hearing such a foolish statement.

"You know," he continued, "we aren't fools. We can see that communism is doomed, that it can't compete in keeping its citizens happy when judged against the West. When it was far away like in

America or Australia, our people couldn't see it. Now they will be able to.

"To stay in power, we must raise their standard of living, or the South will overtake us. Plus, with the demise of Russian communist support, we can't even keep our government in power. The people will rise up if their standard of living falls any further."

I had to take a deep breath before I could ask any questions. This was a bolt out of the blue.

"What are your plans?"

"We have enough income from our trade with Australia to meet our short-term needs. We need a large influx of money to rebuild our infrastructure, which has fallen in disarray ever since the French left."

That was an interesting take on things, I thought they had kicked the French out.

"How much money are we talking about?"

"Several hundred million dollars."

"I don't have several hundred million dollars lying around, but I could come up with fifty million and help guarantee loans from banks in Hong Kong and China."

"That would do wonders for our plans to modernize our country."

And they love power more than communism, I thought. Anything to bury the beast was my next thought.

"I would like to give several more gifts to your country. First, to help buy you a more modern air force and a gift of a small fleet of motor cars for your government."

From their smiles, they all knew they would be getting a new family car. This was my bribe. The air-force modernization was for their protection. Jet fighters could prevent an invasion but not take ground. This would help keep the balance of power in the region. I didn't trust the North or the South.

"We thank you. Your Grace, we would like to invite you to a state dinner tonight. Please wear your dress uniform."

Thank you, Harold, for insisting I bring it along, even though I thought I wouldn't need it.

I spent the rest of the afternoon with the engineering crew overseeing the port construction crew. Not as far along as at Saigon, the port was still making good progress.

Here, not only the docks and cranes to handle the cargo containers had to be built, but the roads leading to them and the support buildings for maintenance and overall harbor control.

The harbor itself was being dredged in parts and resurveyed and re-marked with buoys and modern traffic control for shipping.

I was introduced to the young lady who turned out to be the granddaughter of one of the leaders. She was to be my "date" for the evening. It would have helped if we had a mutual language. She wasn't bad-looking, she just didn't ring my chimes. I don't think I rang hers either as she hid several yawns.

After dinner, I was awarded the Gold Star Award for my help. In private, the chairman told me this was equal to the Hero of the Soviet Union award. Now that was one award I would never receive.

After dinner, there was a dance. I danced with the young lady whose name I couldn't even pronounce. I noticed she kept looking at one young man in particular. I edged us over and exchanged partners with him. Granddad may not have been happy, but the young couple was ecstatic.

What I didn't realize until later was that I had just given a very high-level approval for their being together.

When I got back to England, I would have to check and see if I would be allowed to wear these foreign awards. There were some strict rules, most centering around allies only.

The next morning flying back to Saigon to change planes, I realized the only government left claiming to be fully communist was

North Korea. Could I do something there? I didn't think so; those leaders were stone-cold crazy.

Changing planes in Saigon went smoothly, and the flight back to Hong Kong was the best sort, boring. Harold was in a dither about my two new awards, could they be worn and what precedence would they have? He would have to send some telegrams from Jackson House Asia.

It was late when I got to JHA, so I went straight to bed. After my morning workout, I read my mail while I ate breakfast.

One letter jumped out at me, forwarded from home. It was included with a package of mail that Mum or Dad thought should be forwarded. One of them looked ominous. It was from my local Selective Service Board.

I wondered what it could be about. It started with, "Greetings from your friends and neighbors."

It couldn't be, but it was. I had been drafted.

Chapter 47

My draft letter had the date for me to report for a physical. It was two days from now, crossing the international date line meant it was three days from now.

I debated what I should do. If I didn't report for the physical, I could have legal problems. If I stated I couldn't join the US Army because I was in the British Army, that might cause me to lose my citizenship.

I called Mr. Norman and asked if he had any knowledge of this issue. He told me that he would start working the diplomatic channels, but that, if possible, I should report for the physical.

Next, I called Mum and Dad and told them of the problem. Dad said he would start working on our congressmen and senators. Mum suggested I call JFK. I was reluctant to do that for some reason.

I told her that I would hold it in reserve. I would be flying home at once to take the bloody physical.

It was only after I hung up that I realized that I had no idea what the time was at the other end when I called them.

I called my chief pilot and told him to get the plane ready for a trip back to Ontario Airport as soon as possible.

He told me that he could have everything in place by daylight. I let Boris and Harold know what was going on. It wasn't that late, but I was tired. I toughed it out and called the governor of Hong Kong and let him know that I was leaving for the US on urgent business first thing in the morning.

I then called the Chinese ambassador with the same message and asked him to relay it to the empress.

At first light, we took off for Ontario, California. We would arrive there before midnight today.

The flight as usual was long and boring. I kept thinking about what influence I could bring to bear. I was the head of a multi-million-dollar company. That should count for something.

We landed on time, and there was a limo waiting for me at Ontario. I could have flown my Cessna but that didn't seem wise after my long trip.

At home, my parents were waiting up for me, but we agreed to talk in the morning. Even though I had slept on the plane, I was exhausted.

In the morning things didn't look much better. Dad had talked to the congressmen and senators. They said they would start inquiries, but I should report for the physical.

Mr. Norman called with basically the same message. He did say the queen was not amused.

I had the day to rest, which I did by taking a ride on George to the Forestry Station and hitting a few buckets of golf balls.

The next morning, I reported to the recruiting station where I was loaded on a bus with twenty-some other guys. We rode to some facility near El Toro and were put through our paces.

To no surprise, I was declared fit after my physical, psychological, mental, and moral evaluations. I was told that I had ten days to file for an exemption.

I tried to tell them who I was and what I had been doing. No one wanted to listen. The only time I even raised an eyebrow was in the psychological evaluation. I was asked if I would have trouble killing someone in defense of my country.

I told the shrink that it had never bothered me to kill before, so I didn't think it would now. That caused a whole series of questions. In the end, I think he wrote, "No problems; will kill." I had been forged in fire.

It was a long bus ride home. I listened to the other guys talk. You could tell they didn't have a clue about military life or just about any life for that matter.

At home, Dad didn't have good news. A request for a deferment was being resisted at a very high level of government. Both the senators from California had talked to the Pentagon and were told that I had no political influence to avoid the draft.

The Kennedys had me in a corner for not complying with their every wish. This was confirmed by a call from Mr. Norman. The State Department had informed the British Foreign Office that no exemption would be granted to me.

The queen was not amused.

I received another call. It was from the empress of China, Empress Ping. She was not amused.

I think the diplomatic pressure on the US had to be mounting.

The phone calls kept coming back and forth for the next ten days. I received a letter telling me when and where to report for basic training.

This would be interesting. From a colonel in the British Coldstream Guards to a draftee in the US Army. In a way, I couldn't wait for the time we had to appear in uniform with our medals. It wouldn't be smart, but it would be fun.

I could flee the country, but that wasn't a good answer. I wasn't about to call the White House and give in to whatever demands they would make.

What I could do was up economic pressure on them. I had press releases put out telling how new jobs were being created by Jackson Enterprises in China, North and South Vietnam, Australia, and further expansion in Europe.

The gains to these economies would be a billion dollars a year. What wasn't said was that that billion could have gone to the US economy.

On the appointed day and time, I was on the bus for Fort Lewis, Washington. I think I was in shock about how this all came about. Not that serving in the Army was a bad thing, but the politics were so hardball.

I decided to compartmentalize things, get through basic training, and then take care of the Kennedy boys. I wonder what they had against me. I hadn't refused them that much. There had to be more to the story.

I tried to talk about it with my parents, but Mum brushed me off. I mean she shut the conversation down. That told me that she was involved in whatever was going on.

I could make a couple of guesses, but I didn't want to.

I had read enough about basic that the events from getting off the bus to having our haircut, uniforms issued, being shown how to put our gear away, and making our beds were no surprises.

Even getting awakened in the middle of the night was nothing unexpected, at least to me.

They had us take the AFQT tests. I suspected I scored high and should be considered for OCS, but nothing was said. Later, I found that I would be considered too young.

My interview about my experience was a hoot, at least for me. When asked about special skills, I was a licensed pilot, with several hundred hours in jets.

My educational background included a year at Oxford University until I was kicked out.

Asked about any other experience, that gave me the chance to say I was CEO of Jackson Enterprises, a billion-dollar corporation.

When asked if I had prior military service, I told the officer interviewing me that I was commissioned as a Colonel in the Coldstream Guards regiment of the British Army and that my commanding officer was Queen Elizabeth.

I think it was the last that got me sent to the brig.

An army-appointed lawyer came to see me. It appeared I was going to be court-martialed. He questioned my statements and asked why I told such lies.

I asked him if he had checked up on anything I had told them. He looked non-plussed when he said no.

Why don't you do that, and is it possible for me to have civilian representation?

"Yes, but it would be expensive."

"What do I have to do?"

"I will call whoever you tell me, and they will contact a lawyer for you. I will work with them to turn your case over."

I gave him Dad's office phone number.

The next day he came back and told me that a lawyer by the name of F. Lee Bailey would be here tomorrow.

I didn't know the name, but I knew he would be the best.

He was.

His first question: did I just want out, or did I want to cause embarrassment?

"Embarrassment, the more the better."

My Army lawyer was sitting there with his mouth open.

"So, this is all true?"

"You will see."

The papers were filed for a full court-martial. I was being charged with insubordination in not giving truthful responses to an officer's questions.

My first defense witness was my chief pilot, who testified that the hours in my logbook were correct and that I now had several hundred hours as a pilot of a 707 jet.

Next was the Chancellor of Oxford University, stating that I had attended for a year before being sent down. He also stated that he may have been hasty in his decision and that I was welcome back.

Dad, as acting president of Jackson Enterprises while I was in the Army, testified that I was the CEO of the company and the holder of the patents, which were the company's strength.

As each bit of testimony was given, you could see the officers of the court becoming more uncomfortable.

The president of the court was a major. The rest were captains and lieutenants.

When my general from Coldstream came in, I thought they were going to have a heart attack.

He was sworn in and asked to make a statement before he answered any questions.

He was allowed.

"I have been commanded by my Supreme Commander, Queen Elizabeth II of Great Britain, to find out why Colonel the Duke of Hong Kong Richard Jackson is not being tried in a court of his peers."

That ended the trial. The major knew when the potato was too hot. He passed it upstairs to the base commander, who being no dummy bumped it up the chain of command.

It didn't hurt that those court-martials were not held in secret. Dad had his TV, radio, and newspaper organizations there. There were media representatives from all over the world, including Britain, China, and the Vietnams.

The United States Army was made to look foolish because they had put me on trial without checking my story.

Dad made certain that the Kennedys got thrown under the bus.

I asked him why they were trying to get me.

"They weren't Rick. They were trying to get at your Mum. She kicked old Joe Kennedy where it hurt when he tried to force his way with her."

"They started it; I'm going to finish it."

"Rick, you have been in China. You must have heard Confucius's saying on revenge."

"You mean the one about if you start for revenge, you should dig two graves?"

"That one; don't do it."

The next day I was out of the US Army. It was like I had never been in. There were no discharge papers, as all my entry papers appeared to be gone.

Chapter 48

I had to give in and be interviewed, if nothing else, to pay Dad back for having all his media there.

I told my story to the gathered group of reporters on the bleachers set aside for such an event outside of Jackson House. As Mum said you never let them inside, they might piddle on the floor.

Along with my story, there was an information packet with a copy of all the correspondence back and forth, as well as notes on times and dates when phone calls were exchanged.

After my statement, the questions started. The first question was.

"Is there anything else you should have told them during that interview?"

"That I speak Russian, Mandarin, and Spanish?"

"What about your full title and medals?"

"You mean Colonel Duke of Hong Kong Richard Jackson GC, KG, OBE, KCVO, LoH, NOVKCO, GS?"

I had to explain the two, the National Order of South Vietnam Knight Grand Cross and the Gold Star award from North Vietnam. I took great delight in telling them the Gold Star was equal to the Hero of the Soviet Union.

"Yes, those honors."

"He had me taken to jail before I could."

Knowing that someone would have to pay a price, I knew that lieutenant's career was over before it started.

When asked if I had contacted any of the high-level people that I knew like the queen of England or the president of the United States, I told them they would have to ask them.

I had given serious thought to what Dad and Confucius said. If I tried for revenge, I would have to dig two graves. Instead, I would bide my time; events would overcome the Kennedys. That or Mum would get them first.

Why they were trying to avenge the damage done to their father who earned it, I didn't understand. I wasn't going to make the mistake of continuing a feud.

After that interview, I had some housekeeping details to take care of. I called Mr. Norman in England and updated him on the whole turn of events. He told me that the queen wouldn't be taking questions on the event.

I contacted the Bank of Guangzhou to guarantee a line of credit for the North Vietnamese.

I did receive a call from the White House. It was the president's chief of staff. He wanted to know how mad I was at the Kennedy brothers. I told him I wasn't; I was going to ignore the whole incident.

"Then you won't be moving new business offshore?"

"I said I wasn't mad, not stupid. If they tried something like this once, they will try it again. I don't know what they have against the Jackson family, but remind them about Confucius's saying on revenge."

"What is that?"

"Look it up."

"So, you are moving business offshore?"

"Once again, I'm not moving existing business offshore, just any new expansions or new ventures."

"What new ventures?"

"If I come up with any new ventures!"

"Okay, I get it now. Next, are you going to support anyone who runs against JFK?"

"I haven't made up my mind yet."

"You are no help at all."

"Says one of the guys who tried to mess with my life."

"Nothing personal."

"Please understand this, with me everything is personal. Try me again and find out. Now good day."

What I hadn't said was if Richard Nixon was to run against JFK, I wouldn't support him. I had dealt with him when Ike was in office. I just didn't care for him.

After that phone call, I placed a call to my house in Spain to see how things were going. They were doing well and had held a thanksgiving mass to celebrate my escape from the Soviet Union and again for my escape from the US Army.

People were getting the wrong idea; the US Army is an honorable institution that I would serve in if circumstances warranted. They had been subverted for political purposes.

I then called Nina to see how she was holding up under the glare of publicity. I ended up talking to her dad. I had forgotten that she had started college.

He told me she was doing fine and that she seemed to be adjusting to college life with no problems. He asked how I was doing with all my recent adventures.

"Surprisingly well, Mr. Monroe. Unlike with the Soviets, I didn't have to burn anything down to get out of the army."

"That's good. I hate to think how that would have turned out."

"I was kidding, but it was in bad taste. How are things in the movie industry?"

"I'm glad you asked, we have a movie coming up in which I would like you to do a cameo appearance."

"What is the movie?"

"Its working title is *Escape from Siberia*."

"You got to be kidding!"

"The story, or the cameo?"

"Both!"

"Your escape from Siberia has gained a lot of attention. This is not meant to be a documentary. It is a story based on your escape."

"That I get. Now, why would I want to do a cameo?"

"Because it is a B-movie, and I can't afford your pay scale for it."

"You can't afford my pay scale. Does this mean it is a studio project?"

"Yes."

"Let me buy into the movie for points and I will do the cameo for free."

"We need ten million to make the movie. The studio has five with no problem. I'm about to talk to the bankers about the rest."

"For fifty percent, I will front the other five million."

"Deal."

"How soon will this start?"

"I want to put some footage in the can before year's end."

"I will be in China for the next couple of weeks but will be back here for Christmas. It would be good to get my scene in then."

"Thanks, Rick, you are a good guy."

"Not everyone would agree with you. Tell Nina I called, and I wish her well."

"I will. I'll get the papers over to your attorney."

"He's my next call."

I did make that the next call. It would be embarrassing to forget a five-million-dollar commitment.

I also asked Jim Williamson to get me an update on the dig and park in England.

At dinner, I told Mum and Dad about my call from the White House and how it went. They thought I had handled it as well as I could. The ball was really in Kennedy's hands. If they wanted to continue a feud that made no sense, they could.

It was like RFK's fight with the Teamsters union. Why would he fight his natural allies? Not that I would want Jimmy Hoffa as an ally.

The next morning, I was up early for my flight to China. I was getting the flying hours in. I might be able to take a check ride with the FAA on this plane if I kept it up.

Almost twenty hours later, we landed in Beijing after refueling in Tokyo. I had eaten and gotten eight hours in my logbook, plus eight hours of sleep. This was the way to travel.

I was met at the plane by one of the empress's staff. They had the latest model Cadillac limo. With those fins, it looked like it could take off. I'm not sure what they added, but they looked neat.

We went to what was now my usual room at the Forbidden Palace. Nina was right; my life was different. I was given a while to freshen up, and Harold had a new suit for me to wear. I put it on but refused a tie at this time of day.

I was led to a private audience with the empress.

"Richard, it is good to see you looking well. I was fearful for your life when the Soviets captured you.

"We had our agents trying to find which Gulag you had been sent to. If we could have identified it, I would have troops sent in to bring you out.

"I'm glad you didn't. They still had nuclear bombs then."

"It would have been messy, but we owe you too much."

"I'm free now, and the Soviet Union no longer exists. All their former satellites are forming their governments now."

"I heard a rumor that you wanted to break Siberia off from Russia to deny them their raw materials."

"I did, but I was told that is a bad idea."

"It would be if an outside force invaded Russia, but what if there was an internal group that wanted to break away?

"That would work. The UN would have to stay out of it. The key would still be the Trans-Siberian Railway."

"I have it on good authority that the Buryats and their Mongolian cousins would feel more comfortable separated from

Russia. Recently, there has been a large influx of young men from here in China who are interested in helping the Buryats and the Mongols separate from Russia."

"It would have to be done carefully."

"Some of the people from the Ministry of State Security would like to have your help in understanding the Trans-Siberian Railway and how the Russian armed forces are distributed along with it."

"Only if they pay me one yuan."

"Why?"

"So, the next time the CIA drags me in for questioning, I can tell them I work for the MSS."

"You are a bad boy."

Once she said that, she looked at me again.

"I was wrong, you are a bad man."

Chapter 49

My conversation with MSS was interesting. They had me tell my story while recording it. They thanked me for my time. Their next step would be to have various groups listen to it and come up with a list of questions.

This was much better for me than having to go over it multiple times. It sounded good until I was handed the list of questions two days later.

It took me another two days to come up with answers, which resulted in another list of questions. By the fourth time through, I thought I liked the CIA and MI6 method of sitting you down and going through it until they wrung you dry.

It took them three days, while the MSS process took over a week, and I don't think they got any more information than the first two groups.

Where it got interesting was when they asked my opinion of how to conquer Siberia. I told them the railway was the key. Whoever controls it controls a good portion of the world.

I would plan to capture the major port city of Vladivostok. This would prevent reinforcement by sea and would also gain control of the largest airport in the region.

I would choose how large of a chunk of Siberia I wanted, presumably up to the Ural Mountain range. I would put as large of a blocking force in place there as I could manage.

I would then collect every Red Army position one at a time, starting at Vladivostok and moving west, defeating them in detail.

That was it for my strategic overview. I threw in thoughts about making sure the rolling stock kept rolling, as it would be needed for logistical support.

When asked how long this would take. I replied, "The average speed of the Trans-Siberian Railway is a grand twenty-five miles an hour. You do the arithmetic. Control of each station along the way gives control of that area."

"In theory, this would be a week. In reality, I would allow two months.

"If nothing else, it will take time to rebuild the tracks and remove damaged engines and cars from when the Russians bombed them. Even running at night, they will give you a hard time.

"I think your biggest problem will be running out of rails and engines before you control the entire stretch.

"Anything you could do to take out the Russian bombers and their airfields first would be to your benefit.

"That is all I can think of. Now you should let your general staff come up with a real plan."

My MSS questioner chuckled at that.

"You have not been told."

"Told what?"

"The empress has appointed you to the general staff of the Chinese Army. She ordered you to be questioned in this manner so that we could get your thoughts without being intimidated by all the generals."

Oh great, now I'm in the Chinese and British Armies and just kicked out of the American. There has to be a jailable offense somewhere in this mess.

I soon had my answer in an audience with the empress.

"Queen Elizabeth has seconded you to my army as an observer of our practices. She also asks that you answer any questions we may have on your recent Soviet journey."

She handed me a document from the Coldstream Guards which confirmed my secondment. At least I wouldn't be going to jail. That is, unless the UN caught on to what was happening, and then I would be tried by the World Court.

I would probably end up in Spandau. At least I would have the time to learn German.

I did attend general staff meetings, where I was ignored. I would have ignored myself too.

They were assembling the invasion force in Manchuria. I went there as part of my observation duties. I learned quickly why a land war in Asia is unthinkable.

The Chinese had committed a million troops to the effort. It was like watching a stirred-up anthill.

They had built new airfields for the initial parachute drop into Yekaterinburg. This city is on the western slope of the Urals. The next stop on the railway going west is Perm, about two hundred miles away. The troops had orders, once they took Yekaterinburg, to tear up as much track as they could towards Perm.

I wondered how they could do this. None of their aircraft could fly that far without refueling. It was explained to me that there would be several parachute drops. They would drop troops to seize an area, then engineers with their equipment to build runways.

These were to be bulldozed dirt runways to start. Speed was of the essence. Fuel would be flown in for the planes to get to the next dump.

I didn't understand how that many men could be moved in a reasonable amount of time. It turns out that two hundred planes carrying fifty troops each would put ten thousand men on the ground in no time.

They planned for failures, so there would be three hundred planes involved.

These airfields were in Mongolia to shorten the distances. Other troops were lined up to blitz Vladivostok.

Twelve hours before kickoff, I asked the empress if I could call the US president and give him a heads up so they wouldn't overreact.

After a discussion with her advisors, she told me to make the call. I got through to the White House, but I was no longer on the list to put my calls through to the president or even the chief of staff.

It took me two undersecretaries and a director to get to the chief of staff.

"I need to talk to the president."

"What about?"

"A revolution in Russia is about to happen, and the Chinese are going in on the side of the rebels."

"How do you know this?"

"I have been seconded to the Chinese general staff as an observer for the British Army."

"I knew we should have kept you as a private."

"I hope that was a joke."

"Take it as you will. Here is the president."

I explained what was going down and the US may want to put its forces on alert but not get involved.

"I will take advice from my staff."

"Good idea. You just don't want to tangle with the one million troops the Chinese have involved unless you are prepared to go nuclear in violation of all your treaties."

"I don't like you, Rick, especially when you are right."

"Okay, gotta' go, got a war to observe."

Yeah, I'm not that mature.

I found out that things never go as planned in war, that sleep is a thing of the past, and that you never even have time to sleep.

The first part of the invasion went off without a hitch. Yekaterinburg was secured within the first week. That sounds like a long time, but it was far ahead of the Russian response.

Moscow wasn't even aware they were in a war for the first two days, so the first forward airfields had been constructed and were useable. Paratroopers dropped on Yekaterinburg on the third day, which was the first the Russians knew they were under attack.

The city fell quickly.

The Chinese commander on site rounded up all the rolling stock he could and went towards Perm. Twenty-five miles from the city he had his men work backward pulling rail and loading it on cars as they went.

Ants can accomplish a tremendous amount. No one of them can do much, ten thousand of them a lot. Reinforcements were being flown into Yekaterinburg daily. I think by the eighth day they had thirty thousand troops in the zone.

The rails were pulled back from Perm by the tenth day and all bridges dropped. The Russians now would have a logistical nightmare to get men and supplies across the Urals. It was also now winter, so General Winter would be against them. The Chinese would have until spring to consolidate.

Vladivostok surrendered the city as soon as the first troops came into sight. The Russian warships in the harbor steamed away immediately. If the Chinese had a navy to speak of, they could have captured them all.

As it was, the Russian East Asian fleet got free but now had to steam over halfway around the world to get back to a Russian port.

Of course, this was a Chinese invasion. I had given up talking about the so-called rebels except for my calls to England and the US to update their leaders on how things were going.

Along the Trans-Siberian route, towns and villages with railway stations were surrendering as soon as a train with white flags flying pulled into the station. This is despite a "die-in place" order from Moscow. No one ever said the average Russian was stupid.

If the troops at a station refused to surrender, about five hundred soldiers would disembark from the following train, and using mortars, they would take the station with its fifty defenders in an hour.

Towns without railway stations seldom had troops there, so they were bypassed.

One thing the Chinese troops were careful about was not to damage any track. If they did so, they had been told they would have to march.

If reports back were to be believed, there were very few atrocities. There were some reported robberies and rapes, but they were dealt with harshly.

It is a shame that any happened, but if you had this many troops together from any army in the world, it would be the same.

Chapter 50

The Chinese objective was achieved. They controlled all of Siberia, which is almost two-thirds of Russia. They had the Ural Mountains as a buffer.

It would take the Russians at least a year to replace the track that had been torn up between Perm and Yekaterinburg. That is if the Chinese didn't keep tearing it up.

A rebel government for the area was set up. They approached the UN for recognition. Russia vetoed the request. The rebels formally allied with China.

China started a build-up at Yekaterinburg, ready to invade Russia. The Russian government which had been hardline on the issue was overthrown.

The Russian people realized two things. They had lost Siberia, and they couldn't beat an entrenched Chinese Army. So why die for the bosses?

A three-way peace treaty was signed between the Russians, the Chinese, and the rebels. I never bothered to learn the name the rebels gave their government. It was all a sham.

For me, I was happy that not only was the Soviet Union gone, but that the Russian bear had its fangs and claws pulled for the foreseeable future. They didn't know it, but they had lost their raw material resources. Their leaders had wanted to fight no matter the odds, but the people didn't believe *Pravda*.

That is what you get when you lie enough, even the truth isn't believed.

I was a trigger for the fall of the Soviet Union, but they had set themselves up for failure. They forgot one basic. Life can be good until you run out of other people's money. By ruining their productive middle class, they had destroyed their ability to make money. After that, it was all downhill.

The general staff decided to tour the former war zone. I was invited, commanded, to accompany them. It seemed like a waste of time, but not dangerous.

It wasn't dangerous until we reached the outskirts of Yekaterinburg. Here our convoy was ambushed by a large group of Russian partisans. While a peace treaty had been signed, it didn't mean that sporadic fighting wasn't going on.

Luckily, they didn't have any heavy weapons, or it would have been all over. All I had was a sidearm, the same as the staff.

The ambush wasn't set up correctly as we were able to move our vehicles in a semi-circle. We were crouched down behind our cars when I heard the cries for help.

Four Chinese soldiers were wounded and lying outside of our protective circle. Without giving any thought, I rushed out and grabbed a soldier, and pulled him back to safety.

This so surprised our ambushers that they didn't fire at me. They did on my second trip. They weren't good shots, but I felt bullets fly around me. One did hit me in the left arm. It was a through and through, with a lot of blood flow. It didn't hurt at once, but it would soon.

On my third trip, my arm started to hurt like hell as I pulled another soldier to safety. It would be soon matched by the other bullet, which glanced off my ribs. That one knocked me down, and in doing so probably saved my life, as they now had a machine gun in action.

It stitched the air above me. I crawled back to safety pulling the wounded trooper with me.

I was ready to go out a fourth time when I was held back. I fought for a moment and then realized they were saying the fourth guy was dead.

We heard trucks and tanks in the near distance which meant they were our troops. This was confirmed by the ambushers melting away.

Medics in the relief column patched me up. While painful, nothing vital had been hit. After bandaging me I was given a shot of morphine.

"That is good stuff. I recommend it to anyone who has been shot."

My doctor agreed. Of course, I was off my head when I said it.

I was airlifted back to Beijing, where I spent the next week in bed in a private room in some hospital. On the second day, I had a visitor, the empress.

"Rick, I wish you would stop playing the hero. It is embarrassing to us mortals."

I had time to think about what I had done and didn't regret my actions.

"No one has told me. How did the guys I pulled in make out."

"They lived because they received medical attention in time. Their families are burning joss sticks for you."

"That makes it worth it, not the joss, but that they lived."

"There are some other people here that would like to see you."

It was Mum and Dad. Once they were assured that I was okay, they asked me why I had to keep playing the fool. My luck would run out someday.

"I guess as long as other people are in danger, I will always be a fool."

"We know, Rick. We just get so scared for you."

Is my mum showing a weakness?

Dad spoke up, "I have a question from Mary. She wants to know if while you are recovering, would you like to play some gin rummy?"

That gave us a laugh and broke the tension.

"You know there will be more awards after this?"

"I hadn't given it any thought. What more can they do?"

"I'm sure the empress and the queen will come up with something."

"Why would the queen care?"

"Aren't you attached as an observer for the British Army?"

"Yes."

"So, what you did was while on duty in a war zone."

I immediately saw where this was going and had a hard time accepting it. The Victoria Cross should only go to heroes. Those who show exceptional gallantry in the face of the enemy.

Oh my god.

"Hong Kong will be presenting their highest award, the Grand Bauhinia Medal for this and the all-around help given to the colony."

"Great Britain is creating a National Independence Medal for Northern Mongolia."

"Who?"

"You don't even know who you helped gain independence?"

'I guess not. It is all a sham anyway."

"What do you mean Rick?"

"They are going to ask to become part of China. I came up with it to keep the UN out of it."

"You did, did you?"

"Yes, it was part of the invasion plan I presented to the empress."

"Being as it may, you were the only Briton involved, so you will be the only person ever to be allowed to wear the medal or ribbon."

"At this rate, it is going to ruin the hang of my uniform."

"Harold has already expressed concern. He is having tunics made with internal support."

"Now there is my hero."

"Now to the important award. The empress is creating a new order of chivalry, The Order of the Golden Dragon. You are to be its first Knight Commander. It will be a medal on a chain around your neck or can be worn on a sash."

"China will also be awarding you a Hero of China star, its highest military award.

Dad said, "The strange part is, none of the countries have an equivalent to the US Purple Heart.

My parents stayed with me throughout my ordeals. Not the recovery from my wounds, the awarding of medals in China and Hong Kong.

The empress told us in a private audience that as arranged, Northern Mongolia was asking to become a part of China.

I asked her what she thought the immediate ramifications would be.

"Rick, the raw material will be a godsend. The important thing is that it will take population pressure off China. We are awarding land to every soldier in the campaign. We don't even have to take any away from existing Russian settlers.

"Young men will be starting families, and our population will grow again, but now we can handle it. I think it will be a hundred years before we face this problem again.

"This makes you a true savior of China. We can never do enough for you. Those in the know are aware of this."

"You know I only did all this because the Soviets were stupid enough to kidnap me."

"I'm well aware, and trust me when I say China will never try to kidnap you."

This gave us a good laugh.

In Hong Kong, I was given my award and had to attend a state dinner in my honor. It was boring until I spotted the young lady across the room. She was the beauty that I had seen at my last reception here.

I asked who she was. I had to point her out.

"Oh, that is the granddaughter of Empress Ping. She has been attending university here. She started before the empress came to power, and now wants to finish here."

I looked up again, and she was gone.

In the morning, we flew off to England. It took over twenty-two hours. I gave up my bed to Mum and Dad and slept in one of the small extra cabins in the hold.

As I thought would happen, I was awarded the Victoria Cross. Rather than make a fool of myself, I kept my mouth shut.

Later in a private conversation with the queen, she let my parents and me know that the Russians were thinking they needed a tsar again or a tsarina.

She had been approached and had to make up her mind. This was beyond the scope of the British government and would change a lot of relationships if she accepted.

The Russians were doing it because they were in big trouble and needed an autocratic leader to pull them through.

"Rick, do you have any plans?"

She started laughing, "You should have seen the look of sheer terror on your face!"

I stuttered and stammered.

"Me, the Tsar of Russia. No way, Jose."

Chapter 51

Elizabeth told my parents and me that she was torn about becoming the Russian tsarina. It would help the Russian people and she felt her family owed them that. At the same time, any aid would have to be from her fortune, as they had no claim on the British treasury.

Mum told her good luck with all that. The Jackson family wouldn't be involved. Russia had caused enough mischief in our lives that we were well rid of them.

We flew home for Christmas. As the parents flew home, they dropped me off in New York City. I had some serious Christmas shopping to do.

Mum and Dad were easy. I bought Mum a Steinway Concert Grand Piano, their Model D.

Steinway was reluctant to guarantee delivery by Christmas Day. I made it simple by scheduling my jet to fly to New York to pick up the piano and the installation crew, and then return the crew to New York.

I was fortunate that they had one new Model D in stock that wasn't spoken for. At the same time, I was able to buy a Steinway upright for Denny's suite.

Dad's present was a coin I bought at an auction at Sotheby's. It was an 1894 S Barber Dime.

I would take care of Eddy's present when I got home. I was going to buy him a complete ham radio setup for Jackson House.

He had shown great interest in learning Morse code in Scouts and had talked about getting a ham license. I was going to have a full setup installed.

This served two purposes. Eddy would be able to be an amateur radio operator and at the same time, we could send and receive messages all over the world.

I would go to a local radio club and hire an Elmer to help Eddy learn how to operate the equipment and pass his exams.

Mary was the problem, what do you buy an eight-year-old millionaire? Not that she was allowed to get at her money; it all went into a trust.

Mum and Dad gave her an allowance of twenty dollars a week. This was a fortune for a child, and not bad for a teenager. She would get larger amounts for special events, but on the whole, they didn't let money disrupt her life.

I had various thoughts: how about a Monopoly set with real money? a role in the movie based on my escape from Siberia? a three-quarter-sized playhouse? a lion?

Then it dawned on me. She had mentioned that her pony Misty was getting older and that she thought she was ready for a horse.

I called Mum from New York and asked her about buying Mary a horse. I was too late; that was their present to her.

However, the horse was a jumper, and Mary would need a trainer and all the equipment that would go with it.

The plane was to fly back for me and the two pianos; in the meantime, I would stay at the Waldorf in the suite that I had bought there.

It was getting hard to keep track of my places to live: hotel suites in London and New York; a beach house in LA; my parents' houses in England and California, and then there was my house in Spain plus my newest house, Jackson House Asia in Hong Kong.

While at the Waldorf, I had dinner with President Hoover. He had left word with the front desk that if I showed up, he would like to speak with me.

After we exchanged pleasantries, he wanted to know about my Siberian adventures, his words not mine.

Then he requested an update on the Chinese involvement in Siberia. While I was shopping, the news came out that Northern

Mongolia was requesting to be made part of China. China had brought this to the UN. The diplomats of the world were in an uproar. They were presented with a fait accompli.

They hated things like that, nothing to debate for weeks on end.

Mr. Hoover asked me what I had to do with all of this. Without telling a direct lie, I tried to say nothing. He didn't buy it.

"A change of subject then, why are the Kennedys so upset with your family?"

"Because old Joe Kennedy tried to rape my mum, and she let him have it. They can't let it go, as though their father's actions are my mum's fault. She scares the heck out of them, so they pick on me."

"That sounds like the old bootlegger. Please don't hurt America because of them."

"I would never hurt America."

Mr. Hoover replied, "Just the Soviet Union."

"Those guys, any day of the week. They started it with them trying to nuke the US."

Me and my big mouth, maybe he didn't know about the aborted attack by the Soviets a few years ago.

"I had heard rumors; you just confirmed them. Right or wrong, I can understand why they were unhappy with you."

In for a penny in for a pound.

"Then they went and kidnapped my little sister Mary."

"The heads in the bowling ball bags?"

"Yes."

"You Jacksons play hardball. As I asked earlier, please don't hurt the US."

"I have no intention, and if they do come after me some more, I will go back at them and not the country."

As I was falling asleep, I wondered what I had become.

The pianos and I flew back home. I was able to find an Elmer for Eddy and hire a Mum-approved trainer for Mary, who agreed to select all the equipment that she would need to learn to jump in shows.

Jackson House was decorated for Christmas. Professional decorators had put up trees in almost every room in the house, except our private suites.

Mum was holding a Christmas dinner and dance for charity. Us kids were all drafted to help. Mary was going to be allowed to stay up beyond her normal bedtime to attend the dance.

I escorted a young lady to dinner and danced with a dozen others. None of them interested me. They all seemed immature and vapid to say the least.

One at least got my attention.

"Please dance us over in front of the photographers. I need a picture dancing with you to win a bet."

As I twirled her in the right direction I asked, "What was the bet?"

"I bet twenty dollars that you are so dumb you would dance with anyone, including me."

What do you say to that?

"I hope you collect your money. Why am I dumb for dancing with you?"

"You could dance with the richest, most beautiful women in the world, and here you are with me."

"You and many others will never understand. I don't need beauty and wealth. I need a friend and a life-mate. Read the headlines about all those high-profile marriages and then the divorce. That is not what I'm looking for."

"Oh."

After that, I faded from the scene, went to my room, and changed into comfortable clothes. That was the day before Christmas Eve.

On Christmas Eve we gathered as a family in the library and put up our Christmas Tree. The others were done by professionals. On this one, we used the ornaments that had been in the family for years and held memories for us.

Mary and I made paper chains earlier in the afternoon, while Denny and Eddy popped corn and made strands. I was tall enough to place the angel on top.

Later, we gathered around and exchanged presents.

Rather than drag a horse into the house or an Elmer, we made cards describing the presents.

My present from the whole family was a Napoleonic French Marshal's baton. It was a blue cylinder with eagles dating to the First French Empire.

It is inscribed, "*Terror belli, decus pacis*", which means "terror in war, ornament in peace".

I'm not sure what they are trying to tell me.

We sang some Christmas carols. Thankfully, only Dad and I had the "Jackson" singing voice. We kept it soft. The rest were rather good. Mary especially. Her pitch must be perfect.

We retired for the night. Christmas morning there would be tons of presents to open. But we had already had our real Christmas.

Mum loved the piano. We had managed to sneak it in, set it up, and tune it without her knowledge.

Mary had on her riding costume and was ready to jump six-foot-high fences this afternoon.

Eddy was talking about bouncing radio signals off the new satellites circling the earth. He had read about it in *Boy's Life*.

Dad had the dime in hand to show us, then set it down, and forgot where he put it. That was a mad scramble.

I made a miscalculation about Denny's piano. His room was next to mine and the walls weren't as soundproof as I thought.

What a wonderful Christmas.

Chapter 52

The day after Christmas is Boxing Day. Mum, like all British with servants, gave them presents. I don't know what she gave them, but it was in the form of a check. I suspect it was at least a month's pay from the cheerful thanks that I heard.

I had envelopes made out to my only servants Harold and Boris. I asked Boris to take care of the staff at Jackson House Asia. Thinking of what Boris and Harold had done for me, I gave them a six-month bonus. Boris for his help saving my life, Harold for all the globe-trotting he had done for me. I also sent a check to Rod Bell for teaching me archery.

I received a phone call from the studio. They wanted me to do my cameo shot this week, if possible. That couldn't have worked out better.

I had no lines. All I had to do was stand between two boxcars and shoot an arrow. They would show the arrow hitting a thug who was about to stab the star of the movie.

I did try to ham it up a little by winking at the camera after I released the arrow, but they edited it out. It was a bit much for a serious scene, so I understand.

I hung around the set for a little while. I was able to say "hi" to some people I had worked with before. I thought their star would have wanted to talk to me about what it was really like, but he headed to his trailer as soon as his work was done.

A couple of his hangers-on were still there and asked who I was and why was I on the set. When an assistant told them, they laughed and stated that I should stay and see how a real man performs.

At one time I would have been upset, or even in a fight. Today I just gave a small laugh and turned to walk away.

"Hey, Buddy, we are talking to you."

I kept walking. Not being stupid, I walked in front of a klieg light that was still on. Anyone coming up behind me would have their shadow cast towards me.

"Stop right there; we want words!"

That did it. If they wanted words, they would have them, except my fists would do the talking. As I turned, they arrived. They were in the process of taking a swing at me.

Using the momentum of my turn, I drove a fist into the stomach of the one on the right. A kick in the shins of the other guy settled it down quickly.

Studio guards were on the scene. Plenty of witnesses told how these guys chased me down and took a swing at me. I put them down so quickly they almost didn't see it.

The studio cops knew me, so I was allowed to proceed. The two guys wouldn't be charged as the studio didn't want bad publicity, but they would be banned from the lot.

Mr. Monroe was called immediately, as procedure. He drove up in a studio golf cart.

"Rick, are you okay?"

"Yes, but I'm not sure I want my cameo in this movie."

"Why not?"

"I don't want to do anything that will help that jackass star of yours."

"Your decision; however, it's your money in the film."

"Oh, heck, I forgot about that. Okay, go ahead, but if that actor has friends like that, he is going to be trouble."

I didn't let that sour my mood. I was in California, the weather was great, and no one was seriously trying to kill me. Those guys didn't count.

At home, there was a package waiting for me. It was a portrait of the Chinese imperial family. They are good-looking, but the person who made the picture for me was May-Ling, the granddaughter of

Empress Ping The fact that the empress had a granddaughter was a surprise to the whole world. For her safety, her existence had never been revealed until now. She was absolutely beautiful.

I could see where her beauty came from. Her father Crown Prince Chia-Hao was exceptionally tall for a Chinese. Her mother Ann, an Englishwoman whom Chia-Hao had met at Oxford, was tall and beautiful by any standard in the world. May-Ling was a little taller than her mother and had all her features.

Her older brother Chun-Chieh took after his father in stature and looks.

Her uncle Prince Haoran had never married so he had no other family in the portrait. He started out looking like a smaller version of his older brother, but he had grown fat by leading a dissolute life. I had heard nothing good about him.

The portrait would go up in my suite so I could see the beautiful May-Ling whenever I wanted to. I could end up dreaming my life away.

In China, a different scene was playing out. An angry Prince Haoran was breaking lamps and anything loose he could get his hands on.

He had just read the proclamation his mother the empress had issued, giving land to the soldiers who had gone to Siberia. He had promised it to his clique. These peasants didn't deserve the land.

They should be fighting for the rest of Russia and dying, as that was all they were good for. His brother had agreed with his mother. He had argued against it, but they told him it was for the good of the Chinese people.

What about him and his dreams? He could run China better than they could. Maybe it was time for a change.

Finished for now.

Back Matter

To be continued in Book 13: Regicide[1]
For updates go to: enelsonauthor.com[2]
For information on hiring Janet E. Rupert to edit your fiction project, email: janeteditorrupert.gmail.com

1. https://www.amazon.com/Richard-Jackson-Saga-Book-Regicide-ebook/dp/B09BRH1L9L

2.　　https://www.enelsonauthor.com/

Other books by Ed Nelson

The Richard Jackson Saga

Book 1 The Beginning

Book 2 Schooldays

Book 3 Hollywood

Book 4 In the Movies

Book 5 Star to Deckhand

Book 6 Surfing Dude

Book 7 Third Time is a Charm

Book 8 Oxford University

Book 9 Cold War

Book 10 Taking Care of Business

Book 11 Interesting Times

Book 12 Escape from Siberia

Book 13 Regicide

Book 14 What's Under, Down Under?

Book 15 The Lunar Kingdom

Book 16 First Steps

In the Richard Jackson World

Mary, Mary

Stand-Alone Story

Ever and Always

Cast in Time Series

Book 1: Baron

Book 2: Baron of the Middle Counties

Book 3: Count

Book 4: Earl

Book 5: Earl of the Marches

Did you love *Escape from Siberia*? Then you should read *Regicide* by Ed Nelson!

Coming of age stories don't have to be all teenage angst; they can be fun-filled adventures that become more serious with age. With humor, we follow a young man's coming of age in the late 1950s. Starting in the summer before his freshman year, the series follows him through high school and beyond. He finds wealth as an inventor and fame in Hollywood as he searches for a girlfriend. Wealth and fame prove far easier than girls.Regicide the 13th book has Rick running into serious problems as he nears full adulthood. Danger, fame, and adventure come his way as he stays close to the Chinese imperial family. His actions have caused a change in history as we know it. Not all actions result in good outcomes as he learns. While trying to protect the Imperial family, his company continues to grow. The new research division makes a breakthrough in placing transistors on silicon chips. Then his new space division takes off. This tongue-in-cheek saga is all true, give or take a lie or two.

.

www.ingramcontent.com/pod-product-compliance
Lightning Source LLC
Chambersburg PA
CBHW070311260626
47160CB00003B/807